THREE IN ONE
ANIMAL STORIES

THE WINGED COLT OF CASA MIA

When Charles unexpectedly goes to stay with his Uncle Coot he spends as much time as he can with the horses on the ranch, but things take an extraordinary turn when a neighbour tells them about a colt that has just been born – with wings.

STORIES FROM FIREFLY ISLAND

Settle on the beach with the other animals from Firefly Island and listen to Tortoise's wonderful tales . . .

FARTHING WOOD, THE ADVENTURE BEGINS

There had always been otters in the stream running through Farthing Wood and it had never been a problem. But now, when there is a shortage of fish in the stream, the otters have come ashore. Suddenly the other animals are competing for food.

Other Red Fox Story Collections

Cool School Stories
Three in One Ballet Stories
Completely Wild Stories

THREE IN ONE
ANIMAL STORIES

RED FOX

A Red Fox Book

Published by Random House Children's Books
20 Vauxhall Bridge Road, London SW1V 2SA

A division of Random House UK Ltd
London Melbourne Sydney Auckland
Johannesburg and agencies throughout the world

1 3 5 7 9 10 8 6 4 2

The Winged Colt of Casa Mia first published in Great Britain by
The Bodley Head 1974, *Tales from Firefly Island* first published in
Great Britain by Julia MacRae 1992, *Farthing Wood, The Adventure
Begins* first published in Great Britain by Hutchinson Children's
Books 1994

Red Fox edition 1998

Printed and bound in Great Britain by
Cox & Wyman Ltd, Reading, Berkshire
Papers used by Random House UK Ltd are natural, recyclable
products made from wood grown in sustainable forests. The
manufacturing processes conform to the environmental regulations
of the country of origin.

Random House UK Limited Reg. No. 954009

ISBN 0 09 926583 4

CONTENTS

THE WINGED COLT OF CASA MIA

Betsy Byars

BEST IN THE BUSINESS

We stood at the railroad station and looked across the tracks at each other. He was a boy in a dark suit with his hair combed down flat. He was holding a *Mad* magazine. I was a man in dusty boots and dusty pants with a scar down the side of my face that no amount of dust could hide.

I said, 'Charles?'

He said, 'Uncle Coot? Is that you?'

'Yes.'

He tried to grin. 'Well, it's me too.'

We kept standing there, and then I stepped over to his side of the tracks. Charles was looking up at me, and for a second I could see the Texas sky mirrored in his eyeglasses, the big white clouds. He cleared his throat and said, 'I guess you heard I was coming.' He started rolling and unrolling his magazine. 'Or you wouldn't be here.'

'I got your mom's telegram this morning.'

'Well, she'll probably send for me in a few weeks or something,' he said. 'I won't be here forever.' He made a tight roll of the *Mad* magazine and held it in his fist.

'Well, sure,' I said. 'She'll send for you.' We stood

11

there a minute more, and then I said, 'We might as well stop standing around and get in the truck.' We both tried to pick up his suitcase at the same time. Then I got it and carried it over to the truck and we got in.

We drove out of Marfa and neither of us said anything for a mile or two. My truck's old and makes a lot of noise, but it seemed quiet this morning. Once I cleared my throat, and he snapped his head around and asked, 'Did you say something?'

'I was just clearing my throat.'

'Oh, I thought you said something.'

'No.' I probably would have said something if I could have thought of anything to say, but I couldn't. We rode on for a few more miles. I was looking straight ahead at the road. He was looking out the window at the mountains. We passed a peak called Devil's Back.

I said, 'I reckon this is different from back East where you were in school.'

'Yes.' We drove another mile or two, and then he said suddenly, 'I've seen you in the movies.'

I said, 'What?' because he had spoken real quiet.

He turned his head toward me. 'I've seen you in the *movies*.'

'Oh.'

There was another silence, and then he said, 'I especially remember you in a movie called *Desert Flame*.'

'Well, that's over now,' I said. Up until this spring I had been in California doing stunts for western movies. I had been doing stunts – or gags, as we call them – the biggest part of my life, and I can tell you that the stunts you see in the movies are real and they are dangerous. There are tricks, of course – fences and barn doors made of soft balsa wood to break easily, ground that's been dug up and softened, rubber hose stirrups – but most of the horse stunts you see are not faked, and stunt horses have to be special animals.

Charles said, 'You were riding a white horse.'

I said, 'Yeah.' Then I added again, 'But that's over now.' I wanted the conversation to end.

'Did the white horse belong to you?'

'Yeah.'

'What was his name?'

'Cotton.' I tried to make a period of the word. There's a phrase stunt men have about horses – 'the best in the business' – and that suited Cotton. In a stunt horse temperament is the important thing, not looks, and I had found Cotton on his way to the slaughterhouse because of a badly wounded leg. There was something about the horse that I liked, and I had taken him and started training him. First I let him fall in a sawdust pit so he would get used to it; then I got him to fall when he was walking, then trotting, and finally to fall in a full gallop, a beautiful fall you've probably seen in a dozen movies.

Maybe you remember the movie *Desert Flame* that Charles was talking about and the scene where the white stallion falls in the desert. That was me and Cotton. I rode Cotton right to the top of a dune, reared him, pretended to take a shot in the shoulder, fell backwards, and me and him rolled head over hoof all the way down that dune without bruising either one of us. Stunt men still talk about that fall sometimes.

'Do you still have that horse?' Charles asked. 'I'd like to see him.'

'No, I don't have him any more.'

'What happened?'

I didn't answer.

'What *happened?*' he asked again.

I said, 'Nothing,' and began to drive a little faster.

What happened was something I couldn't talk about. That spring Cotton and I had been taking a fall for a movie called *Bright Glory*. The fall wasn't anything special, just a battle scene, and we were to come toward the camera in a full gallop and drop just before we got there. It wasn't anything unusual. Cotton and I had taken that same fall dozens of times with neither of us the worse for it. But this one fall my timing was off. It wasn't off more than a second, but we went down – not in the soft drop area, but beyond it – and crashed into the camera. I got up but Cotton didn't. His front legs were broken.

It took something out of me. Cotton and I had been together for twelve years, and when I knew he was going to have to be shot – I knew it right when I scrambled to my feet in the dust and he didn't – well, I decided then that I wanted to go back home to Texas. The land called me. I wanted to look at the mountains again, to ride through the valleys, to have that bright blinding sky over me. I wanted to be by myself.

The whole thing came back to me as Charles was talking – the accident, the blood from my cheek falling on Cotton's white neck, the pistol shot. I reached up and rubbed the scar on my cheek.

Charles was still talking a mile a minute. 'And I remember you jumping across a cliff in *Thunder in Oklahoma*. Remember? You almost didn't make it, and you and the horse just hung there practically on the side of the cliff for a moment.'

'Yeah.'

'I stayed to see that part of the movie five times and it got better and better. Everybody in the audience held their breath, and some little kids down in front screamed. Was the horse Cotton?'

I nodded.

'I told everybody that was my uncle up there on the screen – the lady selling popcorn, the man on the aisle, everybody. I don't think half of them believed me. It was the greatest thing I ever saw.'

'It wasn't that great, Charles. The cliff wasn't as high as it looked – they had the camera set at an angle so that it looked higher and' – I hesitated – 'and I had a horse that made me look good.'

'You looked *great*,' he said. 'The boys at my school wouldn't believe you were my uncle it was so great. They ought to put your name up there with John Wayne's so people would *know*.'

He looked at me and his face was shining almost as bright as his glasses. I had never been that great in my life. And at that moment, with the accident still taking up most of my mind, with that one split-second mistake haunting me, the last thing I wanted to hear was how great I was.

'Look, it was just a gag,' I said. I was starting to sweat. There was an edge to my voice, but Charles didn't notice.

He said, 'And I remember one other time – anyway I thought this was you and I always wanted to ask about it. There was this movie called *Son of* something and – '

'I don't remember all of them,' I said.

'But this was such a great stunt you'd *have* to remember. Oh, yeah, it was *Son of Thunderfoot*, and this Indian came riding down a steep hill, and halfway down the hill the horse slipped and – '

'It wasn't me.'

'It looked like you and it was a white horse.'

'Well, it must have been someone else. There are a lot of stunt men and a lot of white horses. Be quiet so I can drive.'

He was still looking at me, squinting through his glasses as if he was looking at a too-bright light. Then he nodded. He turned and started staring out the window. We drove the rest of the way in silence.

THE GUY WHO NEVER GOT HURT

There was a cloud of dust behind us as we stopped at the ranch. 'Here we are,' I said, 'Casa Mia.' I reached over and opened his door for him. Beyond, the buildings looked old and dusty in the bright sunlight.

Charles didn't say anything. He got out of the truck and went into the house with his suitcase. In about five minutes he came out in a pair of blue jeans so new the stiffness was still in them.

I was at the corral saddling up Clay. I wanted to get off by myself for a while, because just talking about Cotton had brought back my loss. Charles spotted me and came over.

He stuck his hands down into his jeans pockets kind of casual-like, and then he pulled out a little square of paper that said his pants had been inspected by Number 28. He crumpled the paper and looked at me.

I said, 'Listen, Charles, I got to go off for an hour or two and – '

He said, 'I'd like to learn how to ride a horse now.' His eyeglasses looked like they had been bought a couple of sizes too big so he could grow into them.

I said, 'Well, sure, Charles, you can learn to ride if you want, but if you're going to be here for a few weeks there'll be plenty of time.'

'I've seen it done a thousand times,' he said.

'Yeah, but seeing it done isn't doing it. Look, why don't you finish reading your magazine or something for a couple of hours. You can unpack. I've got to – '

'I've read four complete books on horsemanship, including the *Encyclopedia of Horses*, both volumes. Have you ever read that?'

'Well, no, but – '

'I even memorized the ten rules of good horsemanship. One: A good horseman controls the horse with his hands, legs, and the weight of his body. Those are called the aids, Uncle Coot.'

'Oh.'

'The most important aid is the legs. You use them to teach the horse to move. If you press the horse with your left leg, the horse moves to the left. If you press the horse . . .'

By this time I could see that nothing was going to satisfy him but getting up on a horse and trying out those aids. I gave up on getting off by myself for the moment. 'I'll saddle Stump for you,' I said.

He stopped talking and blinked his eyes. 'Stump? That's a funny name for a horse.'

'Not this horse.'

I started into the barn and he followed. 'Why, Uncle Coot?'

'You know what a stump does, don't you?'

18

'Well, nothing.'

'Same with this horse.'

Old Stump was a twenty-year-old horse that was known far and wide for not moving. That horse could outstand a tree. He used to be in the movies every now and then when a studio call would come for a horse that would stand without moving – like when a cowboy had to leap off a saloon roof or a balcony onto a horse, because for a gag like that you have to have a horse that won't move. A stunt man can get crippled if he lands on a western saddle just a few inches out of position – and Stump wouldn't move an inch. He would stand for hours with his head down, looking at something on the ground, and you could saddle him and spur him and holler yourself hoarse, and he would still stand there contemplating the ground.

We took the saddle out to him – I knew there wasn't any sense calling him over to us – and all the way Charles was quoting things out of the *Encyclopedia of Horses*. He went on about it so much that by the time we got to Stump I had heard just about all I cared to about horsemanship.

I saddled Stump and gave Charles a boost, and he got in the saddle without too much trouble. Then right away he said, 'I think the saddle is set too far back. It's very important for the saddle to be in the right position.'

'It's fine,' I said. 'It just feels that way because – '

He didn't let me finish. He threw his leg over and sat sideways on the saddle, getting ready, I reckon, to jump down. 'The *Encyclopedia* says that the saddle' – he started, but that was as far as he got because right then Stump started to move.

I wouldn't have believed it if I hadn't been right there because that horse hated to move. To this day I don't know what caused it. You would think that a horse who would stand still when a hundred-and-eighty-pound man landed on his back wouldn't mind a kid sitting sideways on him for a minute or two, but Stump did.

Stump stopped looking at the ground. He tossed his head, jerked around, and took a couple of side-steps. There's nothing gives a new rider a worse feeling than when his horse starts going sideways.

Charles squealed in a high voice, which wasn't one of anybody's rules of good horsemanship, and held on to the saddle with both hands. He got ready to slide off, only Stump came around real quick, kind of dipped under him, and Charles's leg went over the horse and – I was as surprised as he was – he ended up facing backwards.

I've done some backwards riding myself in rodeos, and I tell you it gives you a funny feeling the first time you try it. Charles squealed again and reached out for something to hold, only there wasn't anything there but Stump's tail. As soon as I saw him grab that, I knew he'd made a mistake.

Stump put his head down then and began to double buck, which is jumping up in the air like a goat, hitting the ground, and leaping again. Charles went with him – right up in the air with his arms and legs leaving the horse. I could see the sky between the horse and the boy, but then every single time Charles came right down on Stump again. It would have been a blessing for him to go ahead and get thrown, only he couldn't seem to do it.

Then Stump started hitting the ground with his legs as stiff as posts and his back legs kicking out be hind like a mule's. I ran after him, but before I could get to him, he started going around the corral backwards, twisting and turning. Then he finished by throwing himself down on his side, with Charles's left leg underneath. It worried me for a minute, because a man can break a leg getting jabbed by a stirrup after hitting the ground. That's why stunt men use a rubber hose stirrup on the left side.

I don't know what the *Encyclopedia* had to say about that situation, but I hollered, 'Get off, boy!' and Charles dragged his leg out from under Stump and scrambled out of the way, not hurt at all.

He kept going until he was on the other side of the corral fence. Then he stood there looking at Stump on the ground. After a minute he said, 'Is he dead?'

'Stump? No.'

'But he's just lying there.'

'He'll get up in a minute. That's the first exercise he's had in fifteen years.' The air went out of Charles then, and he looked smaller than ever. I said, 'Let's get back to the house.'

We started walking, him limping and me walking about the same way because of an old hip injury I got in a movie called *Guns of Navaho* that never bothers me in the saddle, only when I walk a distance. So we limped along, and I tried to think of something nice to say. Finally I said, 'You really stayed on that horse though.'

'I thought I never would get thrown.'

'Me too.'

'Actually I *wanted* to be thrown.' He hung his head and said, 'It probably seemed very funny to you.'

'No, it didn't seem funny.'

'I mean, you being such a great rider and all. I've seen you in the movies and I *know*.'

'Charles, didn't you ever get on a horse before?' I asked, changing the subject.

'No.'

'Didn't your mom ever – '

'*No.*' We took a few more steps and he said, 'Actually I haven't seen much of my mother.' His mom, my sister Jean, was the greatest trick rider I ever saw but not much of a mother. She had put Charles in school in the East – I guess more to get him out of the way than anything else – and then a month ago she had broken her shoulder in a rodeo in Phoenix. Money was scarce after that, and so she had sent Charles to me. She had said in her telegram it would be for a couple of months. Charles had said a couple of weeks. Knowing my sister, I was afraid the boy was here to stay.

'Well, that's the way Jean always was,' I said finally.

'Looks like at least she would have taught you to ride a horse.'

He stopped then – we were almost to the steps – and he put one hand on my arm. Behind his dusty eyeglasses his eyes were very bright. He said, 'But I'll learn. I'm going to be just like you.'

He kept looking at me, and I suddenly realized that all he knew about me he had learned from the movie screen. I was the man who did the impossible. I was the big hero, the guy who could leap cliffs, cross roaring streams, take forty-foot jumps into lakes, and fall a hundred times without hardly getting dusty. I was the guy who never got hurt.

And while I was standing there, trying to think of something to say, something that would show him what I really was, the lady came up and told us about the colt with wings.

SOMETHING WRONG AT THE MINNEYS'

This lady, Mrs. Minney, was another unexpected thing that had happened that spring. She and her husband had come to Texas from New York and had bought an old worn-down place across the road. They had come, Mrs. Minney told me, because she was writing a book about the cliff dwellers who used to live in the mountains around here, and she wanted to investigate the caves. Her husband was an artist who was tired of painting buildings and subways and was going to paint horses and cattle and mountains for a change. The Minneys had had a good bit of trouble getting settled because neither of them was a practical person. I don't think a day went by without Mrs. Minney's driving over in her truck to ask me about one thing or another. As soon as I saw her coming, I said to Charles, 'Well, something's wrong at the Minneys' again.'

He turned his head to watch the truck. 'Who are the Minneys?'

'That's Mrs. Minney coming now – the smartest woman I ever met to be so dumb.'

Mrs. Minney stopped her truck and got out. Her shirttail was flapping, and her hair was rising, and she came running over so fast Charles and I backed up a few steps. Even when she came to a halt, she still seemed to be going somewhere.

I said politely, 'Mrs. Minney, this is my nephew Charles.'

She said, 'Mr. Cutter! Mr. Cutter! Do you know anything about cutting the wings off a colt?'

I said, '*What?*'

She repeated it. 'Do you know anything about cutting the wings off a colt?'

I just stood there. I thought about this old Appaloosa I used to have with a map of Mexico on his side. It was my first stunt horse, and he could take as good a fall as you ever saw. And then one day – I hadn't had Mex a year when this happened – when we got ready to fall he just planted his feet and braced his neck and *stood*. I couldn't believe it. I knew Mex was telling me he was never going to fall again, but my mind couldn't take it in. Now Mrs. Minney had brought me up short in the same way.

'What?'

She sighed. 'Wings! Little wings about that long on either side of his shoulders.' She shook her head. 'I just don't know what to do about it. I've never seen a colt with wings before.'

'I haven't either, Mrs. Minney,' I said. 'But whatever those things turn out to be, I can assure you that they won't be wings.'

'Why not?'

'Because they *couldn't* be.'

She looked at me closer. I must have had an

amused look on my face, because she said, 'This is no joking matter, Mr. Cutter. I told you when we bought the mare that we wanted her and the colt for the grandchildren. I trusted you not to sell me a horse that was going to have a colt with anything extra.'

I lowered my voice, the way I do when I'm trying to calm an excited animal. 'Mrs. Minney, I believe there's just been a little mistake here.'

You can soothe a horse with your voice sometimes, but not Mrs. Minney. She got louder. 'If there's been a mistake, it's yours for thinking I'm going to stand for this.'

'Now, Mrs. Minney – '

'I tell you I am *frantic*. I went out this morning to load my truck, and there was the colt. It had been born during the night, and while I was standing there with my heart in my throat – there is nothing as moving as new life – well, then I saw the wings. And I tell you I haven't been the same since. Frank has been in the bedroom with the shades drawn. With his sensitive nature he's not even able to paint.'

'Mrs. Minney, there is no such thing as a horse with wings. There never has been and never will be.'

'But there *could* be.' Charles said. His eyes had gotten big with interest. He stepped right in front of Mrs. Minney. All his aches and pains seemed forgotten.

I said calmly, 'I beg your pardon, Charles, but I have seen horses and known horses since the day

26

I was born. And there never has been such a thing as a horse with wings.'

'There's a vase from Mycenae – it's in the National Museum in Greece – and there's a winged horse on it. Some people say that it's a scene from mythology, but others, including me, believe that there actually *was* a winged horse and – '

'Charles!'

'And then there are the horses from Pech Merle – that's a cave in France,' he continued in a rush.

'I am familiar with that cave,' Mrs. Minney said. I could see that she was far more impressed with Charles's knowledge of horses than with mine.

'And there are horses painted on the wall' – Charles went on – 'and above the horses are hand-shaped marks like wings.'

'That's true!' Mrs. Minney said. 'I never thought of it, but those marks *are* like wings.'

'And do you remember the skeleton found in the diggings at – '

'*Charles!*' He shut up long enough for me to say, 'Now that is enough! Mrs. Minney doesn't want to hear you trying to prove something that is impossible.'

'I do,' Mrs. Minney cried.

I ignored her. 'Mrs. Minney is worried enough without your adding to it. She doesn't care what's been painted on vases and cave walls and – '

'I do!' Mrs. Minney cried again.

'No, you don't!' She stepped back for a moment. 'What the three of us are interested in right now' –

I continued as calmly as I could – 'is what has been on this earth, actually been on this earth. And there has never been a horse with wings and never will be. Never!'

They both looked at me without speaking. Then Mrs. Minney sat down on the porch steps. She said, 'Well, actually, it is a relief, Mr. Cutter, to hear that.' She sighed and patted her face with her shirttail. 'Nobody knows what a relief it is to think you have a horse with wings and then find out you have a horse with – ' She broke off and looked at me. 'What would it be that the horse has?'

I did not want her to get excited again so I said, calmly, 'Well, since it's not wings, it will have to be something else. I think we can all agree on that.' I glanced from Mrs. Minney to Charles.

'Well, if it's *not* wings.' Charles said, 'then of course it *will* have to be something else, but I still think – '

I rested my hand on his shoulder so firmly that he choked down the rest of his words. 'What I am going to do, Mrs. Minney,' I continued, 'is come over to your place now, look at the colt, and tell you what he has.'

'Could I come too, Mrs. Minney?' Charles asked. 'I'd like to see this for myself. It is quite possible, you know, that this is the first winged colt in the – '

'Charles!'

'Of course you come.' Mrs. Minney took a deep breath and sighed. 'I feel better now. My trouble is that I get excited too easily. Another woman, seeing she had a colt with wings, would probably have the wings removed in a sensible way and go about her business.'

We climbed into the truck, and she said, 'The trouble is that all I can think about just now is investigating the caves, and when something happens to distract me, I get upset.'

'Your reaction seems normal to me,' Charles said. 'A colt with wings would be exciting and upsetting to anybody.'

I nudged Charles and said to Mrs. Minney, 'Anyway, everything's going to be all right *now*.'

Mrs. Minney backed the truck around and almost went in the ditch. Then she said, 'Yes, we'll look at the colt, find out what the trouble is, and then go in the house and have some lemonade. Would you like that?'

'I would,' Charles said.

'And tomorrow I'll be back at work. You cannot imagine what excitement there is in entering a cave where men lived hundreds of years ago and finding bits of sandals and bows and arrows. Even a bit of pollen centuries old can tell what plants these men had. A piece of bone can tell what diseases they suffered from. You, young man, with your knowledge of caves, probably know something about this already. You' – she leaned forward and looked at me – 'probably don't.'

'No'm.'

She drove for a few minutes. Then she shook her head and said, 'Still and all, I will feel easier in my mind when I know what those things on the colt are.'

I thought I heard Charles say 'Wings' under his breath. I wasn't sure, but I nudged him again anyway. That kept him quiet for the rest of the drive.

A SURPRISE

We stopped in front of the barn and got out. Mr. Minney stuck his head out the back window of the house, and Mrs. Minney called to him, 'Don't worry, Frank, those aren't wings on the colt after all.'

'They looked like wings to me,' he called back.

'Mr. Cutter says no.'

'What are they then, Mr. Cutter?' he asked, still leaning out the window.

'I'll let you know in a minute.' I took off my hat and waved it at him. This was a thing I used to do in the rodeo. It always seemed to give the crowd a lot of confidence in what I was about to do, but not Mr. and Mrs. Minney.

Mrs. Minney waited without speaking until my hat was back on my head, and then she said, 'Frank and I don't like this, Mr. Cutter. We don't like it at all.'

'Yeah, I got that feeling, Mrs. Minney.'

'We had such happy visions of the grandchildren riding around the ranch. Come on in the barn.' She took me and Charles in an iron grip and led us down to the last stall. We stood there for a moment because it took our eyes a while to see in the dim barn.

Peggy, the mare, was a fine chestnut with a white mane and tail. I reached over and scratched her muzzle and said, 'Good girl.' I couldn't see the colt – nothing but the spindly legs because he was on the other side of his mother, drinking her milk. Then Peggy shifted to the side, and there was the prettiest little Palomino colt you ever saw. The sun was coming through the window behind us, and it shone down on the colt. He was pale gold like wheat, and his mane and tail were silver. There was a white spot on his forehead.

As I watched he moved closer to his mother on his long awkward legs. I said, 'Why, there's nothing wrong with that colt. Look at him, Charles. He's perfect.'

'You're not going to get away with that,' Mrs. Minney said. 'There's something wrong and I know it. And don't think for a minute that you're going to give me a few comforting phrases and walk out of this barn like you're not responsible.'

I leaned forward and looked again. 'There are no wings on that colt.'

Right when I was saying that in a loud voice, the colt gave a little sidestep, nuzzled up against his mother, and kind of lost his balance. That was when something came fluttering out from his sides. It was a quick movement, so light and fast I almost didn't see it.

'I'd like to know what you call those,' Mrs. Minney said in a hard voice.

'Wings,' Charles said.

I said, 'Now hold on a minute. Horses don't have wings. That is a known fact.'

'This one does,' Charles said in a voice hushed with excitement. He turned and looked at me. His whole face was lit up.

For a minute I had a funny falling sensation. Like one time when I jumped a horse off a forty-foot cliff into a Missouri lake. When I jumped I was so scared I had a knot in my stomach as big as a cannon ball, and I thought that cannon ball would probably take me all the way to the bottom of the lake. I never made a jump like that again.

Charles turned to Mrs. Minney. 'Did you notice the shape of the wings, Mrs. Minney? They seem to have the same structure as those of the newborn swift and may never be really strong enough for flight.'

'I'm glad to see there's at least one person with brains in the Cutter family,' Mrs. Minney said.

'On the other hand,' Charles continued, 'the wings could increase in strength until they are quite capable of lifting the weight of horse and rider, which I estimate to be about fifteen hundred pounds.'

'The boy knows more about horses than a lot of other people in this barn,' Mrs. Minney said coldly. She had been a city lady for so long that she still carried over her shoulder a big leather handbag.

Now she kind of struck me with it so there wouldn't be any doubt who it was that didn't know much about horses.

'Mrs. Minney, listen, I am just as surprised as you are. There is an explanation for this though. I do know that.' The cannon ball in my stomach was so heavy I thought it was going to bring me down to my knees in the barn.

'Huh!'

'A perfectly logical and sensible explanation.'

'Ho!'

'I've been working with animals all my life, and I know there is always a logical and sensible explanation for everything.'

Without giving me a chance to try to think up this explanation, she nudged me again with her handbag. I said, 'All right, Mrs. Minney, if you'll just calm down a minute, I will step into the stall and have a look at the colt and find out what has happened.'

'I think I already know what has happened,' Charles said eagerly.

Mrs. Minney folded her arms in front of her. 'I think we *all* know what has happened,' she said. 'Only one of us is too stubborn to admit it.'

'What occurs to me,' Charles went on, 'is that this could be a throwback in the gene structure. Or perhaps the result of some drug that the mare took during the gestation period. Uncle Coot, did you give the mare any drugs?'

'No.'

'Did she have access to any strange foods?'

'Will you hush and let me try to find out what has really happened here?'

I opened the door of the stall, went in, and rubbed Peggy's neck. You have to move gently with a colt that's a few hours old. I usually try to handle them from birth to get them used to me. I knelt down and ran my hands over the colt. I turned to see him in a better light. Now the wings were the most obvious things in the world. I couldn't understand why I hadn't seen them earlier.

'Well?' Mrs. Minney said.

I put my hands on the colt's sides, and the wings came out and fluttered against my hands. I couldn't say anything because I felt like I had a wad of cotton rammed down my throat. I stood up slowly.

'Well?' Mrs. Minney said, louder.

I took off my hat and ran my hand over my hair. I shifted my pants up an inch or two and jammed my hands in my back pockets. I looked down at the colt and still I couldn't speak.

'Well?'

'Mrs. Minney.' I swallowed and the sound of it was like a gun going off in the quiet barn. 'Mrs. Minney, I don't know why and I don't know how, but you have got a colt with wings.'

TEXAS PEGASUS

As soon as I said that, Mrs. Minney took the leather handbag and brought it down hard on my head. It was like getting hit with a saddle. Then she started saying, 'I knew it, I knew it,' and 'You're not getting away with this. You're not, you're not, you're *not.*' I never saw such a mad woman in my life.

'Mrs. Minney, Mrs. Minney, ma'am, wait a minute. Listen!' I was trying to get out of the stall without upsetting Peggy and the colt and to shield my head at the same time. Mrs. Minney drew back and watched me. Her eyes were such little slits I couldn't even see what colour they were. 'Now, *listen,*' I cried again.

'I'm listening,' she said, taking a deep breath, 'but it better be good.'

'I just don't think you realize what you have here, Mrs. Minney, that's all I want to say. A horse with wings is a valuable thing. If you have the only winged horse in the country, in the world actually, then you've really got something.' She didn't look impressed. 'A winged pig would even be great, a winged squirrel, but a *winged horse*!'

'Actually there really are winged squirrels,' Charles said, 'only the wings are more like folds of skin.'

'Will you shut up, Charles?'

'I just thought you'd want to know about the flying squirrels.'

'Thank you.'

Charles said, 'And there are also flying lizards in Indonesia, but actually they only glide from tree to tree, and there is also some kind of creature called a flying fox, but I believe – '

'That's enough, Charles! Mrs. Minney is upset enough without your alarming her even more with these wild stories of flying foxes and lizards.'

'The thought of flying lizards in Indonesia is much less alarming to me,' Mrs. Minney said, 'than what is happening here in this barn now.'

'Well, sure,' I said. 'I never worried about those lizards much over there either.'

'You never even *knew* about those lizards!' She wasn't going to let me get away with a thing.

I said in a firm voice, 'The point is, Mrs. Minney, that this colt is quite possibly the most valuable colt that has ever been born.'

'All I want – ' she said. And she opened her eyes wide enough for me to see what colour they were. They were a cold grey. 'All I *wanted* was a horse that I could sit on and ride when I felt like it and that my grandchildren could sit on and ride when they came out to visit.'

'I know, but this – '

'And if you think we are going to get on any

horse with wings, you are mistaken.' She leaned forward and looked at me real close. I had a horse named Bumble Bee used to do that before she bit. 'If it's got wings,' she said, 'then it just might *fly*!' She pulled back and looked at me with her arms folded over her handbag.

'Mrs. Minney,' I said, 'what is it you want me to do? Whatever it is – just tell me and I'll do it.'

'That's more like it,' she said. 'I want one of two things. Either you remove those wings and leave no trace they were there – and frankly I don't think you can do that – or you take the mare and the colt back and refund my money.'

'It's my duty,' Charles said, 'to tell you that this time, Mrs. Minney, my uncle happens to be right. A horse with wings is valuable. The public is always eager to see something unusual and – '

Mrs. Minney put her hands on her hips. 'I thought better of you, young man, than that. If what you are suggesting is that I run some sort of carnival side show and exhibit this poor unfortunate animal – Why, I'd as soon turn babies out of their carriages.'

'I wasn't suggesting a carnival exactly, but television appearances would be a possibility. You could become famous.'

'What do I care for fame? What is fame except people recognizing you, and everybody I want to recognize me does so already.'

'But I mean really famous, *world* famous.'

'Young man, if you become famous because of something you have done, that is one thing.

38

Becoming famous because of something you *own* is another matter. Now I don't want to hear another word.' She turned to me. 'Are you taking the colt and mare back or not?'

I looked down at the little Palomino nuzzling against his mother. I wanted the colt all right. I wanted him a lot. I don't guess a man can be a stunt man for half his life and not want a winged colt.

'Well?' she said.

'I would be pleased to take the colt and mare back.'

'And no *forcing* this animal to fly either,' she said. 'I don't want to turn on my television some night and see you forcing him to fly.'

'No'm.'

'I want you to be good to this horse. He'll fly if he wants to.'

'Yes'm.'

'Shake on it.'

I put out my hand and we shook. Then she got a firmer grip on my hand and leaned over and said, 'And there better not be any tricks.'

'There won't be.'

Charles and I took a last look at the colt, and then the three of us went out of the barn. Mr. Minney was still leaning out the back window. I tried to pretend I didn't see him and kept walking, but he called, 'Mr. Cutter! Mr. Cutter!' I kept walking and he called, 'Mr. Cutter, did you find out what those things were?' I kept walking. 'The things we thought were wings – what are they?'

'Mr. Minney's calling you,' Charles said. 'He wants to know what – '

'I heard him.' I shifted my hat and said in a low voice, 'They're wings, Mr. Minney.'

'What?' Mr. Minney called.

'*Wings!*' I shouted. '*Wings!*'

'But I thought you said – '

'He was *wrong*,' Mrs. Minney said behind me. She sounded real satisfied.

We hesitated a minute, but she didn't say anything about the lemonade or driving us home in the truck, so Charles and I began walking. I was too stunned to talk, but Charles ploughed right in.

'You know, I thought of something else,' he said. 'There's a statue in one of the French museums of a horse with wings and also – '

'There is no such thing as a colt with wings,' was all I could manage to say.

'Also there was Pegasus – he was the most famous flying horse in the world – and do you know how they tamed him, Uncle Coot?'

'There is no such thing as a – '

'With a golden bridle. And I also remember reading an article in *Time* magazine about this man who believes that Greek myths like Pegasus really did exist, that they were super beings from other planets. So maybe there *was* a winged colt at one time, and this colt is a descendant!'

'There is no such thing as – '

'And there's another statue – I think it's Egyptian – and – ' Charles kept talking about flying horses all the way to the ranch. I thought he never would run out of things to say. I thought he must have spent the biggest part of his life reading books. Finally I interrupted and said, 'Wait a minute. How do you know all this stuff, Charles?'

'I read.'

'Well, yeah, sure, everybody reads, but they don't know all that stuff.'

'Well, I read a lot. I once decided to read every book in the school library – that was because I had a lot of extra time, you know, like during vacations when everyone else had gone home?' He looked up at me. 'But anyway, getting back to the statues, if there *was* no such thing as a flying horse, well, then why doesn't *one* of those countries have a flying bear or a flying dog? You never see statues of flying dogs.'

'I don't know, Charles. The only place I ever saw anything about a horse with wings was on a gas station sign, and I can't even remember which one it was now.' The truth was I was starting to feel dazed. It was like the time I did a gag for a movie called *Riders of the Plain*. They tied this rope around my chest, and it was about two hundred feet long and six men were holding the other end of the rope. Well, I got on my horse and started out, full gallop, until the rope was played out, and then I was yanked backward from the saddle. It was supposed to look like a blow from a rifle had knocked me from my horse. It doesn't sound like a bad gag – I'd done worse – but when I slammed into the ground, my knee rammed into my forehead. I wandered around for the rest of the day feeling dazed and stupid. That was the same way I felt now. I had seen that colt. I had looked right at him. The wings had touched my hands. I still couldn't take it in.

'I wish,' Charles was saying, 'that I was close to a really good research library, because I would like to look into this matter in my spare time.' He stumbled in his excitement. 'Hey, you know what I'm going to do? I'm going to start a record of the colt and keep notes on everything he does. Tomorrow I'll take pictures with my Polaroid and – what time can we get the colt?'

'Afternoon.'

'He'll be walking by then?' He looked up at me. His eyes were as round as quarters.

'He'll be walking,' I said. 'He may even be flying.'

And Charles leaped up in the air and hollered, 'Yeah!' I guess I would have joined him if it hadn't been for my hip. I resettled my hat and kept walking.

After a minute Charles said, 'Oh, yeah, Uncle Coot, I just thought of something else. There's this Etruscan vase – it was dug up near Cerveteri – and on this vase is a wonderful flying horse. It –'

THE STORM THAT WENT ON AND ON

We got home with the colt the next day, and I began to realize right then that my past experience with horses wasn't going to help me as much as I'd thought.

This colt was different. It wasn't just his wings. It was something in his nature, something that made him shyer, less predictable than other colts. And he was lightning quick. It took me the best part of two days to ease a light halter on him, and after two weeks I was still trying to teach him to back up on command.

All this time Charles was writing down everything the colt did in a notebook. I never saw anybody write so much. It wasn't the kind of thing a person would casually take down about an animal, but real scientific things, measurements and behaviour and all.

I was in the notebook too. Everything I tried with the colt during those first weeks was written down. And if I'd stop for a minute he'd say, 'How're you doing, Uncle Coot? Is anything wrong?'

I'd shake my head. 'Nothing more than usual, Charles.'

'What do you mean?'

'I just mean that it's not going to be as easy to train Alado as you're thinking.' Alado was what Charles had named the colt because *alado* means 'winged' in Spanish.

'Oh, I know it's not going to be easy, but you can do it. You've already haltered him.'

'Yeah, but it's almost like working with a different kind of animal, Charles, it's – '

'I know, Uncle Coot. That's why it's so lucky that you're the one training him. Nobody else could do it.'

'Yeah.' And I'd hear him click his ballpoint pen so he'd be ready to write down what I tried next.

Those first weeks had a strangeness about them. There is something about a new and unknown horse that usually brings up the spirit in a man. When I was a boy there were wild horses on the range, and there was something about seeing an untamed horse tossing its mane and running like the wind – didn't matter if it was a shining black, a great mustang, or a flea-bitten pinto – that made the blood rise in me, that made me feel free and wild too, even though I was nothing but a skinny, patched-pants boy.

I should have felt that way even more about Alado, because he was wild and free in a way that I had never imagined, but I didn't. I felt about the colt the same way I had felt about the boy when he turned to me that first day with his face shining and said, 'I want to be just like you.' It was a sort of worried, uneasy feeling, as if something was going to happen that I couldn't control.

It showed in the pictures we took with Charles's Polaroid. I had a stiff, strained look. The colt was a pale unnatural blur. And Charles looked like a kid who had just discovered Christmas. To look at those pictures, you would know that there was going to be trouble, and the trouble came in August with as bad a storm as I ever saw.

Southwest Texas has always had a lot of storms. I remember when I was a boy there was one so bad that my grandad lost five head of cattle and two horses on the range in one afternoon. The lightning just seems to pour down from the sky like arrows, hitting whatever's in the open. And I remember that afternoon my grandad got so mad that he stood up and hollered, 'All right, lightning, go ahead and strike me and the boy too and be done with it. Go ahead! Strike us!' It scared me, standing there beside him, and one time later when I did get hit by lightning on the range – got thrown out of the saddle and came to lying on the ground with my mouth filling with rain water – the first thing I thought of was my grandad yelling at the lightning.

The horses were restless that afternoon, sensing that a storm was coming. The air was so full of electricity that little balls of electricity like peas were flashing on their ears and tails.

Late in the day the horses came up closer to the house, stood in a restless bunch for a while, and ran away. Then they came back and did the whole thing again.

'Shouldn't we do something?' Charles asked in a worried voice.

These storms make me as uneasy as the horses because weather out here is usually an excess. If it rains, it can rain six inches in one hour; or if it's dry, there won't be a drop of rain for two months; or if it's hailing, balls of hail will make dents in trucks and raise knots on people's heads. There just doesn't seem to be such a thing as a gentle storm in south-west Texas.

'Nothing we can do,' I said.

He looked to the horizon, which was black and streaked with lightning. Then he looked at the horses moving nervously around the corral, pawing at the ground, running in spurts.

Alado was the worst. He would run first this way, pause to listen, then run the other way. The rumblings of thunder caused his ears to flatten against his head and he tossed his mane in the air again and again. The sound of thunder doubles over the mountains and rumbles down twice as loud as you ever heard it anywhere else.

'My main worry,' Charles said finally, 'is the colt.'

'The colt's all right. He's with his ma and they've got a shelter.'

'But, Uncle Coot – '

'These horses stay out on the range all winter. They can take care of themselves.'

'But – '

'They're all right.'

We went into the house and had a supper of fried beans and bread. Charles didn't do more than push his beans around on his plate. 'I've heard of lightning striking animals,' he said finally in a low voice.

'It'll do that occasionally,' I admitted.

'And one stroke of lightning can measure more than fifteen million volts.'

'I guess. I never measured one.'

He didn't say anything else for a minute, and I thought that the trouble with him was that he knew too much for his own good. He got up, pushed his plate away, and went to the window. If the horses were close to the house he could see them from there. I watched him leaning against the glass. Then he looked down at his hands and said what he had been working up to all along. 'We could bring the colt into the house.'

It was only seven o'clock now, but black as night. Everything was still. The wind hadn't started to blow yet, and for the moment there was no thunder either.

'I think Alado's all alone by the fence. I think all the other horses are in the shelter.' He turned around and started stammering, 'Uncle Coot, please! I know I'm not supposed to bother you. Mom told me how you hate to be bothered, but if you'll just do this one thing I'll never ask you for anything again. I'll stay completely out of your way. You won't even know I'm around.'

'Now, hold on, Charles. Be sensible.'

'I *am* being sensible. The colt's not like any of the

others. He's got wings and if the wind gets strong enough – well, anything could happen. He's *got* to come in the house.'

I could see that he wasn't going to be able to sleep a wink with the colt out in the storm. I didn't imagine I'd sleep too well myself. I said, 'All right, I'll get the colt.'

It was a mistake and I knew it, but I pulled on my poncho, yanked my hat down on my head, and started out the door. 'You stay here though. Understand?'

'I will, and thank you very, very much.'

'Just stay here.'

'Yes sir, and I promise I will never, ever be any trouble to you again as long as I live.'

He would have promised anything to get me out the door. He was all but pushing me. I stepped out onto the porch, and right then the lightning struck somewhere to the west. I was ready to turn and go back into the house. If I'd had good sense I would have. Only I looked back at Charles in the doorway, and I stepped off the porch and ran for the corral.

The wind came up as I got halfway across the yard. It came up quick and strong at my back and doubled me over. I ran in a crouch to the corral. I couldn't see the horses anywhere, but I started struggling to get the gate open against the wind.

Right then there was another crash of lightning. This one had a human sound. It was like somebody had screamed in my ear, and I felt like somebody had hit me on the head with a sledge hammer at the same time. The pain went all the way through me, down to my toes, and then I blacked out.

When I came to, I was crumpled up against the fence like a piece of uprooted weed. In a movie called *Six Outlaws* I was once thrown right through a balsa wood fence. It was so real-looking that when the movie was shown, people in the audience would let out a moan when I went through that fence. It was nothing, though, I can tell you, compared to slamming into this real fence. Every bone in my body hurt.

I tried to get to my feet by holding on to the fence post, but my legs and arms were like rope, and my head must have weighed a hundred pounds. Finally I gave up and slumped to the ground and bent my head over my trembling knees.

The storm lasted for another hour. There was a hard blistering rain and deadly lightning and wind and some hail thrown in for good measure. I just lay there. I couldn't do anything but pull my poncho over my head to keep the worst of it off my face and wait. I didn't know then, and I still don't, whether it was getting hit by lightning or being slammed against the fence that shook me up. Whatever the cause, I was in bad shape.

After a bit the rain slackened, and Charles came running out with a black umbrella he had brought with him from school. The wind tore it out of his hand first thing and tumbled it out of sight. He ran over to where I was, zigzagging in the wind. He looked so frail I half expected him to go blowing away after the umbrella.

'Are you all right?' he hollered, bending over me.

I couldn't do more than nod.

'Where's Alado?' He was looking over the fence now, trying to see where the horses were.

I reached out and grabbed him, and he helped me to my feet. It was hard getting to the house with him looking backwards the whole way. But we finally made it, and I sank down on my bunk.

'I'll get you some dry clothes,' Charles said, but I shook my head. He hesitated and then covered me up with a blanket.

'Did you see Alado out there anywhere?' he asked in a worried voice, tucking the blanket around my shoulders.

I shook my head.

'Do you think he's in the shelter?'

I nodded.

'Do you think you'll feel like going out in a little while and making sure he's all right?' Before I could shake my head there was the sound of the wind getting stronger. Charles glanced toward the door. 'I think another storm's coming.'

It was the last thing I heard because I closed my eyes and fell asleep. When I woke up it was dawn. Charles was slumped over by the window, his face on the sill.

He woke up as soon as I stirred and came over. 'How are you this morning, Uncle Coot?'

'Well, I'm better,' I said. 'A little sore and stiff

maybe.' Actually I was like a board. If I bent, I would most probably break.

'It's my fault,' he said, looking down at his feet.

'Well, don't let's get into that.' The last thing I wanted right then was an argument about whose fault my condition was.

'No, it *is* my fault,' he continued. 'I thought about it all night. Anybody else but you would probably have been killed.'

'Yeah.' I was just too tired and sore to argue. I got up, moved my arms a little, and shook my legs. I expected my hip to be hurting more than anything else because that's my weak spot. Instead it was my shoulders. I started over to the dresser, moving real slow, to get some clothes, and when I passed the window I stopped and looked out.

In the pale light of dawn the whole place had a strange look. Water was still lying on the ground because too much rain had fallen to be taken into the earth, and everything had a faded, colourless look. On the horizon the huge orange sun was just coming into view.

Charles came and stood by me and said, 'I don't see the horses.' He grabbed my arm in both his hands and yanked. 'I don't see the horses!'

'Now, don't get upset.' I limped out on the porch and stood at the edge of the steps. Charles came out and grabbed my arm again.

I said quickly, 'Don't yank my arm, Charles, because my shoulders are – '

'Where's the *colt*, Uncle Coot?' he asked, yanking

51

my arm harder. His voice broke and I thought my shoulder had too. 'Where's Alado?'

THE SEARCH THAT DIDN'T
GO ON LONG ENOUGH

A person can see for miles from my front porch, but the only horse in sight this morning was Stump. He was standing about a hundred yards from the fence looking at a puddle on the ground.

'Where could the horses be?' Charles asked in a funny voice. The gate had blown off its hinges during one of the storms, and I figured the horses had left some time during the night.

'Now, don't go getting upset.'

'I can't help it. They're gone.' He looked at me. 'Alado's gone.'

'I can see that.'

'Well, what are you going to do?'

I sighed, and even that hurt my shoulders. 'What I'll do is ride out this morning and find them.' I made it sound easier than it was. In my condition even lifting the saddle wasn't going to be a cinch.

'I'll go too,' Charles said.

'Charles, look, I think you'd be better off staying here.'

'But I want to go. I want to help.'

'I know that.' The plain truth was that Charles

hadn't caught on to riding. He'd tried – I'll give him that – but he just hadn't gotten the hang of it. He was always yelling proudly, 'Look at me, Uncle Coot,' and I'd look just in time to see him bounce out of the saddle or something.

I said, 'Well, Charles, I'd like your company, but there's only one horse and that's Stump, and – '

'I could ride behind you.'

' – and I'd make better time alone.'

He ducked his head and said, 'Oh, well sure. I should have thought of that.'

'Let's get some breakfast.'

I went into the house, changed my clothes, and scrambled some eggs. We ate without saying anything. Charles kept getting up from the table and going to the window to see if the horses had come back. I don't think a bite of food went into his mouth the whole meal.

After breakfast I saddled Stump, mounted, and sat there. For the first time I knew how that horse felt, because right then I could have sat in the saddle looking down at the ground for about ten hours, not moving once.

'Good luck, Uncle Coot,' Charles called. He was on the porch, watching us with one arm wrapped around the post.

'Right.' I finally got Stump to take a few steps.

'Good luck!'

I nodded to him – I would have waved if I could have – and very slowly Stump and I set off.

There's something about this land that always stays

the same. I thought about that as I rode. A lot has happened here. A lot of people have come and gone – Mexicans, traders, Comanches, ranchers, outlaws – but they didn't change the land. It's just too big, I guess, too hard. It's the kind of land, though, where a colt could disappear without leaving any more of a trace than the people.

It was a long morning. I came back to the ranch about noon with Clay and two other horses, and Charles was waiting right there on the porch where I'd left him. His face, when he saw I didn't have the colt, got a little tighter-looking.

'Didn't you even see Alado?' he asked.

'No.'

He paused, swinging one foot out over the steps. 'Would you tell me if you had?'

He looked at me, and I knew he wanted to know if I had found the colt dead. I said, 'When I find him, dead or alive, you'll know about it.' And I saddled Clay and rode off again.

'Good luck, Uncle Coot,' he called.

'Right.'

By the end of the week he was still calling 'Good luck' as I rode off, but luck was running out. I had gone over my ranch and most of the land beyond, and I had found every horse and colt but Alado.

I was keeping my eye on the sky now, watching for vultures more than anything else. I found myself thinking about a scene in an old movie called *The Red Pony*. In this scene vultures flew down and ate the dead pony. The way they did that was to tie

55

strips of raw meat onto a dummy pony. Then they got some real hungry vultures and let them loose, and the vultures flew right down in front of the cameras and began to tear off pieces of flesh. It was a real-looking scene, and it kept flashing in and out of my mind as I rode.

By now I knew I wasn't going to find Alado. I figured he had died somewhere up in the mountains or drowned in one of the swift streams that form in the arroyos after a heavy rain. The only good thing about the situation was that Alado had been weaned, so he might not starve to death; that is, if he *was* still alive.

I kept looking long after I knew there was no hope, because in my own way I felt as bad about losing the colt as Charles did. Alado hadn't been my whole life, of course, the way he'd been with Charles, but I sure hated it that he was gone.

There was one other thing too. Charles had a lot of confidence in me, in the fact that I *would* find the colt. He kept saying over and over, 'You'll find him. I know you will,' and I could see he believed it. A couple of times I said, 'Look, maybe I can find him, but more likely I can't, Charles.'

He would always answer, 'You can. Uncle Coot, you can do *anything*.'

Finally, though, I had to give up. I didn't say anything, but one morning at the time I usually saddled Clay and went off, I started fixing the fence instead.

Charles came running out and cried, 'Uncle Coot!'

I said, 'What?' I looked at him but I didn't stop working.

'Aren't you going out to look for Alado?' He paused, and I couldn't see his eyes because the sun was shining on his glasses. To tell you the truth I was glad of it.

I stopped what I was doing and said, 'Charles, look, I want to explain something to you.'

'Aren't you going?'

I thought suddenly how I must have looked standing there — not a big man, dusty, scarred face, leaning to favour my bum hip. I wondered why he couldn't see me like I was. He had told me once the first time he ever saw me was in the movies, and I was leaping a forty-foot canyon. I reckon an impression like that stays with a boy.

I rubbed the scar on my cheek. 'Now, listen to me, Charles,' I said.

'Are you going or not?'

I paused and let my breath out in a low sigh. Then I said, 'No.'

He shifted and the glare left his glasses, and I could see his eyes then. They had a blank look as if he hurt too bad to understand what was happening.

'Charles, I'm not giving up because I don't *want* to find the colt. Don't think that. It's just no use. I've gone over every mile of ground ten times and —'

'You don't have to explain.'

'If I thought there was any way in the world to

get Alado back I would be out there every day. It's been over two weeks, though, and no trace of him. You're smart enough to know what that means.'

He kept looking at me for a moment, and then he turned away. 'Wait a minute, Charles, I'm not through.' He stopped, but now he was looking at the mountains instead of me. I said, 'If there was any way to get the colt back I would. Now that's the truth.'

He didn't say anything.

I said, 'I know what the colt meant to you, but you're too bright a boy to hope for the impossible.'

'It's not impossible for you,' he said in a low voice. He looked at me. His voice rose. 'Anyway, you don't have any idea what the colt means to me.'

I looked into his eyes. I thought of myself when I was ten years old, and my grandad, who I was living with, led my horse Sandy away and sold him. I ran after my grandad that day and struck him and tried to pull the rope out of his hands, and finally they had to lock me in the corncrib. I can still remember yelling and throwing corncobs at that locked door.

Charles said, 'Can I go now?' He started digging up dust with one foot. 'I've got something to do.'

Without waiting for me to nod, he started walking toward the house. I let him go. When I went in for lunch the first thing I saw was that all his notebooks and papers about Alado had been put away. The table where he kept them was cleared and pushed against the wall. The Polaroid pictures of me and him and Alado had been taken from the mantel.

I wanted to say something, but I couldn't find the right words. We sat down, ate, and I went back to work. Neither of us said much of anything for the rest of the week. And when we did start talking we just said things that needed saying like, 'Pass the beans,' or, 'I need some help with the pump.' Neither of us mentioned the colt.

Time kept passing and I kept thinking that things would get back to normal before long. But it didn't happen. I think Charles wrote his mom the first of September and asked if he could leave the ranch and go back East to school. I don't know for sure he did that – he wouldn't have told me about it anyway – but one day he got a letter from his mom that made him look like he didn't feel good.

I said, 'Any news from your mom?'

'Nothing special,' he said.

'How's her shoulder?'

'Fine. She'll probably be sending for me before long.'

'Sure.'

Without looking at me he added, 'But I guess I'd better go ahead and start school here, just in case.'

'Sure.'

The canyon between us was wider than anything I ever jumped in the movies, and it would have taken a better stunt man than I ever was to get over it.

SOMETHING WRONG AT THE
MINNEYS' AGAIN

It was the last of September and Charles was in school. This left me on the ranch alone now during the day, which was what I had wanted when Charles first came. But for some reason being by myself didn't make me feel as good as I had thought it would.

I was saddling Clay one morning when I looked up and saw Mrs. Minney's truck coming up the road. It was about nine o'clock in the morning, and she was moving like a freight express. The cloud of dust behind her shot straight up in the air and stayed there.

The truck made a half turn in front of the house, skidded in the dust, and came to a stop. I could see that Mrs. Minney was really upset this time, because it took her four tries to get the door open.

I hurried over and said, 'Let me do that for you, Mrs. Minney.' I put out my hand and she struck at it through the open window.

'Don't you touch my door!'

I drew back and waited. She tugged the handle around and finally kicked the door open with her foot. Then she got out of the truck and stood looking at me without saying a word. Her face didn't have any more give to it than hardened dough.

I thought about this black steer my grandad used to have that got bogged down in a quicksand stream once. My grandad and me tried to pull him out, but we couldn't. He was stuck too deep. There wasn't any danger of him sinking lower and drowning though, so we left him overnight and came back the next morning with the mules. We knew in advance he was going to be mad because he was always bad-tempered, and standing overnight in quicksand wasn't going to improve him any. We roped him, pulled him out with the mules, and cut him loose. When he got to his feet he stood there glaring. Right before he started after us his eyes were as savage as anything you ever saw in your life. They looked a lot like Mrs. Minney's eyes right now.

Mrs. Minney reached out her finger and poked me in the chest. 'You ought to be whipped,' she said.

'What?'

'Whipped!' she shouted. 'You ought to be whipped and run out of town.'

'What are you talking about, Mrs. Minney?'

'You think you can get away with anything, treat people and animals any way.'

'I don't know what you're talking about.'

'Huh!'

'No, I really don't.'

'Ho!'

'Mrs. Minney, if you'd just calm down and explain.'

'Ha!' By this time she had me backed up against the side of the house, and her finger had almost poked a hole in my chest. I never saw such a mad woman. 'You don't fool me,' she said.

'But Mrs. Minney, I don't know what you're talking about. I really don't. You probably won't believe me, but I'm as dumb as that old horse over there.' I pointed to Stump.

She looked from Stump to me. 'At least,' she said coldly.

I sighed. 'Now just start at the beginning, Mrs. Minney, *please*.'

She folded her arms and looked at me. Her eyes were real narrow. 'Well,' she said, 'last night Frank and I went to bed early. He had been painting all day and I had been getting soil samples from caves and we were tired. It was about twelve o'clock and we were lying in bed, listening to the wind – did you ever hear such a wind? And then, just when the wind reached a peak, there was a terrible, ear-splitting crash on our tin roof.'

'A crash?'

'The most terrible racket I ever heard. Mr. Minney and I sat up in bed and looked at each other. He said, "Something's on our roof." My heart stopped. We listened a minute more and he said, "It's a cougar. A cougar has jumped onto our roof from the mesa and – "'

'I have never seen cougar around here, Mrs.

Minney,' I interrupted. 'It couldn't have been that. There are bobcats sometimes, but they wouldn't make a hard sound like you're describing.'

'Don't try to be smart with me, hear? Frank heard the noise and he thought it was a cougar and I heard it and it sounded like a cougar to me too. You, who didn't hear a thing, are now becoming an expert on it.'

'I'm sorry.'

'Well, if you don't keep quiet, I'll just go into town and find the sheriff. I imagine he'll listen without giving me a lot of unnecessary talk about bobcats.'

'I won't say another word.'

She gave me a hard look before she continued. 'So Frank said he would go and see if he could get the cougar off the roof, but I said, "No, if anybody goes after the cougar, it had better be me," and finally he agreed.'

'I imagine so.'

'I got the broom and the rifle and the flashlight and went out the back door. All this time there was such a clattering on the roof you wouldn't believe it.' She began to wring her hands. 'I was shaking like a leaf. I couldn't even push the button on the flashlight, Mr. Cutter.' She began to wring her hands harder than ever. 'And then the moon came from behind a cloud and I looked up on the roof and I dropped the flashlight *and* the rifle *and* the broom.'

'What was it, Mrs. Minney?'

'Because there on my roof – ' She broke off to get her breath.

'Yes, Mrs. Minney?'

'There on my roof – '

'Mrs. Minney, *what was on your roof?*'

She looked at me. 'The winged colt.' And when she said that, she reached out and poked my chest so hard I thought there would be a place left in my skin for the rest of my life, like a hole I have in my leg where a steer horned me.

'The winged colt?'

She nodded.

'But that couldn't be. Mrs. Minney, the colt was lost in a storm in August and we haven't seen him since.'

'He was on my roof last night.'

'But, Mrs. Minney – '

'He was on my roof last night, and as soon as I saw him I called Frank, and Frank said that one of us was going to have to climb up and carry him down.'

I was so stunned I couldn't speak.

'What appeared to have happened, Mr. Cutter,' she went on, 'was that the colt was over on the mesa, and during the wind storm he got blown onto our roof. He was pathetic, scared as a rabbit. I said to Frank, "Well, if anybody's going to climb up there it better be me since I've been climbing cliffs for two months now".'

'And he agreed.'

She nodded. 'So we got the ladder and I started

up. A roof is not as pleasant a place as you'd think, I can tell you that. But I inched over to where the colt was and I grabbed. For some reason, Mr. Cutter, even though I slipped over easy as a snake, it scared him. And then – I tell you, Mr. Cutter, it makes my heart stop to think about it even now – and then those wings came out and the colt flew off the roof. It was awful. He flew to the ground and I, having no wings, just fell right off like a sack of grain and lay there for twenty minutes.'

'And the colt?'

'He was fine. He landed about twenty feet from the house.'

'Where is he now?' I said quickly. 'Do you know?'

'By this time I was able to get up and go in the house,' she continued. 'I got an apple and came back and held it out to the colt. He came over in the light and he was pitiful, Mr. Cutter, half starved. I could count his ribs.'

'But where is he *now*?'

'Later I said to Frank, 'I should think that man' – meaning *you* – 'would take better care of his animals than this. I should think he would look after his colts and not let them fly all over the countryside scaring people out of their beds!'

'Mrs. Minney, where is the colt *now*?' By this time I was ready to take her and shake an answer out of her, like my grandad did to me when I was a boy and got a nickel caught in my throat – just turned me up and shook until it plopped out in front of everybody in church. '*Where is the colt?*'

She looked at me. 'The colt is in my barn.' She held up one hand. 'But before you come get him, I want some assurance that this sort of thing is not going to happen again. Frank and I need our sleep at night. We cannot be crawling up on roofs to get colts in the middle of the night and then have them flying around the yard like birds.'

'Yes'm.' I wasn't going to give her an argument about anything now.

'And so I'm going to ask for your promise that this is not going to happen again.'

'I promise.'

She looked at me hard, and then she nodded. 'I'm going to give you one more chance, Mr. Cutter. I just hope I won't regret it.'

'You won't.'

'Well, then, you can come get the colt this afternoon.' She started walking back to the truck.

'Mrs. Minney, one thing before you go.' She turned and looked at me. 'Just thank you, Mrs. Minney, that's all.'

'Huh!'

'No, I mean it. Charles has had a bad time over this. He cared a lot about that colt.'

'Too much, if you ask me.'

'Yes'm, and he sort of blamed me for what happened.'

'Well, I should think so.' She looked at me. 'Of course it's none of my business, but that boy's mother ought to be taking care of him.'

'I know that.'

'An uncle is no substitute for a mother.'

'Yes'm.'

She looked at me again. I thought her eyes could see all the way through me. 'Still,' she said, 'I guess you're better than nothing.'

'Well, I'm trying to be.' She got into the truck and looked at me while she was turning the key. I said, 'Thank you again, Mrs. Minney. I really mean it.'

'Huh!' she said and drove off in a cloud of dust.

TO GET A COLT

When Charles got home from school that day I was waiting for him by the truck. I said, 'Put your books down and get in. We got an errand to do.'

Charles set his books on the edge of the porch and got in the truck. 'Where are we going?'

'To get a colt.'

He didn't answer, just looked straight ahead at the road. I had offered Charles one of the other colts after Alado was lost, but he had said no. And I had sold the colts about a week ago.

'Why are you getting another colt?' he asked. 'What kind is it?'

'Palomino.'

He looked at me when I said that. 'Palomino?' he asked in a funny voice. For a long time we had been real careful what we said to each other. Never once had we mentioned Alado. Even the word 'Palomino' was out. Still, the colt had always been right beneath the surface of both our minds. Now it was out in the open.

'Palomino,' I said again.

'Where is it?'

'Over at Mrs. Minney's. It got up on her roof last

night, and she came over this morning all upset about it.' I said this with a real straight face, and he looked at me and didn't say anything. 'What she figured happened' – I went on – 'was that the colt kind of got blown over from the mesa, carried by his wings, and – '

When he heard that, he grabbed me by the arm. 'Is it our colt? Is it Alado?'

'Yeah.'

'Is that the truth?'

'Yeah.'

'Uncle Coot, is that the *real* truth?'

'*Yeah*.'

'Don't kid me, Uncle Coot. Is that the real *honest* truth?'

'Yeah, it is the real honest truth.'

'I don't believe you.'

We went on like that all the way to Mrs. Minney's. Finally, when we drove up in the yard and Charles saw Mrs. Minney standing there waiting for us with her hands on her hips, he began to believe.

'Where's the colt?' he asked. He got out of the truck so fast he went down on his knees in the dust. He scrambled up and stood there. He looked like he'd stopped breathing.

'He's in the barn, young man, but I want to tell you one thing before we get him, the same thing I told your uncle. A colt is to be taken care of and not allowed to fly over people's houses in the dead of night.'

'Yes'm. Can I – '

'If you can't take care of a colt, you don't deserve to have one.'

'No'm, can I see him now?'

She gave both of us a good long look and then she said, 'Come on,' and led the way into the barn.

Alado was in the back stall, standing quietly, but as soon as he saw us, he started moving around. I said, 'Stay back, Charles,' because a colt can injure himself real easy in the first year of his life. You even have to be careful of a nail sticking out of the stall because a colt will just go wild sometimes. 'Let's stay back.' I took Charles by the arm and held him, because he was bent on running right into the stall and throwing himself on the colt.

He stayed but he didn't like it. We waited a bit, the three of us, while I talked to the colt and gradually we moved closer.

I had been feeling mighty good up until this point, but I got solemn fast. The colt was the sorriest sight I had seen in a long time, thin and shaky in the legs, and I could count all his ribs. It worried me. I'd seen it happen before. Colts that have a bad first year never make it up sometimes. They never recover the growth they've lost. You can sometimes spot a colt that's been neglected just by its shape, even when it gets older.

I took the halter I'd brought with me and stepped closer. We had been putting a halter on Alado from the time he was two weeks old. Now he shied and jumped backwards. I calmed him finally and got the halter on and led him out into the yard.

There's a way to lead a colt – you keep his shoulder against your leg or hip and never pull him behind you like a toy. Alado wouldn't stay with me though; he kept pulling away and shying, and it took us a while to get him in the trailer.

Just when we were ready to drive off, Mrs. Minney came to where I was standing by the truck. I said, 'You don't have to say another word, Mrs. Minney. I am going to take the best care of this colt you ever saw,' because I thought she was going to light into me again about the way we'd treated Alado.

Instead she shook her head and said, 'You know, it's a funny thing, Mr. Cutter, but I thought I saw another animal with Alado last night up on the mesa. Could that be possible?'

'Another animal? I don't think so.'

'But Mr. Minney got the same impression.'

'Another animal *with* the colt?'

'Either with him or after him,' she said. 'We couldn't tell which.'

Right then Charles called from the back of the truck. 'Come on, Uncle Coot, Alado's getting restless.'

'I'll be right there, Charles.' I turned back to Mrs. Minney. 'What kind of animal was it?'

'Mr. Cutter, I've told you all I know.'

'Could it have been another horse?'

She shook her head. 'Not big enough.'

'A coyote?'

'I never saw a coyote. Now, Mr. Cutter, that is all I know.'

'Are you coming, Uncle Coot?' Charles called.

'Right away.' I got in the truck and backed around. On the way home I gave some thought to what Mrs. Minney had said, but when we got the colt in the corral, I forgot everything but his condition. He was pitiful, gaunt as a rail.

'He looks so bad,' Charles said, leaning over the fence.

'I know.' Alado was standing on the far side of the corral now. His energy, every bit of it, was gone. His wings had a droopy look to them as if they were too heavy to hold to his sides. His head was turned to the ground.

'Will he ever get strong again?' Charles asked. I knew it hurt him to see the colt in such a poor condition. It sure hurt me.

'Well, we'll do what we can,' I answered. 'We'll double his feed and put an egg in it and some butter. Before you know it, he'll be stronger than Clay.'

'I hope so.' Charles turned. 'I'll go mix up some feed right now.' He left and started whistling halfway across the yard. I stood there staring at the colt. I thought as I looked at him how very vulnerable he was. What an easy prey. I thought about what Mrs. Minney had said. Something was either *with* him or *after* him. If something was after him, he was there for the taking.

A WHITE FORM IN THE MESQUITE

I couldn't get to sleep that night, and so about midnight I went out on the porch, sat in a chair and put my feet up on the railing.

The Comanches called the month of September the Mexico Moon, and I always think of them late on a September night. They used to come through here on their way to Mexico to get horses. Every September they'd come when the nights were clear and mild. Their trail, a long pale ribbon from the buffalo plains down to Mexico, used to come right about where I was sitting.

While I was thinking about this I kept my eye on Alado over in the corral. His wings were still drooping, and the moonlight made them appear to be a load thrown over his shoulders. But then, I thought, maybe that's what they were – a burden.

I leaned back in my chair, crossed my legs, and closed my eyes. The thing that kept flitting in and out of my mind was what Mrs. Minney had said that afternoon. Something was either with the colt or after him.

I couldn't make sense of it either way. First of all there wasn't much danger from animals around here any more. Years ago, a hundred and fifty or so, there were great grizzly bears in the mountains. They could travel forty miles a day, and meeting up with one meant death. Thirty years later, though, every one of them had been killed by hunters.

Even coyotes were scarce now. I remember my grandad telling me about the time he was out herding cattle, and coyotes kept pestering him and keeping him awake. My grandad didn't want to shoot because of the cattle, so he finally threw one of his boots at them. Next morning he found that the boot had landed in the banked embers of the campfire and been burned to a crisp. My grandad held the loss of that boot against the coyotes until he died.

A coyote was about the only thing I could think of that could be after the colt. Usually a coyote eats what it finds dead – gophers or jack rabbits, but it also kills stray sheep and calves on occasion. With the colt's weakened condition it could kill him. I sat there for the best part of an hour, but I still couldn't think of any animal that could be *with* the colt.

I dozed in my chair and awoke abruptly with my hands still folded over my chest. Something had awakened me, but I didn't know what. I leaned forward. I realized suddenly that I couldn't see the colt, and I got to my feet.

As I stood there I heard a high howling noise in the distance, and I felt a chill on the back of my neck. I went down the steps. 'Alado!' I called.

I waited, listening. Suddenly the door slammed

behind me, and Charles came rushing out. He almost ran me down. 'What's wrong?'

'Probably nothing, Charles, but you better get my gun just in case.'

'Your gun? What's wrong? Has something happened?'

'I don't know.'

Without another word he went into the house, came back with my rifle, and put it in my hands. I said, 'Now, stay behind me.' We started walking toward the corral.

For a moment I couldn't see Alado at all, and then in the distance I caught sight of him. He had jumped the fence somehow, and he was running. There was nothing limp or weak about him now. It was a nervous, frenzied run, and Charles and I started after him.

As we crossed the yard, I heard the howl again. 'Is it a wolf, Uncle Coot?'

'I don't know.'

'What do you think?'

I had stopped thinking a long time ago. I said, 'I'll get Clay.'

Without taking time to saddle him I mounted and started after Alado, my rifle in front of me. Charles shouted, 'Wait for me, Uncle Coot, take me with you.'

In the distance Alado was only a pale blur. The sound of the howling came again. 'You wait here, Charles.' I jabbed my feet into Clay's sides, and he set off in a gallop. He was a good range horse, quick and fast. You could turn him on a saddle blanket, and he was going like an arrow now, burning the earth.

He shortened the distance to the colt fast. We went out in front of Alado, circled and came back to head him off. Confused, Alado paused.

The howl came again – louder, closer. Alado threw up his head. Then he started forward, and I saw he was heading toward a mesquite thicket. I spun around and saw a low white form behind the mesquite.

I lifted my gun just in case. Alado moved between me and whatever was behind the mesquite. I waited. Alado whinnied and moved straight for the thicket.

I lowered my rifle. I knew Alado would not be running to meet danger. Slowly Clay and I moved closer. In the thicket ahead the white figure was crouched low. I knew now it couldn't be a coyote or a wolf.

I slipped off Clay's back and walked slowly toward the mesquite. I thought I knew now what it was. I whistled softly. 'Here, boy.' I held my gun ready, the safety off, my finger on the trigger, just in case. 'Here, boy.'

There was a pause. Alado was right at my side now, nervously marking time, moving as if he was being jockeyed for a race. He whinnied and tossed his head into the air. His mane brushed my hand.

'Here, boy,' I said, my eyes on the thicket. 'Here!' I waited.

And then out of the thicket came the thinnest, puniest, sorriest-looking dog I ever saw in my life.

He came out on his belly, crawling, his body as low to the ground as he could get it.

I knelt. 'Come here, fellow.' The dog came within three feet of me and then thought better of it. He writhed with uncertainty. He twisted. He turned his back on me. He made two complete circles. I could feel his agony, his desperate wanting to come, and his fear.

'Here, fellow, it's all right.' Beside me Alado was quiet. I snapped my fingers. 'Here.'

The dog untwisted. He looked at me, but he stayed where he was. I held out my hand. He took two steps and got close enough to smell my fingers. I could have grabbed him and pulled him to me, but I knew better. 'It's all right, boy.' He moved close enough to let me scratch his neck. I knew he wasn't going away after that.

'Good boy.' I looked at Alado and down at the dog. The dog wasn't much more than bones, worse-looking even than the colt. I didn't know how and I probably never would, but he and Alado had somehow come together in the past month. The dog was probably the reason Alado was alive.

I rose after a minute, said, 'Come, boy,' and started walking. The dog hesitated, but he couldn't resist. Somebody a long time ago had probably said that to him. With his head down he slunk after me. Alado watched, and then he started after the dog.

We went along like that, Indian style, until we met Charles running toward us. He said, 'What happened, Uncle Coot? Was there something out there?'

'Yeah,' I said. 'That.'

Charles came closer. 'What is it? A dog?'

'Yeah.'

'But where'd it come from, Uncle Coot?'

'Beats me,' I said. 'Mrs. Minney told me this afternoon that she'd seen another animal on the mesa with Alado. I guess that's what it was.'

'But how did they get together?'

'I don't know.' I glanced back at the colt and the dog. 'I reckon we never will know exactly what happened. The way I figured it is that some time after the storm the colt found the dog or the dog found the colt and they survived together.'

'Maybe the dog was used to horses. Maybe he'd looked after calves or colts before,' Charles said. 'Anyway, we *have* to keep him, Uncle Coot.'

I nodded. I'd decided that myself as soon as I saw Alado following the dog. I said, 'I think at last we're going to be able to train Alado.'

Charles glanced around. 'With the dog?'

'Yeah. I may be wrong, but I've got the feeling I can get Alado to do what I want just by getting the dog to do it first.'

We walked on, and when we got back to the house Alado followed the dog right into the corral. 'See that?'

Charles nodded. He watched them a minute, and then he glanced at me and grinned. 'Too bad you can't teach the dog to *fly*.'

'Yeah, that would be nice, wouldn't it?' Then I took a good easy breath, the first I'd drawn in months. 'Well, we better feed the dog, I guess, and get to bed. Alado'll be all right now.'

'I'll feed him, Uncle Coot,' Charles said. He ran into the house.

I took one more look at the dog and the colt and I went in the house too. I fell asleep dreaming of the colt, not as he was, but as I wanted him to be, strong and sure and able to do anything.

$349 WORTH OF SNAKES

For a while it seemed that my dream was going to come true, because throughout the winter Alado did get stronger and more sure of himself. Training him was easier with the dog, just as I'd hoped, and by spring Alado looked like a different animal. He was still wild, but there was a new certainty in his movements. I reckon he would have been like any yearling if it hadn't been for the wings. And so when we rode over to the butte one Saturday in May, there wasn't a thought in my mind of trouble.

There always have been a lot of snakes in this part of the country. My grandad told me that in 1926 some Mexican cotton pickers went after snakes one summer instead of cotton and five tons of snakes were turned in to the local dealers. My grandad said he made over thirty-nine dollars that year just in his spare time.

Snakes never worry me though. Generally a snake is a coward and a bluffer, and he'll hiss and rattle and give you every warning in the world before he strikes. The last thing I would have expected trouble from that day was snakes.

We had been riding for an hour or two, me in

the lead, followed by Charles on Clay. Alado and the dog were trailing behind. The colt would step off to the side every now and then to investigate something or eat a little grass. Then he would run to catch up with us. A yearling is a beautiful frisky animal, and that was the way Alado was that day. Sometimes when you watch yearlings play and run you get the feeling that they think this is going to be their last free summer and they want to make the most of it.

Charles and I were over in the shadow of the butte, on the north side, and I heard a noise. It wasn't the sound a snake makes, but more of a steady buzzing, like bees swarming. I knew that snakes are generally attracted to buttes because of the crevices between the rocks, but I still hadn't thought about snakes.

I turned my horse toward the sound – I was curious – and Charles came with me. We rode slowly forward, coming up closer to the butte as we rode. Alado had left us and gone over into the brush, frisking and running on his own.

Since I was in the lead, I was the first to see what the noise was, and it stopped me cold. Dozens of rattlers were collected around a hole at the base of the butte. Since it was early May and hot, I figured the snakes were just coming out of their den because they were sluggish and didn't seem to have much life to them. That's the way snakes are when they first come out of hibernation.

'Well, did you ever see anything like that?' I asked

Charles. I knew he hadn't because this was the first time I'd seen it myself.

Charles pulled his horse up beside mine, and both horses whinnied and moved backwards as soon as they saw the snakes. Horses are afraid of snakes and never get close to them if they can help it. In the movies when you see a horse trampling a snake under its hoofs, it's just a rubber snake. It looks real because the rubber snakes are built with a clock mechanism inside that causes the tongue to flick in and out. When they show a close-up of a real snake, they use fake horse legs. They never put the two together.

'Are they rattlers?' Charles asked.

'Yeah,' I said. 'There's nothing to worry about though. They haven't even started getting away from the den. They're still sleepy and sluggish from hibernation.'

'Are you going to do anything about them?'

'Well, I'll probably get some dynamite later and blow up the den. One thing we don't need around here is a bunch of rattlesnakes.'

'Rattlers are very dangerous,' Charles said.

'Yeah.'

I thought he was going to give me some facts and information about the life and habits of rattlesnakes, but instead he shuddered. 'You know, these are the first snakes I've seen in my whole life except in books.'

'Well, it's a bunch of them.' I rested in my saddle, leaning forward. I was thinking that with today's prices, those snakes might be worth about $349. I didn't feel much like collecting them and turning them in though. 'We'll come back this afternoon, and you bring your camera and get some pictures before I blow it up.'

The horses were still nervous, moving sideways and backwards, every way but forward where the snakes were. Charles and I kept looking. It was a real strange sight.

Just about this time I glanced up and saw Alado. I had forgotten about him because of the snakes, and when I looked up he was running straight toward us. Sometimes a yearling will run as if he's in the greatest race of his life, and that was the way Alado was running. The only trouble was that the snakes were between us.

I turned my horse quickly and started around the snakes to head him off. I waved my hat and shouted, but this only made things worse, because Alado moved closer to the butte.

'Back, Alado,' I shouted. The only way I could stop him now was to move right across those rattlers, and that was something I wasn't about to do. Rattlers can be sluggish, but they would liven up if a horse was trampling them.

'Alado, no, no!' Charles hollered. He tried to start Clay forward. I could see he was willing to ride right through the rattlers.

'Charles, get back!'

He heard me, but he kept urging his horse forward. I couldn't move for a moment, and then I shouted, 'Stop, Clay, *back!*' Clay had been trampling the earth nervously, but he stopped at my command. 'Back!' He turned, made a tight circle, and ran fifty yards in the opposite direction.

'Alado!' Charles cried. He was yanking the reins and doing everything he knew to get Clay turned around, only nothing worked.

Alado was coming so fast that he was on the snakes before he saw them. He had known something was wrong from the way Charles and I were acting. He had gotten nervous and skittish, and the fact that he didn't know what was wrong made him run faster. He was at top speed when he saw the snakes.

For a minute Alado acted like he was going to rear. He threw his head back, whinnied, and then he made a lunge forward as if he was trying to jump over the snakes, to clear them. He leaped into the air.

His eyes were wild. His mane was whipping the air. Everything in the world seemed to have stopped except this frenzied animal.

'Alado!' I cried. His wings came out then and beat down one stroke. Then there was another and another. 'Alado!' I cried again, choking on the word. Alado was flying.

FLIGHT

I've seen some terrible-looking things in my life. There's a beauty in a stunt that goes right – no matter how frightening it seems – and a sickening awfulness when one goes wrong.

That's what Alado's flight reminded me of, a stunt gone wrong, because I never saw anything wilder or more unnatural-looking in my life. I thought at the time that he would never get back to the ground alive.

His legs were moving in a sort of awkward, galloping motion, and then one of his wings brushed the side of the butte. This caused him to lose what balance he had, and his left wing dipped toward the ground.

Now he was fighting not only gravity, but being off balance. His wings beat harder, wild uneven strokes, and he rose a few feet. His hoofs were pawing the air with a certain desperation, as if it were a matter of climbing the air rather than flying through it.

Then it was over. In the last moment before his hoofs touched the ground, his body straightened.

His wings stretched out. And he landed on all four hoofs, hard, like a bucking horse.

I was yelling at him by this time, yelling so loud my throat hurt, but he started running. It was as if he was being pursued.

I started after him. I wasn't trying to catch him, just keep him heading in the direction of the ranch, but we went for the best part of an hour before he slowed down. Then it took me another half hour to catch him and get a rope on him. He was just plain worn out then and I was too. After we rested he followed me home, gentle as a lamb.

I was with him in the corral, rubbing him down and talking to him when Charles rode up an hour later. Charles was so tired and saddle sore he could hardly get off his horse. I knew what a struggle he'd had trying to keep up with Alado and me because just ordinary riding wasn't easy for him.

'Are you all right?' I asked.

He didn't answer. He came running over. 'Alado!'

'He's all right.'

'I thought he was going to be *killed!*'

'Yeah, me too.'

The struggle came into my mind, and the unnaturalness of what I had seen stunned me all over again. When you're training an animal, teaching him to do something unnatural like fall, you have to do it slowly. You have to build up to it. The difficulty here was that there had been no way to train Alado to fly. Flight was against his nature, and the whole

86

experience had been one desperate attempt to get safely back to the ground.

Charles rubbed Alado's neck. After a minute he glanced over at me. 'You shouldn't have tried to stop me,' he said. He turned his face away and laid his cheek against the colt's neck.

'What?' I hadn't heard him good because his face was half-buried in the horse's mane.

He lifted his head. 'You shouldn't have tried to stop me.'

'Well, you shouldn't have tried to go through those rattlers. You talk about stupid things – now that *was* stupid. You could have been killed.'

He didn't look at me. It was the first stirring of something, like the brewing of a storm, a change in the air. I wanted to smooth things over because both of us were tired and upset. 'I'm going in,' I said. I patted Alado on the rump and started for the house.

Charles said, 'If you didn't want to save him – that's your business. Only you shouldn't have stopped me.'

I turned around. 'Is that what's wrong? You think I could have saved him?'

He looked at me. 'If you'd cared enough.'

I stood there for a minute. I didn't know what to say. There's not a man who has loved horses better than me. The first thing I ever loved was a horse. The first tears I ever remember shedding were over a horse and dried on a horse's neck. There have been a time or two in my life when a horse was the only friend I had in the world. I thought of Cotton.

I realized suddenly I was rubbing the scar on my cheek. It had been a while since I'd done that. I looked at the mountains in the distance. Then I looked at Charles. His eyes were burning in his dusty face.

I still didn't know what to say. Suddenly everything was confused, beyond what I could understand. I said, 'Just because a horse has wings, Charles, you can't − ' I stopped in the middle because I realized that wasn't what I wanted to say at all.

'It isn't the wings,' he said. 'You don't understand anything. If he was a plain ordinary horse it would be the same to me.'

The colt was quiet now, standing between us, letting Charles rub his neck. Charles was still looking at me. He wanted something from me, I knew that, but I didn't know what. Maybe he wanted a promise that the horse would always be safe. Maybe he wanted me to be the great, wonderful hero he had always thought I was.

We waited, standing there, and finally I said, 'Just don't let yourself care too much about the colt. That's all.' I turned away then and went into the house.

Late that afternoon I rode out with dynamite and blew up the rattlesnake den. I told Charles he could come along, because I figured he would never have a chance to see something like that again, but he said he was too tired and wanted to stay home with Alado. I waited, taking a long time getting started because I thought he might want to change his mind.

He didn't, though, and in the end I rode out by myself.

It was just as well he didn't come, I guess, because there wasn't much to see. There was just a dusty explosion and a lot of dead snakes. I rode around for a while to see if I could see any alive and wiggling, but I couldn't. Then I headed for home.

As I rode I found myself thinking of something Mrs. Minney had told me the other day. She told me she had been up in the mountains, and she'd found an old Indian grave. There was a skeleton curled up in it and the dust of some possessions – a bow and arrows, a blanket. No telling how long it had been there and no one knew about it. For some reason thinking about that brought my troubles down to size.

By the time I got back to the ranch I had started telling myself that Charles and I had just had a little quarrel, which was natural enough under the circumstances. I decided to forget it.

Charles and Alado were in the corral along with the dog when I got there. I said to the dog, 'Well, where were you when we needed you?'

Charles grinned a little. 'I think he was more scared than any of us. Did you kill the rattlers, Uncle Coot?'

I nodded. 'Yeah, I got them all.'

'Well, we shouldn't have any more trouble then, should we?' Charles asked. He asked it in such a hopeful way that I told him what he wanted to hear.

'No, we shouldn't have any more trouble.'

MORE IN THE SKY THAN HAWKS

In this part of the country anything seems possible in the summer. The colours are brighter than any you ever saw and the bare mountains against the sky look like their names – Cathedral Point and Weeping Women and Devil's Back. A desert arroyo, dry for years, rushes with water after a rain, and the Marfa light burns in the desert and no one can find it. A winged colt doesn't seem strange at all in the Texas summer.

June started slow and easy. Charles was out of school now and spending most of his time with Alado. Mr. and Mrs. Minney had gone back East for a visit, leaving with us a painting of Alado flying off the roof of their house that night last September. We set the picture on the mantel, but neither Charles nor I liked to look at it. It showed too plainly what could happen. It made Alado's desperation, the danger of his flying very real, and most of the time we avoided it. Occasionally, however, I would come into the room and find Charles standing there staring at the picture, and occasionally he would come in and find me doing the same thing. We worried a lot in silence.

On this particular day Charles decided to take Alado to the mesa, which was about two miles behind the house. A mesa, which means 'table' in Spanish, is just a flat-topped piece of land with steep sides. It used to be a hill, I guess, only the sides washed away and the top wore smooth, leaving a piece of land like a platform. There was a stream that ran by the mesa after a rain, and that was why Charles had decided to go.

Charles and Alado set out and right away the dog came crawling out from under the porch and started after them. He never liked Alado to go off without him.

The dog was still not much more than a skeleton. We had fed him enough for two dogs; we had given him better than we ate. Still he was bones, and that's what Charles called him. When Bones lay down on the porch it sounded like someone had dropped kindling wood.

At three o'clock I was outside working on the truck, and I happened to glance up and see a glider flying overhead. The glider was low, circling about a mile north of the corral. I straightened up quick.

'Hey, Charles!' I called, in case he had come home without my seeing him. 'Charles!' I wanted him to see the glider because that was all he had been talking about since Sunday, when we had gone into Marfa. The National Gliding Championship was being held there, and since these were the first gliders Charles had ever seen, he couldn't quit talking about them.

A glider, in case you never saw one either, is an

airplane that flies without an engine. These gliders have races and distance tasks, and when the contest is going on, you can see gliders and glider trailers everywhere you look.

Charles and I had gone to the airport on Sunday, and it was an awesome sight. Seventy gliders were all stretched out on the ramp, waiting to be towed up by airplanes. Later it was even more awesome to see them in the sky, seventeen or eighteen of them together, circling beneath the clouds.

A glider, I learned that afternoon, is a lot prettier than an airplane. The wings are real long and slender, and I reckon it comes closer than anything I ever saw to being a bird.

Well, we had gotten into the truck finally and started for home, but Charles couldn't talk about anything but gliders. He knew the name of every glider he'd seen – the Libelle and the Kestrel – and he knew that gliders go up by getting lift from air currents, and he knew what some of the altitude and distance records were. He told me that one of the gliders we saw had flown nonstop for six hundred miles.

Every day since then Charles had spent most of his time outside squinting up at the sky, watching for gliders. He claimed a couple of times that he had seen one over the mountain peaks in the distance, but it had looked more like a hawk to me.

'Charles!' I called again. I knew he was going to be disappointed. After all that watching here was a glider practically over the corral, and he wasn't around to see it. There was a chance he'd seen it from the mesa, I thought, because the glider had come from that direction, but I wasn't sure.

I watched the glider and, from what Charles had told me, I figured that the pilot wasn't doing too well. He had gotten low and was moving from one place to another trying to find some lift so he could get high enough to finish the race.

I watched for a while, but it didn't look like he was getting any higher to me. The glider moved on toward the road. It was almost overhead.

I was getting excited now. In this part of Texas there aren't many places to land a glider because most of the land has yucca and mesquite on it. So sometimes – Charles had learned this at the airport – the pilots land their gliders on the road.

By now the glider was even lower and so close overhead I could hear a funny eerie noise as it passed, a whistling sound. The pilot moved closer to the road. He was really low now, and I got in my truck and drove as fast as I could. I got to the main road just in time to see the glider land.

I went over and helped the pilot pull his glider to the side of the road, and then I looked it over. The pilot leaned in the cockpit and did something to his instruments. Then he glanced at me. I was standing at the back of the glider, by the T-shaped tail.

'You own that ranch over there?' he asked.

I nodded. 'What is this for?' I asked, pointing to a metal thing that was sticking out of the tail. And then the pilot asked something that stopped me cold.

He said, 'What was that thing I saw flying back there at the mesa?'

'What?' I asked. My hand dropped to my side.

'Back there behind your place. I couldn't get a good look at what it was because I was trying to find some lift, but it was flying. It looked as big as a horse. I don't suppose you folks raise flying horses around here.' He laughed.

I got a funny feeling in the pit of my stomach. I said quickly, 'Look, if there's nothing I can do for you here, I better get back to the ranch.' I knew that Charles was in trouble.

He said, 'Sure, here comes my crew now.' We looked up the road at a car pulling a long white trailer.

I said again, 'I better get going.'

I got in the truck and drove back to the ranch as fast as I could. I jumped out and saw Bones coming toward the house. He was just a streak he was going so fast, and his tail was between his legs and his ears were flattened against his head. He ran around the house and went under the steps. I heard him work his way back under the porch where there was a break in the stones. He was wheezing and panting as if his lungs would burst.

'Come here, Bones.'

The wheezing and panting stopped. Even the breathing seemed to have stopped.

'Come here, Bones, *come*.'

As soon as the pilot had mentioned seeing something fly back at the mesa I had known something was wrong. It was confirmed now. Unless something had happened to frighten him badly, the dog would never have left Alado.

Clay was already saddled. I started out as fast as I could in the direction Charles and Alado had taken. I rode all the way to the mesa without seeing a trace of them.

'Charles! Charles!'

There was no answer. I turned Clay and rode to the right. I had the feeling that something had happened to Charles, and I suddenly got a sickness in my stomach. It was like that time with Cotton, only worse. I thought I might fall out of the saddle.

I rode, stopped, and called again. 'Charles, where are you?' I threw back my head and bellowed, '*Charles!*'

I waited a minute, and then I heard his voice in the distance. I rode around the mesa.

'Here I am,' he called.

I looked up and saw Charles clinging to the side of the mesa. He hadn't gotten far, and he appeared to be stuck.

'What are you doing up there?' The relief of seeing him safe made me yell louder than was necessary.

'Uncle Coot?' He hadn't been crying, but he was stammering so badly I could hardly recognize my own name.

'What happened?'

'Uncle Coot?'

'What *happened?*' He swallowed and I said, 'Now,

come on, Charles, what are you doing up there? What's going on?'

'I don't know exactly,' he said, still stuttering a little.

'Well, try to tell me what happened. Start at the beginning.'

'We were coming down to the stream, me and Bones and Alado, just like we planned.'

He stopped and I said, 'Go *on*, Charles. The three of you were coming to the stream.'

'Yes, and just then I looked up and saw a javelina ahead with her babies.'

'Go on.' A javelina is a wild pig. They can be mean, but there's not much danger as long as you let them alone. 'You didn't bother them, did you?'

'No, as soon as I saw them, I started backing up. I was going around to the other side.'

'So what happened?'

'Well, when I stepped back, I stepped right on Bones. He was behind me, see, and as soon as I did this, he let out a terrible howl and leaped forward and landed directly in front of the javelina.' He paused and shook his head. 'After that I just don't know what did happen. It was like a tornado. Pigs were charging – it seemed like there were a hundred of them – and Bones was howling and running – and I was trying to grab Bones and we all rolled right into the path of Alado.'

'And Alado flew,' I said with a sinking feeling.

'It was terrible at first, Uncle Coot. I was never so scared in my life. And then all of a sudden he was flying. It wasn't like at the snake den. He was *really* flying.'

'Well, that's great.' I knew there was something that he hadn't told me yet. 'If Alado can get control of himself, he'll be safe,' I said, sort of marking time. 'We won't have to worry about him.'

'I thought he was never going to stop, Uncle Coot. He flew and flew and *flew*.'

Suddenly a terrible thought came to me. I said slowly and carefully, 'Where is Alado now, Charles?'

At that question Charles's face sort of crumpled.

'Where is he now?' I asked, hitting at every word.

Charles swallowed.

'*Where is Alado?*'

Without a word Charles lifted one hand. He pointed to the top of the mesa. With a sort of sick feeling in my stomach I looked up and saw standing on top of the mesa, about fifty miles above us – anyway that was how it looked – the colt Alado.

THOSE WHO CAN – FLY

Charles raised his head, and we both looked up at the colt for a moment. The height gave him a frailness, and Charles looked away quickly. He said in a rush, 'But he flew real good, Uncle Coot. I wish you could have been here. He really flew!'

'I can see that.'

'I mean he can really *fly*, Uncle Coot. He – '

'I can see that, Charles. There's no other way he could get up on top of that mesa.'

There was a moment of silence, and then Charles said, 'How are you going to get him down?'

All at once I felt tired. I suddenly thought of the early days of movie gags. The stunt men never used to look real in their falls. They would gallop up at top speed, bring their horses to a halt, and *then* fall out of the saddle. I felt like that was what was going to happen to me now. I had come galloping up as fast as I could, and now suddenly I felt so tired I could have just dropped out of the saddle.

It was Charles's last statement that did it, I think, that 'How are *you* going to get him down?'

I sighed. I realized that maybe it wasn't that I felt tired. It was that I felt just like what I was – a man with a lot more than his share of scars and a lot less than his share of brains. I was aware of my bum hip and my scarred cheek, my gored leg, my twice-broken wrist. The years of knocking around rose up and hit me all over again while I was sitting there.

Charles said again, 'How are you going to get him down?'

'Well,' I said finally, 'I reckon he'll have to get down the same way he got up.' To tell the truth I didn't know what to do about the colt. The sight of him up on the mesa had made me feel like I'd had too much sun.

'You mean fly down?' he asked.

'Yeah, I guess he'll have to fly down.'

'But, Uncle Coot, he only flies when he's startled or frightened. He would never just fly on his own. He can't reason that out. You told me yourself that horses can't reason.'

'Well, some horses can probably reason,' I said. 'I'm no expert.'

'You told me that horses do foolish things some-times because they can't reason. I remember you saying this at the table one night, like horses will run straight into a fire instead of away from it.'

'But flying is an instinct with this horse.'

'I *know* he won't fly down.'

'Well, we can wait and see, can't we? We don't have to start risking our lives this second.' I wanted some time, but I could see I wasn't going to get it.

'You can wait if you want to.' Charles started scrambling up the side of the mesa. His position hadn't been good to start with, and what with all the sliding and slipping he ended up even lower than he had started. He looked at me and said, 'Don't try to stop me.' And he started up again.

I stayed where I was. When Charles had slipped a second time I said, 'Now, look, Charles, don't get in such a hurry. Why don't we – '

'I'm not going to wait around for him to fall off and kill himself. I don't care what you do.' He was still making climbing motions, but he had worn through the legs of his pants and skinned both his knees, and that was slowing him down some. He said again, 'There's no need your trying to stop me.' This time he said it like he was trying to give me an idea.

The last thing in the world I wanted to do was get off my horse and climb that mesa, particularly when I didn't know what to do when I got up there. I sat a minute more, leaning forward on my saddle. I shifted, and then before I could say anything Charles blurted out, 'You don't care about Alado at all, do you?'

It caught me by surprise, the way he said it and the way he was looking at me. 'What?'

'You don't care about Alado.' He paused. 'You don't care about anything.'

'Wait a minute now,' I said. 'I care about the horse.'

'You didn't want to get him that night in the storm.'

'The night I almost killed myself going after

him? That night? I'm not Superman, you know, I'm just – '

'You didn't want to go that night and you didn't want to look for him after the storm, and then that day at the rattlesnake den, you – '

'Now, just hold on a minute,' I hollered. He shut up because my voice had gotten loud as thunder. I wanted to say something then – he was listening – but for some reason I froze. All my life I've been troubled by not being able to say what I wanted.

He waited, and the moment for me to speak came and went. He said, 'You don't care about anything,' in a low voice. Then he added, 'Or anybody.'

Suddenly I remembered when I was six years old and I came galloping across the front yard on old Bumble Bee, standing up, arms out, yelling like an Indian. 'Pa, look at me!' Later, when I hit the ground and lay there half dead, my pa came over and started pulling my belt to get the air back in me. He said, 'You want to get yourself killed? Is that what you're trying to do?' It was the first summer I had seen my pa since I was a baby, and I wanted him to notice me so bad I would have tried about anything. Every time I got near him I'd put his hand on my head or his arm over my shoulder or I'd try to climb on his back or swing on his arm. I broke my wrist two times that summer trying to make him show he cared about me.

I said, 'I'll go up and get the colt.'

Charles wiped his nose and climbed down a few steps. I turned my horse to the right. For some reason I felt like my insides had been churned up with an egg beater.

Charles slid the rest of the way to the ground. He said, 'How will you get him down?'

'I don't know.' I rode Clay all the way around the mesa until I found a place where I might, with a lot of luck, be able to climb up without killing myself.

Charles came running over, out of breath. 'Is this where you're going up?' he asked, squinting at the mesa.

'This is where I'm going to *try* to go up, yes.'

'You can make it. I know you can.'

I never felt less like a superman in my life. I said, 'The cameras are not rolling now, Charles.' I got off the horse and slung the reins over a bush.

Charles paused, and then he came over and rested one hand on Clay's neck. He hesitated. He said, 'Maybe we could wait a little while, Uncle Coot. What do you think? Maybe he *will* fly down.'

I started up the side of the mesa without saying anything. I'm not much of a climber. My bum hip bothers me when I have to put a lot of weight on it, and I slipped twice before I went ten feet.

'Uncle Coot, if you want to wait for a little while it's all right with me.'

I kept going. I managed to get about halfway just by going real slow, one step at a time, the way a little kid goes up stairs. I stopped to rest against an outcropping of rock. 'Are you doing all right?' Charles called from the ground.

'Wonderful.'

'You look like you're almost a fourth of the way to the top.'

I had thought I was bound to be a good bit farther than that, but I didn't say anything.

'The rest of the way looks like it's going to be a little harder though,' he called. 'It's steeper and there don't seem to be as many bushes to hold on to.'

So far the total number of bushes I had found was one prickly-pear cactus which I would not advise holding unless it was a life-and-death situation. I rested a moment longer, and I started thinking how much easier things are in the movies. Like sometimes in a movie when somebody is supposed to be climbing up a cliff, they will just let him crawl on his stomach on the ground, and they will film this at a steep angle to make it look like he's climbing. Or when they're filming a sand storm, they throw stuff like talcum powder up in front of big fans and let that blow on the actors.

'Why are you stopping, Uncle Coot?' Charles called up. 'Is there any special reason?'

The hurting in my hip had begun to ease. I looked down at him. 'No, nothing special.' I started climbing again.

I can't tell you exactly how long that climb took me, but it seemed like the longest afternoon of my life. And all the while Charles was calling things about my progress. He couldn't seem to shut up. Once I guess he looked away, because he called, 'What happened? Did you slip?'

'Slip?'

'Yes, I thought you were farther up than that.'

'No,' I said, 'I'm not any farther than this.'

'Well, it just seems like you're lower now than you were, Uncle Coot.'

'Lower in spirits,' I said.

'What?'

'Nothing!'

'What? I couldn't hear what you said.'

'*Nothing!*'

He must have known from the way that 'nothing' rumbled down the side of the mesa that it would be a good idea for him to shut up. He didn't call to me any more, just gasped once when I did slip a little. I looked down at him right before I pulled myself up on top of the mesa, and he was standing there with his hands raised against his chest like a small church steeple.

The top of a mesa isn't anything beautiful – just some dry grass and rocks and a few straggly plants, but it looked good to me. I lay there on my stomach for a moment and then I stood up. My hip was hurting so bad I thought I wouldn't be able to walk. I shook my leg a little, which sometimes eases it, and tried to put weight on it.

Across the top of the mesa Alado was standing watching me. 'Here, boy,' I said.

He came over slowly, tossing his head. He had the reluctance any animal has in a strange situation, and he shied away a few times before he came. I patted him and scratched his nose. 'When you fly, boy,' I said, 'you really fly, don't you?'

'Hey, Uncle Coot?' Charles called from below.

'What?'

'Is he all right?'

'Yes.'

'He's not hurt or anything?'

'*He*'s not.'

'Are you sure?'

'Yes.'

'Well, how are you going to get him down? Have you got any ideas yet?'

'No.'

'As soon as you get an idea will you let me know?'

'Yes.'

I looked at the colt and I scratched his nose again. 'Alado,' I said, 'we are stuck.' Then I shook my leg and rubbed his neck and tried to think of some way to do this impossible thing before dark.

THOSE WHO CAN'T – WALK

The sun gets the colour of desert poppies at sunset out here, but this evening it was something I dreaded seeing. I had been stuck up on the mesa with the colt for three hours, and I was no closer to getting him down than I had been at first. I was also bone tired and hungry and I did not have an idea in my whole head.

When I first got up I had tried to startle Alado a few times by waving my arms at him and tossing my hat under his feet. All I got for my trouble was a crumpled hat. The thing was that Alado wouldn't get near the edge of the mesa. As long as Charles and I had both been on the ground he had looked over constantly, coming right to the edge. Now that I was up here with him, he stayed in the exact centre.

I didn't blame him really. If he went over the side, he wouldn't have to fall far before he struck the rocks, and it turned me cold to think about that. Still, if he got a good running start, I kept thinking – Then I would give him the old hat under the feet a few more times. Nothing doing.

After a while I sat down and picked up little pebbles and tossed them at a weed. Sometimes when

I'm doing something like that my mind works better, but this time it didn't help.

'Uncle Coot?' Charles called from below.

'Yes.'

'Are you still there?'

I sighed and bombarded the bush with every pebble in my hand. 'Yes, I am still here.'

'Well, what are you doing?'

'Thinking.'

He paused and then yelled, 'What are you thinking *about?*'

What I was thinking about was those chutes they used to build in the early days of movies, tilted over the edge of a cliff and greased. The chutes were hidden so they wouldn't show on the film, and once a horse got started down the chute he couldn't stop. He would have to go off the cliff. They got a lot of good pictures that way, but a lot of ruined horses. In my mind I had sent Alado down that greased chute half a dozen times. 'I'm not thinking of anything, Charles,' I yelled back.

'Well, if you do think of something – '

'Yeah, I'll let you know.'

It stays light a long time out here – sunset is usually about nine-thirty – but once the sun drops it gets dark fast. By this time the sun was disappearing below the horizon. I got up, went to the edge of the cliff, and called: 'Charles!'

His head almost snapped off his neck he looked up so fast. 'What is it, Uncle Coot?'

'I want you to take Clay and go on back to the house, hear?'

'I don't want to.'

'Well, do it anyway. There's no need both of us spending the night out here.'

'I don't want to leave Alado,' he said. 'If you could only go ahead and get him down, then we could all go home together.'

'Yes, that's true.'

He looked down at his feet and then back up at me. He said, 'I don't want to leave you either.'

Sometimes a man's life shifts in a moment. It's happened to me more times than most men because I've had a hard fast life. I felt it happening again.

'Did you hear me, Uncle Coot? I don't want to leave you out here either.'

I nodded. We kept standing there and I knew somehow that Charles, looking up at me on top of the mesa, seeing me from that distance, suddenly noticed how little separated us. I wasn't so much of a superman at that moment, and when I looked down at him, I could have been looking back over the years at myself. The truth slithered up to us like a sidewinder. Separated by the height of a mesa, we were the closest we had ever been.

'All right,' I said, 'go home, then, and get yourself a blanket.'

'Thanks, Uncle Coot.' He untied Clay quickly and rode off toward home. I watched till he was out of sight. Then I lay down, put my hat under my head, and tried to get some rest.

'I'm back, Uncle Coot,' he called after a while.

I got up, walked to the edge of the mesa, and watched him spread out his blanket in the moonlight.

'I'll be right here if you need me.'

'Fine, Charles.'

I went back and lay down. There's no getting comfortable on top of a mesa – I had already found that out – but I got settled for a long night the best I could.

Alado was standing near my feet. He was so still I thought he must be asleep. About midnight – although I didn't think it would ever happen – my eyes closed too.

I woke up and it was two o'clock in the morning and I couldn't see the colt. I got up slowly. My hip had stiffened while I was asleep, and I limped forward a few steps.

I whistled and called: 'Alado!' The sky was as bright with stars as I'd ever seen it and the moon was big. I looked around and I still couldn't see the colt. 'Alado!'

For a moment there was silence and then I heard a whinny to my right. I hobbled over and saw what had happened.

On this side of the mesa there was a gentle slope. At the bottom of the slope was a steep cliff, straight down to the rocks, but the colt didn't know this. The moonlight made everything look different, and I could see why he had been fooled. The colt had seen the slope, started down, and now he couldn't get back up.

'Here, Alado, come.'

I reached down to take his halter and lead him back. Sometimes all a horse needs is a familiar hand to help him do something he couldn't do on his own. As I reached down, though, my hip gave way. It just buckled.

I yelled, more with surprise than pain, and then I slipped down the slope. I hollered and scratched and grabbed at whatever I could find. I went wild for a moment. I knew that if I didn't stop I would slip right off the cliff, take the colt with me, and both of us would end up on the rocks below.

My fingers dug into the ground like steel hooks, but I kept slipping. I was right by the colt's legs now, and although I hadn't touched him, he started slipping too. He was scared, I knew that, and for a moment I thought we were both lost. I squirmed around to avoid hitting him, and right then my foot found a rock ledge and I stopped.

'It's all right, Alado. It's all right, boy,' I gasped.

He whinnied now, a loud high whinny. I turned over on my back and looked up. His pale legs were flashing by my face, thumping against the earth. Alado wasn't slipping any more, but the dirt was still sliding down the slope and over the cliff, and that gave him the feeling he was. I tried to reach up and hold him, but at that moment his wings flashed out. The wind from them beat against me. I drew back.

Alado paused a moment, the wings lashing at the

air, covering me when they came down. It was a strange, eerie thing. The wings blocked out the sky, the whole world. I couldn't move and I couldn't speak. The colt slipped again. I was frozen against the ground. Then he slid a few more inches down the slope, and he was in the air.

I managed to sit up then and look down the cliff. For a second the colt seemed to drop straight down. He just sank. The huge white wings flashing in the night seemed powerless. His body was turned a little sideways. It was like a fever dream. Then, at the last moment, just when I thought he was going to crash into the rocks, an updraft of wind rose beneath his wings and he flew.

He flew away from the cliff, his pale wings powerful now, sure. This was the way I had dreamed he would fly. I couldn't move for a moment and it wasn't my hip either. It was the sight of that colt in the air. In all my life I have never seen anything like that, terrible and awesome at the same time. It was something that was going to be with me the rest of my days.

Then Alado landed about two hundred yards away and, without a break, ran off into the night.

I stayed there a moment, hanging on the slope like a kid halfway down a sliding board. I was still too caught up in what I'd seen to move. Finally I made myself turn and work my way back up. I limped over, picked up my hat and put it on my head.

Then I stood there. I knew how Mrs. Minney felt

that night on the roof when Alado went flying off,
however badly, and she fell to the ground like a sack
of grain. I hitched up my pants and started down.

I've heard men say that coming down a mountain
is harder than climbing up, but it wasn't for me.
After I climbed down the first part, which was red
rock, I slid down the rest of the way – or fell sitting
down, whatever you want to call it. I was rolling
down the last part when Charles ran up and threw
himself on top of me. It stopped me from rolling
anyway. I hesitated a minute, and then I put my arms
around him and he started crying. He didn't make
any noise doing it, but I knew he was crying because
his tears were rolling down my neck.

'It's all right, Charles. It's all right.' I patted him
on the back.

He said, 'You could have been killed.'

For some reason his seeing me as I was, just a
plain person, made me feel like crying too. I patted
his back again. 'It's all right.' I waited until he was
through crying, and then I said, 'Did you see Alado?'

He nodded against my chest.

'You saw him fly?'

'Yes.'

We stayed there a minute. 'It was something,
wasn't it?' I said.

'Yes.'

'It was really something.' I took a deep breath and
slapped him on the back. 'Well, let's get Clay
and start for home.' I could see when I raised up
that Clay had walked over to the stream for a drink.

'I'll get him.' Charles went running over to Clay and grabbed at the reins. He didn't get them on the first try, and the horse turned and trotted away a few steps. He looked at Charles. Charles went running at him again, and this time Clay turned and took off in the direction of home.

'Clay!' I yelled, but he was gone.

Charles came back lowly. He shrugged. 'I don't know what I do wrong with horses.'

I grinned a little in the dark. I said, 'Give me a hand up.' He helped me to my feet and I dusted myself off, and we started walking home.

Charles said, 'I never will be the master of a horse, I know that now.' He shook his head. 'Never.'

'You know what the Comanche used to do, don't you?'

'No.'

'He used to find a wild mustang and rope him and throw him, and then he used to put his mouth over the horse's nose and breathe into it. He believed he was putting the controlling spirit into the horse.'

'Well, I've tried everything else.'

We heard the sound of a horse coming toward us and I said, 'Well, old Clay's coming back. We'll be riding home after all.'

I tell you it made me feel a lot better to think of easing myself up on Clay's back. Instead, when I looked, I saw Alado coming toward us. Alado went to Charles and nuzzled him and started walking beside him. I said, 'It doesn't look like you're going to need that old Comanche trick after all.'

'Maybe not.' I could feel he was smiling a little.

We kept walking. It was slow because of my hip. I looked at the colt and the boy. I said, 'I'll tell you something, Charles. One day that colt is going to fly as easy as he walks.'

Charles looked at Alado. Without glancing back at me he said, 'I know.' I knew he was seeing again the pale wings in the dark sky just as I was. Seeing the colt fly like that, being the only two people in the world to have shared that awful and beautiful sight, touched us so much we couldn't speak of it any more. I knew he was thinking as I was, 'One day –'

Suddenly I heard the sound of Clay's hoofs in the distance. 'Clay,' I shouted, 'get over here.' The sight of that horse coming out of the darkness was one of the best of my life. I limped to meet him. 'Am I glad to see you, boy.' I lifted myself into the saddle. Then I turned.

'Here, Charles, take my hand.' I pulled him up behind me. 'Let's go home.' And we rode off together with Alado following behind.

STORIES FROM FIREFLY ISLAND

Benedict Blathwayt

I

FIREFLY ISLAND

On warm nights the animals of Firefly Island would gather on the beach at the edge of the forest and ask Tortoise for a story. Tortoise had many memories and many stories.

'Tell us why the frogs croak at night,' they would say. 'Tell us the story of Lizard's race and of the great storm; about Big Bottle-nose and Brave Pig.'

Tortoise was wise, Tortoise knew almost everything. 'What is the moon?' the animals sometimes asked. 'What are the stars? Tell us why we are here, and where we come from.'

Tortoise would blink and take a while to answer. He was old, very old, but not old enough to know that their island had once been molten rock and bare of any life at all, that the sea had risen and fallen many times, that the land had joined and unjoined. Tortoise had not been here to see the first seeds and nuts arrive, blown on the wind or carried by tides. Grasses, bushes and trees had sprouted from sand-filled cracks in the rock, and eventually insects and birds came to their branches.

Tortoise could tell them only that their ancestors had always been here; that the island was all there was upon the sea; that the sea itself stretched flat, the same for ever and ever, and the sky, too, spread outwards endless and empty.

Tortoise supposed the moon was a cluster of glow-worms and each star a bright firefly asleep on the blackness of the night: surely this was how it was – and it would always be the same.

The animals loved Tortoise. 'Tell us another story,' they said.

'About us!' giggled the monkeys. 'Tell a story about us.'

Tortoise frowned, the other animals sighed, for monkeys meant trouble. But Tortoise told them a story . . .

Many years ago there was a terrible storm, a storm that rocked every branch of every tree and sent waves foaming into the fringe of the forest itself.

With the whistle of the wind howling right through the night, and the rain lashing every hole and crevice, none of the island's animals got any sleep at all.

By morning they were exhausted. The storm died away, the sea grew calm, the sun came out and the whole forest steamed. Every bird and creature dried itself and then fell thankfully asleep, a long deep sleep that lasted until sunset.

Now, while most of the animals were still tired enough at the end of that day of recovery to settle down as usual for a good night's rest – the monkeys were NOT. They felt completely refreshed. They swung through the branches and hooted and howled and chattered and joked. What a noise! They carried on like this until dawn, so that nobody else on the whole island got any rest at all. And the following day, of course, they fell asleep in the hot sun, while the other animals had to busy themselves in their daily search for food.

And when did those monkeys wake up again? Just as the sun went down.

It became a dreadful habit: they slept by day and played by night. The storm had upset the rhythm of the island. The monkeys just laughed when the others begged them to be quiet.

It was all very well for the monkeys: they managed to grab fruit as they swung through the trees; even with a thin moon they could see well enough. *They* didn't go hungry. But the birds couldn't fly at night and it was too dark for some of the animals, too cold for others. Day was the time to feed, night was the time to sleep – it had always been that way.

'What are we going to do?' the animals asked each other in desperation. They settled down to think of a plan.

The finches suddenly had an idea. They told Grass-snake and Lizard. The chipmunks and porcupines agreed; so did the deer and the wild pigs. Everyone thought it a very good plan, everyone except the frogs who no-one had bothered to tell. The frogs seemed to get left out of everything –

perhaps because they lived in far-off wet and boggy places where nobody else wanted to go.

Wild Pig asked the finches: 'When are we going to have this concert?'

'Tomorrow,' said the finches, 'at sunrise.'

The next morning, full of fruit and tired out from their night of fooling about, the monkeys settled down to sleep. The sun was warm, how peaceful they felt.

Then the finches gave the signal to begin. Already gathered beneath the trees where the monkeys slept, every creature on the island began to sing. If they couldn't sing, then they began to squeak, to snort, to bellow, or to grunt. The leaves of the trees shook with the noise of it all. The monkeys woke and held on tightly to their branches. At first they didn't know what was happening. The singing echoed from cliff top to tree top and back again.

'Quiet please!' shrieked the monkeys. 'We're tired, we want to sleep!'

But the animals' concert went on. It was no use the monkeys blocking their ears or moving to a further tree; the orchestra of animals followed below them.

'Please let us rest,' begged the monkeys, 'it's been a long night, we need our sleep.' But the chorus of voices kept singing and the pelicans brought fruit and water for dry throats.

'How long is this going to go on?' groaned the

monkeys. All day, thought the finches to themselves, but they said nothing.

And that's just how long the concert lasted – all day. Towards sunset the noise grew wilder, more ragged and disorganised. But no quieter. The monkeys were desperate from lack of sleep. 'We shall go mad!' they whimpered.

As the sun dipped into the sea, bit by bit the singing faded. The exhausted animals shut their eyes and fell asleep. And as the last voice died away, the monkeys too were finally able to sleep.

Such a hush and stillness fell over the island that you might have wondered if anything lived there at all. But there was still one remaining noise – a bubbly, piping sound from the island's damp places. It was the frogs. No one had told them about the concert, they had been asleep all day, too deep in the mud to have heard anything, and they were now just waking up.

But it was not an unpleasant noise and the other animals were too tired to be annoyed. One thing was certain: they could not spend another whole day singing, just so the frogs would sleep at night. Once was quite enough.

All the animals, including the monkeys, slept right through the night. And when the sun rose, they all awoke. Except the frogs of course, they were just falling asleep!

And that's the way it has been ever since.

II

BRAVE PIG

Wild Pig blushed — somebody had asked Tortoise for the story of Brave Pig.

'Do you mind if I tell it?' asked Tortoise kindly.

Pig shrugged, he didn't really mind; after all, it had happened a long time ago.

So Tortoise told the story . . .

Once, long ago, Wild Pig had been a bully. He was a mean, spiteful, self-satisfied show-off. He thundered through the ferns and grasses of the island's forest frightening the jungle-fowl and chipmunks out of their skins. He would only laugh at the flurry of feathers and their terrified squeaks. Pig, after all, was afraid of nothing.

The lizards and squirrels, deer and porcupine, all disliked this particular wild pig. They could never curl up safely in a patch of sunlight on the mossy forest floor, for it was quite likely that Pig, with a snort and delighted squeal, would come galloping through the undergrowth and leap right over them — or, more often, leap not quite far enough and land

122

right on top of them. Pig's hooves were hard and his tusks very sharp.

He never seemed able to apologise for his clumsiness. By night or day, scaring the island animals out of their wits seemed to him to be one huge joke. According to Pig, no-one was as fearless and intelligent as himself; no-one could run round the island quicker; no-one was quite as sensible, agile or handsome as he.

Pig thought he was absolutely perfect.

One dark night, with a broad piggish grin on his snout, Pig woke up one of the shy deer as she slept peacefully in a clearing. He chased her in and out the tree trunks, slashing at the ivy and creeper with his tusks, this way and that, squealing as only a wild pig can.

'Afraid, eh?' he cried with a laugh. 'Coward! Coward!'

To the deer he seemed like a bad dream come to life. Quail and Pheasant comforted the little deer when at last she stopped running in circles. Her black nose twitched and her dainty legs quivered in fear.

'If only there was a way we could show Pig up, in front of all the other animals on the island,' said Quail, 'if we could just make him see what it's like to be made a fool of.'

'What we need to do is to frighten Pig,' said Pheasant.

So, bobbing and pecking on the forest floor, they hatched a plan.

Quail did not roost at sunset that evening. When it was dark she went to a clearing in the forest where she knew the glow-worms gathered.

'I badly need your help,' she said to them, as the little beetles moved among the leaves, their tails glowing bright green, 'we are all being terrorised by Wild Pig.'

But the glow-worms didn't seem very interested in her plan. Quail became quite severe. 'Normally,' she said, 'we jungle fowl are asleep by now, so we don't have the opportunity to eat you glow-worms. But, if that were somehow to change . . . and staying up late became an unfortunate habit . . .'

'We'll help,' said the glow-worms, quickly. 'We're ready when you give the call.'

Pheasant, meanwhile, had been to see one of the monkeys; they were known to be clever with their hands. Monkey thought Pheasant's plan a good joke and he also agreed to help.

Finally, Quail talked with the young deer who had been badly treated by Pig and asked her if she was brave enough to lure Pig down to the big rock by the drinking pool.

'Flatter him,' said Quail. 'Say how brave and strong he is; ask him to escort you to the pool because you are thirsty – yet afraid of the dark and of monsters and dream-beasts that may lurk in the shadows. He is so vain he will be unable to refuse you.'

The young deer said yes, she too would help in curing Pig of his nastiness.

The next afternoon, on the slope of the big rock by the drinking pool, Monkey painted an enormous face; a face with jagged teeth and horrible eyes. No-one could see the face because Monkey had drawn it with a pointed stick dipped in wild honey, but the glow-worms would easily be able to find the sweet sticky lines of the drawing.

Now every part of Quail's plan was ready.

That night there was no moon. It was very dark. 'Good luck everyone,' clucked Quail.

The young deer looked for Pig. He was easy to find, snorting and grunting as he nosed the ground in search of tender roots.

'What do *you* want?' he asked gruffly when he saw the deer.

'Oh, brave handsome Pig,' said Deer meekly, 'I need your help. It's a hot night and I'm thirsty, but it's so dark that I'm quite lost and unable to find my way to the drinking pool.'

'Well, you'll have to stay thirsty,' said Pig rudely, 'I'm busy.'

'I only asked,' Deer went on, 'because your courage is well known to all of us. You are strong and wise and scared of nothing.'

'That may well be true,' said Pig, looking up for a moment, 'but a pig has to eat. I told you, I'm busy. Go away.'

'You see,' said Deer, not giving up yet, 'I have asked everyone else to lead me to the pool and no-one will help. The forest is too dark tonight and they are afraid of what terrible unknown things might lie in wait.'

'A lot of nonsense!' snuffled Pig.

'Oh, if only I was as brave as you!' sighed Deer.

'Just a hoof-load of old stories,' said Pig, 'invented in order to keep youngsters at home.'

'Oh Pig,' said Deer, 'if only I could convince myself of that. Of course,' she added, 'the others did say that even you would refuse. On a night as black as this, they all said, even Pig will feel a little afraid and stay in his lair and tell you to leave him in peace until morning.'

'Oh,' snorted Pig, thoughtfully, 'they said that?'

'Yes,' sighed Deer, in mock despair, 'and I suppose they were right; it was just too much to ask after all; one couldn't expect it, even of the bravest Pig.'

Deer began to wander away into the shadows.

'Wait a moment,' grunted Pig, 'you are obviously such a nervous weakling that I've decided to change my mind. Follow me.'

So Pig set off, his snout searching out the scented forest trails that led to the drinking pool. As Deer followed, she noticed Pig seemed slightly on edge. Sometimes he would stop and listen. 'What's that?' he'd ask; the merest rustle of leaves or flutter of moths made him jump.

'Oh Pig,' whispered Deer, 'I am so afraid.'

'No need,' snuffled Pig, 'no need.' But he didn't sound very sure of himself.

'Are you certain that there are no such things as

monsters of the night?' asked Deer, as she followed him.

'Of course,' Pig replied, his tusks chattering a little, 'of course I'm sure.'

They came into the clearing by the drinking pool. All was quiet except for the gurgling of the spring at the foot of the smooth rock face; except for the 'cluck' from a quail roosting somewhere in the Rizzleberry tree. Pig himself felt rather uneasy; he was secretly glad that Deer was there with him.

That quiet call from Quail had been a signal to the waiting glow-worms: they had already taken up their positions on the lines of honey drawn by Monkey; the whole of the rock-face was thick with them. On hearing Quail's signal, all together they lit their tails.

There, out of the blackness, towering above Pig and Deer, a huge and hideous green face appeared!

Pig's scream echoed round and round the island. Everyone heard it. He was off, crashing blindly through the undergrowth, tripping and skidding, his little hooves carrying him away from the terrible glowing beast faster than he had ever been before.

Many of the animals who had hidden in the bushes around the drinking pool began cheering and laughing: what a sight it had been, Brave Pig in a panic! He would never live it down.

Tortoise had found Pig the next morning, cowering miserably in his lair. Although Pig knew it had all been a tease, his teeth still chattered. What disgrace he felt.

'Never mind,' said Tortoise, 'cheer up. I'm sure that if you can forgive us, then we can all forgive you.'

Pig had looked up then, with a glimmer of hope in his moist eyes. 'I am going to change,' he said.

And he did.

Tortoise had come to the end of his story.

'You can all see,' said Pig, rather embarrassed, 'that although I'm still a bit clumsy, I am nevertheless a completely new and likeable animal – considerate, brave, modest; improving all the time.'

Tortoise smiled. 'Dear Pig,' he said, 'I don't know what we would do without you.'

III

SNOW

Tortoise loved the moon, and he loved the sea. On moonlit nights the foam washing in on the edge of the waves seemed as white and rounded as snow.

On just such a night, when the animals had followed Tortoise down to the beach, one of the chipmunks was reminded of his favourite story: 'Tell us about snow, Tortoise,' he squeaked, 'please tell us.'

It had only snowed once on Firefly Island, as far as anyone could remember; as far as Tortoise could remember anyway — and wasn't he the oldest and wisest of them all?

So Tortoise settled down in the damp sand and told them the story of the snow.

In a burrow under the toadleaf tree there once lived a fat chipmunk. This chipmunk didn't join in the great games of chase and tag that were carried on by the squirrels in the lower branches of the trees. Nor did she seem to want to play hide-and-seek in and out the boulders and burrows of the forest floor.

The truth was she felt shy, and could never find

enough courage to join in. And because she didn't *ask* to play, the others thought she didn't *want* to play – so they never bothered about her. She ended up being left out of everything. 'Hi, Sleepyhead!' was the most anyone ever said to her.

Leading a solitary life was very boring. She had nothing to do all day long but follow her instinct for collecting and hoarding. Soft berries and fungi she couldn't resist eating on the spot, and that was why she grew fat, but dry nuts and seeds she stored in the trunk of a huge dead tree that stood at the foot of the mountain. At the bottom of this trunk was a hole hidden by a stone. Much higher up was another hole, and this was where she poked the nuts and seeds she had collected in her dry mouth pouches.

Since there was always food of one sort or another available on the island, such an enormous store was quite pointless. But filling it occupied her lonely days; growing fatter and fatter, she ate and collected and slept, every day was the same.

When the other squirrels grew tired of playing, which wasn't often, they too would idly store away a bit of food. But their hoards were usually in damp or obvious places: the mice and crows would raid them or sometimes Pig or Porcupine would stumble upon them and that would be that. More often than not the squirrels simply forgot where their stores were hidden, and the nuts and seeds rotted or sprouted when the rains came.

★

One day, during the cool season, the unsettled weather grew more than usually cool – it grew very cold indeed. The sky over the sea became heavier and greyer by the hour. The finches perched silent in the trees, as if they had some foreboding of disaster.

The cutting wind came first, from the shadow side of the island. The leaves spun, showing their silver undersides. 'It's going to rain,' said Pig, knowingly; the cold penetrated his bristly fur. He shivered.

The wind increased in strength, the tree tops heaved; fruit and berries fell to the forest floor: *tump, tump* they went as they hit the ground. The squirrels came in from their playing and huddled together underground. How the wind seemed to search and search down their long burrow tunnels.

The gale blew the nuts from the trees and bushes; they fell like hailstones, *putt, putt, putt* against the leaves. Porcupine huddled in his tiny cave; the deer sheltered behind the rocks by the drinking pool, and the air was filled with wind-tossed blossom.

But it wasn't blossom time! These petals were snow-flakes, and now the deer had cold white noses.

Already littered with nuts and berries blown from the trees, the forest floor filled up with snow. Deeper it grew, so that the squirrels' burrows became muffled and dark. And still it snowed. And still the icy wind blew.

'What is it?' said the animals. 'What has happened?'

The wind blew all that night. The snow heaped up in drifts around the tree trunks. Even if the

131

squirrels had remembered where their stores lay hidden they could not have got at them.

At first light everyone was cold and hungry. The wind had dropped but the sky hung heavy and grey and the forest lay deep in snow. The branches were bare of food. The monkeys were hungry, the deer were hungry, the mice and finches were hungry. Pig was hungry.

'We're going to die, aren't we?' said Hedgehog to Tortoise. Tortoise felt too cold and slow to answer. He stared out over the endless sea. But it was true, for if the small animals and birds didn't get any food soon they would probably die – some of them that very day.

The squirrels tunnelled desperately in and out of the snow looking for their hidden supplies. They blamed wild pigs and crows for stealing them.

The fat and lonely chipmunk woke cold and hungry like everyone else. Hedgehog's snout came snuffling at her burrow entrance hoping for a snail or worm.

'Good morning,' said Hedgehog, 'you've missed out on everything as usual.'

He told Chipmunk all about the storm and how the cold blossom-like snow now covered everything; he told her how the birds and animals would soon starve to death one by one, beginning with the smallest, which meant mice and squirrels like her. 'If you don't believe me, come and see the snow for yourself,' said Hedgehog.

Chipmunk, barely awake, followed Hedgehog out

of her burrow. It certainly was cold. The snow beneath her paws woke Chipmunk up. 'There's no need . . .' she muttered to herself.

'There's no need . . . what?' asked Hedgehog.

'There's no need to starve,' said Chipmunk, suddenly bright-eyed. Then she told Hedgehog why.

Hedgehog grew very excited. 'Come on,' he fussed, 'what are we waiting for! Let's go and find this tree of yours.'

As they set out for the dead tree at the foot of the mountain, Hedgehog told everyone about Chipmunk's secret store.

'If this is a joke, then it's a very cruel one,' said the other squirrels. But they followed her all the same for anything was worth trying.

Soon there was a fluttering and hopping procession of birds and small animals going towards the edge of the forest. Tortoise and Pig had helped to flatten some sort of a path through the deep snow. It wasn't long before they had all gathered at the foot of the tall bleached tree that stood among a jumble of boulders at the bottom of the mountain.

At first Chipmunk couldn't find the stone that blocked the lower hole of her food store. The others helped to clear away the snow. When at last they found it, the stone wouldn't move. Pig swung at it with his tusks; the whole clearing held its breath.

And then the stone spun aside. Out of the hole spurted a wave, a flood, an avalanche of dry nuts, golden seeds and hard-skinned berries. The foot of the tree swarmed with mice and squirrels, jungle fowl and finches while the larger animals waited their turn. There was plenty for everyone. As quickly as they cleared the food from in front of the hole, more flooded out. There was sufficient dried food stored in the height of that huge hollow tree to keep them all going for many days.

Tortoise wasn't keen on wrinkled berries, but he chewed on them patiently and soon he felt better. Pig stuffed himself with nuts; they were his favourite food.

'We've got a lot to thank you for, Chipmunk,' chattered the other squirrels. But, as usual, Chipmunk was barely able to say anything and turned away tied up in knots of shyness.

The snow melted in a few days. The sun shone and the forest dried out. The squirrels went to Chipmunk's burrow every morning and asked her to play. On the fourth day she came outside and watched. On the fifth day she joined in.

It never again snowed heavily on Firefly Island, though sometimes in the cool season the top of the mountain shone crisp and white. The rotten tree eventually blew down, but it was quite empty, for Chipmunk never kept a store again – she was too busy playing. And with all the hiding and chasing she became quite thin and nimble.

'What is it like to be dead?' the squirrels asked Tortoise, when he had finished the story about the snow and everyone almost starving to death.

Tortoise watched the ribbon of waves coming up over the sand. He was not sure. 'I look at the fallen leaves and shrivelled mosses,' he said, 'and I see them ever so slowly become earth. The trees and bushes and plants feed from the earth and we, in turn, feed from them. In this way, the leaves and moss are never lost; they are part of us. How much of me is leaf and moss; how much of me is Tortoise?'

The tide was coming in and frothing around his legs. The squirrels ran further up the beach.

'I cannot see,' said Tortoise, puzzled, 'exactly where anything begins or ends.'

IV

THE UNWELCOME VISITOR

Firefly Island had been buffeted by many storms, so it was no surprise that Tortoise had stories to tell about the winds and high seas he had seen.

The winds came from far over the ocean and soon disappeared again; but often the seas would leave behind strange things on the sand: shells and oddly shaped branches – and other things that Tortoise didn't understand at all.

'Tell us the story of Big Bottlenose,' said the Pelicans.

The story had begun on this very beach, so Tortoise closed his eyes and tried to remember how it had been.

Once there was a tremendous storm. All night the island had been pounded by steep breakers and heaving surf, but by morning the wind had dropped and a watery sun rose over the white sands. There on the beach lay an extra rock, just where the stream ran out of the forest and down to the sea.

The pelicans discovered it first. It was an enormous black boulder, seven times as big as Tortoise.

'But it's not stone at all,' said one of the pelicans, looking closer, 'it's got two eyes and a mouth.' And it had.

'I want to go back in the sea,' said the bottlenose whale unhappily. But she was firmly stuck, high up the slope of the beach where huge waves had washed her the night before.

'Why don't you roll and flap down to the sea like we do?' said the seals. But she couldn't. The finches flew into the forest and sounded the alarm: 'Come and help, come and help!' they twittered.

All the animals tried to roll the whale back into the water – but, even with Tortoise and the pigs helping, it was hopeless.

'It's so hot,' groaned the whale as the sky grew bluer and the sun rose higher. She had to get back into the sea soon or she would die. Everyone thought hard.

Then the monkeys had an idea: 'Remember that wall we built across the stream when it was so hot?'

Pig remembered: the monkeys had made a lovely cool pond under the shade of the trees.

'And remember when we broke down the wall?' said one of the monkeys with a smile. They remembered.

The animals set to work at once. On the edge of the forest, where the little stream ran down the sloping sands to the sea, they began to build a dam. The curving wall grew higher, the stream became a pond; it grew deeper and deeper.

Meanwhile, to keep Big Bottlenose cool and

moist, the pelicans went back and forth to the sea's edge and scooped up water in their beaks. They poured the water over the whale's back.

'Thank you,' she sighed, 'that's lovely.'

It was a tremendous dam. The monkeys wove rushes and creeper in and out of the tree trunks. They carried branches and rocks to build the wall. Pig shovelled mud and blocked up any gaps with tussocks of grass. Tortoise helped roll the bigger boulders into place. They made sure that the centre of the dam had a weak spot – it was part of the plan.

As the pond filled, its water stretched back into the forest. Before long the dam was as high as it could be and the water started to flow thinly over the top.

'We're ready,' said the monkeys. They began to pull out the stones from the centre of the dam. Below the dam lay the stranded whale, and down the slope of the beach lay the sea.

The monkeys took away as many stones as they dared: they were frightened that before they could jump clear, the dam would burst and the flood of water wash them out to sea.

Tortoise tucked in his head and charged at the weakened wall with his heavy shell. It began to give way and water spurted through gaps in the stones. Tortoise took a deep breath and dug his claws firmly into the sand. Would the monkeys' plan work?

With a rumble the dam collapsed. A wall of green water curled down the beach, swirled around the poor hot whale, lifted her up and rolled her down to the waiting sea like a great black log. With a flap of her broad tail she finally pushed herself out from the shallows into the deep waters of the lagoon.

The animals cheered. The whale blew a whoosh of spray from her blow-hole. 'Thank you,' she called, 'thank you. How can I ever repay you!'

Thinking that it would be the last they'd ever see of Big Bottlenose, the animals waved and shouted goodbye.

The bottlenose whale, the twisted logs, the shells and seaweed – they were not all that the sea washed up on the night of the storm.

Clinging desperately to a floating jumble of drift-wood came another creature. Only a solitary finch, sleepless on his wind-tossed perch, saw it arrive, but he was unable to follow it in the dark.

After the animals had freed the whale and returned to the cool of the forest, they had a feeling of unease: the finches and chipmunks were puzzled as to why some of their friends were missing. As the day wore on they sensed that something was terribly wrong: there had been strange pouncings in the under-growth and hidden panic in the lower branches of the trees.

'There's something after us!' the finches sang.

'Yes, something attacked us too!' chattered the squirrels.

A foreign smell hung in the air. A few feathers were found and strange footprints in the wet earth of the forest paths. The deer said they would follow the trail.

It didn't take them long to find the intruder. He was crouching under a bush, a wide smile on his face.

'What do you want?' one of the deer asked him. 'Why do you bring fear and trouble to Firefly Island, where do you come from?'

But the cat didn't answer, he only smiled in a knowing, self-satisfied sort of a way. A finch's feather hung from his whiskers.

The deer went back and told Tortoise and the others what they had seen. Pig was furious, his teeth chattered in rage and he set off along the path at a gallop, determined to skewer this strange animal with his tusks. But when Pig arrived and skidded head-over-heels into the bush in a fountain of leaves, the cat sprang gracefully onto a low branch and settled down to cleaning his paws as if nothing had happened.

The animals asked Tortoise what they should do. They had to get rid of the intruder. How awful if one day the trees stood bare of birds; if sunrise and sunset were empty of singing.

'Unless we do something,' said Dormouse, 'there will be no-one smaller than Porcupine left alive.'

'Better to act sooner rather than later,' agreed Pig, who was still a bit dazed.

Tortoise turned away and dragged himself down to the sea's edge to think. His head was empty of plans. Why should an intruder have to spoil every-thing! As Tortoise lay there worrying, a nose and a pair of eyes appeared out of the water. It was Big Bottlenose.

'I thought you were long gone,' sighed Tortoise.

'No,' replied the whale cheerfully, 'your island is as good a place as any to wait for some of my own kind to pass by again. The ocean is a big place to be alone.'

'It must be,' agreed Tortoise, who suddenly felt lonely too.

'You seem very miserable,' said the whale, 'what's happened?'

Tortoise told the whale their troubles.

'How did this creature get here?' asked the whale. The others had gathered round Tortoise, but only one bird knew how the cat had arrived.

'I saw,' chirruped the finch, 'on the night of the storm! It came in with the waves, on a jumble of strange logs.'

The whale was thoughtful; it didn't take her long to shape a plan.

'If the creature came from over the ocean,' she said, 'then that is where we must return it. All we need is a fresh offshore wind and a small, but brave volunteer.'

Before she could stop herself, Dormouse opened her mouth: 'I'll do it,' she squeaked, 'I'll do it, really I will.'

Nobody slept well that night – and having heard the whale's plan, Dormouse slept worse than any of them. She prayed that by morning there would be a stiff wind blowing in from the sea, and the plan would have to be abandoned.

At first light a silent procession of chipmunks and finches, mice and lizards, hedgehogs, frogs and rabbits – and every other animal and bird smaller than Porcupine – followed Pig to the cave set deep in the rocks by the drinking pool. It was damp and dark inside. Pig and Tortoise stood guard at the entrance. 'We're safe here,' said the squirrels.

'Maybe,' jeered the rabbits, 'but who wants to spend the rest of their lives in a mouldy old hole like this.'

Tortoise watched the leaves high above the cave entrance. He smiled. The wind was blowing down from the mountain. It blew across the mossy tree tops and on out to sea.

'Dormouse is out there alone,' sniffled Pig, 'I wonder how she's getting on?'

Dormouse was looking for the cat. The pelicans had flown back and forth over the forest and reported the cat's position. The cat lay asleep in a patch of sunlight not far from the sandy bay. Everything was perfect.

Dormouse crept up to the cat as he slept and pulled one of his whiskers. A big green eye stared at Dormouse. 'Oh, sorry to disturb you,' squeaked Dormouse, pretending to be horrified, 'I thought you were Rabbit.' At once she moved off, dragging one of her legs behind her as if she was lame.

The cat, so surprised at what had happened – and so curious to know what this fool of a mouse was up to – held back from catching and killing the dormouse straightaway. The cat had a few questions to put first: 'Where is everyone?' he asked, in his slow silky voice, 'I woke up hungry this morning, but found the island suddenly empty of anything worth eating – save for one rather dim, lame dormouse, of course!'

'Well, they've gone,' shrugged Dormouse.

'Gone? But where?' asked the cat.

'Not telling,' replied Dormouse and dragged herself off into the undergrowth.

This mouse was easy to follow and the cat had more questions. He placed a heavy paw on her tail and held her fast.

Dormouse pretended to be terrified. 'Oh please don't eat me,' she begged. 'If you eat me you'll never find the others; I would be your very last meal – my secret would go with me.'

'What secret?' said the cat, cautiously.

'The secret of where the others are hiding,' said Dormouse.

'Do you mean,' said the cat quietly, 'that I could find the others? That they haven't gone far?'

Dormouse nodded her head and lowered her eyes. 'And you're going to help me, aren't you?' said the cat sweetly.

Dormouse bowed her head as if full of shame. 'Follow me,' she said, in a whisper.

Still limping, Dormouse led the cat towards the sandy beach at the edge of the forest. Their progress was painfully slow, and the cat grew hungrier by the minute. When it came to crossing the stream they faced a great delay for the cat was terrified of getting his fur wet and Dormouse, with her pretend bad leg, made a show of being unable to leap or climb over anything. In the end Dormouse hung on to the cat's back as it sprang across a narrow stretch of water downstream.

Now they were on the beach, the sand hot on Dormouse's pink feet. She led the cat to the very edge of the sea, where rounded boulders and spits of sand jutted out into the deep water. A warm wind from the forest ruffled the surface of the lagoon so that it was difficult to see the shell-strewn bottom easily.

Dormouse limped out to the very end of a jetty of sand, and with a sigh she slumped down in the shade of a large trunk of driftwood washed up by the tide.

'I don't see anything at all,' said the cat, joining Dormouse. He was determined the mouse shouldn't slip away but he was nervous of the deep water lapping on three sides of them.

'Don't panic,' said Dormouse, with another little sigh, 'have a rest, relax. We're very close now.' But truthfully she already had the cat just where she wanted him.

The cat could not relax. Water made him jittery. And hadn't he felt something of a tremor in the sand and rocks beneath him? Yes, there it was again!

It was too late to run away. At that moment Big Bottlenose propelled herself out into the lagoon, with the cat, the log, and Dormouse balanced on the patch of her back which remained clear of the water. Most of the sand and seaweed with which the pelicans had disguised her was washed away.

Dormouse waved goodbye to the car and then threw herself into the water. A sharp-eyed pelican, who knew the whale's plan, landed at once on the waves beside Dormouse and scooped up the sodden little creature in its beak. Big Bottlenose, meanwhile, sank lower and lower in the water so that the cat had no choice but to jump onto the log and hold on.

The whale dived into the glassy blue depths and away. There was the cat, dry but alone. The pelicans, who were kind birds, had wedged a wad of fresh fish into a hole in the log, so that the cat would not starve.

The wind blew the log further and further from Firefly Island, until, to the animals watching from the beach, it became only a black speck on the wide turquoise sea. And then it was gone.

Everyone congratulated Dormouse as she dried herself on a hot rock. They had come rushing from the cave as soon as they'd heard from the pelicans that the cat was adrift on the log. But where was Big Bottlenose? They had not had a chance to thank her.

'Where had she gone?' the finches asked Tortoise, when he had finished the story. But Tortoise didn't know. He wondered what it was like to live in such emptiness. Firefly Island was surely the best, the only place to be.

V

THE CAVE OF THE COLD WIND

One evening, when the animals of Firefly Island had gathered on the beach to hear Tortoise's stories, somebody mentioned Bear.

'This has been just the sort of hot and horrible day that Bear would have hated,' grumbled Wild Pig, rolling in the damp sand.

'Bear?' asked some of the younger animals, puzzled. 'Who is Bear? What is Bear?'

Tortoise was one of the few animals old enough to remember Bear. 'Bear is no longer with us,' said Tortoise. 'He is here on Firefly Island but we don't see him.'

'Tortoise is telling us, in a gentle way, that Bear is dead,' said one of the rabbits.

'No, I am sure Bear is not dead,' Tortoise replied quickly, glancing up at the steep mountain that stood at the centre of their island. 'If ever you could find the Cave of the Cold Wind, then I am certain you would find Bear, too.'

The animals stared at the faraway mountain rising above the trees. Its jagged ridge of honey-coloured rock came straight out of the sea on one side of the island, reached a sharp summit in the middle, and then fell back steeply into the sea on the other side. Goats lived on its lower slopes; their hooves had worn giddy little paths between the ledges where they fed and the caves where they sheltered. Above them was high country that belonged only to the eagles. No grass or scrub grew there. Vicious winds blew over the sharp ridge; the air was thin and cold and bare rock sparkled with frost. The mountain was a barrier to whatever lay beyond.

'The mountain has so many caves,' sang the finches, suddenly curious to see Bear. 'Which is the special cave where Bear lives? Which is the Cave of the Cold Wind?'

'You won't find Bear,' grunted the rabbits, 'the caves are hot and airless and they stink of goat droppings. No-one would want to live up there: not even this bear, whoever or whatever he is.'

But Tortoise was not listening to the finches or rabbits. Thinking of Bear had reminded him of a terrible time on Firefly Island long, long ago.

'If it had not been for Bear,' he said quietly, 'I think that none of us would be here this evening.'

A sudden hush fell upon the animals.

'Once,' said Tortoise, 'the sun shone like it did today. But it shone hard and hot every day, for countless days. We enjoyed it for a while: such cascades of flowers there were; such smells from the dry forest floor; such warm comfortable nights. But the rains that usually come after the blossom has fallen did not arrive. No clouds billowed up over the horizon. The day of the shortest shadow came and went; and still it had not rained.

'The precious Rizzleberry fruit hung hard and shrivelled as pink seashells and across every green leaf in the forest crept a bitter brown stain of dryness. The smaller streams ran dry and their muddy bottoms opened up into deep cracks. The waterfalls that had once roared white and achingly cold became silent: only thin trickles of tepid water snaked over their slimy rocks. The bog where the frogs lived turned slowly into a bowl of dust. Those were bad times,' sighed Tortoise, 'terrible times for all of us. But especially bad for Bear.'

'Why?' asked the rabbits.

'Because Bear was a big animal,' Tortoise replied, 'and his fur was thick and black, and quite soon he was dreadfully hot and uncomfortable. Normally he would have lain blissfully beneath one of the waterfalls or swum in a pond deep in the forest. But it wasn't long before the only fresh water left on the island was a little dribble running from the foot of the cliffs into the drinking pool.'

'Why didn't he go for a swim in the sea?' asked one of the rabbits.

'Because,' said Tortoise, 'the salt water made Bear's skin itch, and when it dried, his fur stood up fluffier than ever. Poor Bear was miserable, he lay in the shade by the drinking pool with his chin on his paws and dreamed all day and all night of slipping down the pebbly edge into the clear cool water.'

149

'Why didn't he just jump in?' asked the rabbit.

'The pool was for drinking, not for swimming in,' Tortoise replied. 'During the day I stayed on guard. The animals had to queue up to drink; I was there to make sure nobody stirred up the mud or drank more than they needed.' Just telling the animals about it all made Tortoise's mouth feel terribly dry.

As the drought worsened, the animals became very frightened. Was this the end? Had it come so soon? They had often grumbled or complained about their ordinary lives but now they seemed precious and wonderful. They didn't want to die.

Bear felt more uncomfortable than afraid. One night, hot and sticky, he could put up with it no longer. Making sure that everyone was fast asleep, he padded delicately to the edge of the pool and as quietly as possible, nose first, he slid into the moon's perfect reflection.

Ah! how deliciously cool it was, what a relief; his hot sweaty fur soaked to its roots at last. He lay on his back looking up at the firefly stars, determined not to worry about tomorrow. Who would ever know he had done this? He could take a secret swim every night. It was a lovely thought.

But the next day, when the animals lined up and took their turns to drink, there was uproar.

'Ugh! the water's bad!' said Badger.

'It's revolting,' said the monkeys.

'It tastes of damp fur,' said Wild Pig.

'It tastes of *Bear*!' said Porcupine.

'Oh Bear! How could you do such a thing,' cried all the animals together.

They were furious. They shouted at Bear; they insulted him; they promised never ever to forgive him.

Bear was a bit taken aback: was it such a terrible thing that he had done?

'We don't want you any more,' said the other animals, 'we never want to see you again.'

There is no feeling so awful as when everybody hates you. Even in the hot dry air Bear's eyes became rather moist. He turned his back on them all and lumbered off into the forest. Their hate followed him like a smell; like a swarm of angry honey-bees. He wanted to get as far away as possible from their cross faces and dislike. He wanted to find a place where he would not be disturbed.

Bear travelled right through the forest until he reached the great wall of Firefly Mountain. One of those caves up there would be a good place to hide, he thought, as he set off up a narrow path made by the goats. Soon he was high above the forest. He didn't care if he fell. His clumsy paws sent stones clattering down into the tree tops.

But when he reached the caves they were hot and smelly, so Bear climbed higher and higher always hoping he might find a better one.

And he did.

One of the caves was lovely and cool. Good, thought Bear in his misery, I shall find the back of the cave and curl up in a big ball and go to sleep – and with any luck I shall never wake up again.

But this cave ran deep and dark into the mountain and Bear could not find the back of it. There were alcoves and smaller caves leading off the main passageway but these smelt stale and uninviting. A cold breeze ruffled Bear's fur, he was sure he could smell trees and ferns. His black nose led him on. Normally, Bear might have been afraid in such complete darkness, but though he could see nothing, the wind blowing through the cave grew sweeter and cooler. He could smell wet moss now, and wasn't that the roar of the sea?

A faint light began to show on the rock walls of the passageway; and then round a bend, perhaps a thousand paw-lengths away, Bear saw a tiny circle of daylight.

The cave had narrowed now so that Bear's bottom brushed the roof and sides. Nearer and nearer came the end of the tunnel and then suddenly he was out in the open.

Bear couldn't believe what he saw: below him a steep green landscape of stunted bushes and white waterfalls led away down the mountainside to the tree tops of a dark forest. And curved around the edge of the forest was the sea.

Bear had come *through* the mountain; he had found a secret way. He was now the other side of Firefly Island.

The ledges of rock beside him were cushioned with old snow. The sun never reached this face of the mountain nor even the forest below. The plants and trees were different here: they liked the coolness and the shade – just like I do, thought Bear happily. He plunged his muzzle into an icy stream and took a long, long drink. Silver fish darted in the pools and larger fish leapt the waterfalls. The shrubs were heavy with ripe berries; some bitter and some sweet. This is the place for me, thought Bear, the perfect place.

He had just set off down the mountainside to enjoy his new world when suddenly he remembered the other animals – they were back there, on the other side, baked and blistered and without water. Bear made up his mind to forget them all; they had not forgiven him so why should he forgive them. Bear felt quite indignant.

But the memory of the parched animals followed him, like the shadow of a horrible bird. He felt uncomfortable and ugly inside. The memory stopped him enjoying the dew-wet berries and the clouds of cool mountain mist. Remembering the thirsty animals spoiled everything – and Bear realised that it always would. So he turned around and headed back up the slope to the small dark mouth of his secret cave.

The next day, back at the empty drinking pool, Lizard and a few of the chipmunks were licking the last damp patches of mud to cool their tongues. The other animals lay around the pool in what shade remained. The sky was clear and cloudless – there was no hope of rain. The end of everything seemed near.

And then Bear crashed through the bushes scattering flocks of tiny birds. 'Where's Tortoise?' he demanded. 'Where are Badger and Pig? I've got some important news.'

'Oh, Bear,' said Pig, with a mean sneer in his voice, 'nice to see you again, Bear. Have a swim, we really don't mind. Go on, enjoy yourself.'

Bear looked at the empty drinking pool and the circle of miserable animals. 'I've got something very important to say,' Bear growled and he told them what he had found.

The animals followed Bear up the zig-zag of the stony goat tracks. First the deer and then Coati; then Pig and the porcupines; then the monkeys and Lizard and Grass Snake. The pelicans and partridges followed, and a long way behind struggled the rabbits, dormice, squirrels and a fluttering of finches.

Pig felt giddy under the glare of the sun. Sometimes his hind hooves slipped off the edge of the narrow path and kicked for a moment in thin air. He muttered to himself, 'If this is some sort of cruel joke of yours, Bear, I will never, ever . . .' But Pig could not think of anything sufficiently awful with which to threaten Bear: things couldn't get worse than they already were.

'How will you know which cave it is?' panted Porcupine.

'I scratched the rock outside with my claws,' said Bear. 'I'll know which cave it is when I get there.'

And he did.

Here were the claw marks, and here the cold wind blew. There was a lot of bumping of noses and pulling of tails along the dark passage of Bear's cave. Nobody wanted to lose touch with those in front. Only Mole felt completely at home. The squeaks, grunts and chattering of the animals echoed strangely up and down the cave.

The tunnel narrowed so that the deer had to lower their heads. And then a glimmer of light glistened on the damp rock, and rounding a corner the animals saw a far-off circle of sky.

A booming, scraping sound in the tunnel behind them alarmed the finches. 'Quick!' they cried out. 'The roof's falling in!' But the noise didn't come again and the animals hurried on towards the daylight.

Then, there they were, tumbling from the cave mouth out into Bear's secret country. How wonderful the water tasted, how sweet the berries.

'Thank you, Bear, thank you, Bear!'

The finches pecked at his ears in gratitude, the dormice jumped up and down on his paws. Bear enjoyed being a hero. Everyone thanked him; everyone except the pelicans who were busy flying from the stream to the cave and back again. Bear wondered what errand they were on.

High above the summit of the mountain soared two eagles.

'You knew all this water was here,' shouted the

monkeys, 'and yet you never told us. How could you not tell us?'

But the eagles, as always, gave no hint that they had heard.

Soon night shadowed the mountain. It was very cold. A burr of frost crisped the edge of each leaf and blade of grass; stones by the stream's edge became slippery with ice. Bear felt warm enough with his thick coat but the other animals were chilled. They huddled around him to keep warm; the finches and partridges fluffed up their feathers; the squirrels and dormice burrowed deep into Bear's fur. The deer browsed patiently, their breath hanging like mist in the frosty air. Nobody wanted to sleep next to Porcupine. Pig grunted in his sleep and his little hooves twitched as – in his dreams – he ran from a pack of angry bears.

The next day the animals moved down the mountain and into the dark green woods. It was warmer here and the forest floor was springy and brown. The tall trees had needle-like leaves, the berries on the bushes were large and tough; the river crashed powerful and white between huge rounded boulders. It was big country, best suited to big animals. Bear felt completely at home but the other animals did not.

Every day, Bear sent one of the energetic monkeys to look over the other side of the mountain to see if it had rained yet. For a long time they were disappointed, but one evening a monkey came back and said he had seen great clouds boiling up on the far horizon; and a warm moist wind blew from that direction, too.

The next day the monkey bounded down the mountainside, tripping and rolling over in his excitement. He told them that the far-off clouds had now gathered low over the island on the other side and raindrops as big as rizzleberries drummed from leaf to leaf; the streams ran muddy but full, and already the brown clearings had sprouted a green haze of new shoots. The drought was over and it was time for the animals to go home.

But Bear was staying. He was happy here: out of his misery had come great contentment. So he said his goodbyes, one by one.

'Did you say goodbye?' asked one of the rabbits when Tortoise had finished telling the story of Bear. Tortoise seemed uncomfortable; he didn't reply.

'We were always told,' said the rabbit, 'that there was nothing but sea and sky the other side of the mountain. How wonderful to have actually *been* there. You really do know everything, Tortoise.'

But Tortoise looked rather embarrassed. 'I didn't say goodbye to Bear,' he confessed, 'though I wish I had. There was a reason why I didn't.'

'What was the reason?' asked Rabbit.

Tortoise cleared his throat. 'Do you remember I told you how the finches heard a scraping noise and they thought the roof of the cave was collapsing? Well, the tunnel grew narrower and narrower as it neared the other side . . .' Tortoise paused for a moment, ' . . . and I got stuck!'

The animals on the beach couldn't help laughing, but Tortoise didn't mind. 'That was why the pelicans were flying up to Bear's cave with beaksful of fresh-water – I was terribly thirsty.'

'Did you ever get unstuck?' asked another rabbit.

Tortoise smiled. 'Of course I did. But it wasn't very funny at the time. The tunnel was full of animals who had said goodbye to Bear, and I was blocking their way. I don't go very fast when I'm going for-wards, but I almost never have reason to go backwards: I was very out of practice.'

'I would love to have seen Bear,' sighed the rabbit, 'I wonder if he's still there.'

'I'm sure he is,' said Tortoise cheerfully. 'I'm sure he's very happy.'

The sky slowly turned red and then a deep dark blue as day disappeared over the sea. That night, as Tortoise slept beneath the rustling leaves on the edge of the forest, he dreamed of Bear. And in his dream, Bear hugged Tortoise with his warm leathery paws: a great big hug that was both 'goodbye' and 'hello'; a hug that told Tortoise everything was going well.

VI

KING BADGER

At the end of one hot and sultry day, as the animals gathered together on the beach, a distant rumble filled the sky: a sound like a huge tortoise's shell being scraped against a boulder. The clouds far over the sea lit up with flashes of white light.

'There's a storm brewing,' said Wild Pig, knowingly. The smaller animals began to get nervous and fidgety.

'Don't be afraid,' said Tortoise calmly. 'In all my life I have only known thunder and lightning hurt one animal – and even then, not very seriously.'

'Tell us about it, Tortoise,' the animals said, 'we are all listening.'

'All except Badger,' said the rabbits, 'he's gone off somewhere.'

'In the circumstances that is not surprising,' Tortoise said with a smile, 'for in fact my story is all about Badger.'

Peacock was partly to blame for what happened to Badger.

Peacock was moulting and very worried about

159

losing his good looks. One morning he stopped Badger in his tracks. 'Tell me I'm still beautiful,' he begged, 'all my feathers are falling out.'

'Don't worry, you look quite splendid,' said Badger, who like all badgers was terribly short-sighted; he was the last person Peacock should have gone to for an opinion.

Peacock, feeling generous in his new hope, began to flatter Badger, 'Well, you yourself are an unusually handsome badger, you know.'

'Thank you,' said Badger, thoughtfully. He'd never bothered very much with his appearance and in fact he was a rather flea-ridden bramble-torn specimen. But from that day on, a feeling of being superior began to grow in Badger. He became discontented with the noise and bustle of family life; of sleeping below ground in a cramped hole with his argumentative brothers and sisters. I am too good for all this, he thought, I want to be free of the drudgery of being an ordinary badger. In his determination to be something special, Badger left home.

He went first of all to visit a sleek and beautiful badger who lived on the other side of the forest. For a long time Badger had only dreamed of daring to ask her to be his mate: now he felt both brave enough and handsome enough. He was a bit puzzled when she refused even to look at him. Never mind, thought Badger, I will try again another day when my appearance has improved still further.

But he didn't manage very well on his own. He was cold at night and whenever it rained he got soaked through. His ragged unkempt claws were in too poor a condition for him to dig a nice dry burrow all by himself. He wasn't even very good at snouting for worms and roots. Badger gradually fell into a dreadful state.

One day, bumbling along a path through the undergrowth, Badger bumped into a rabbit crying her eyes out. 'What's the matter?' he asked.

'The deer are kicking us off the Big Clearing,' sniffed the rabbit. 'It has the sweetest, richest grass and we've always been allowed to graze there and now they say we can't.'

In general the badgers and the rabbits didn't get on together, but Badger was glad of company: even miserable company was better than none at all. 'Come along,' he said reassuringly, 'we'll go and sort it out.'

So they found the Big Clearing and peered out from under the bushes to see what was going on. It was true: whenever a rabbit hopped out of the circle of trees onto the grass, the deer would push it away with their foreheads or even kick out with their small black hooves. They were being very possessive about the grazing.

Badger ruffled up his fur so as to look especially fierce. 'You big bullies,' he growled, rushing out into the open, 'why not pick on somebody your own size.' He ran in wild circles, grunting and grumbling, nipping at their heels. The deer were terrified and bounded off into the shadows of the trees not knowing what had attacked them.

Badger glowed with pride. He was a hero. The rabbits said they couldn't think of any way to thank him. Badger couldn't think of anything either. But then the rabbit who had been in tears found a large juicy worm and brought it to Badger as a present. That one worm was the beginning of all the trouble that followed.

'Thank you,' said Badger, pleasantly surprised, 'I am very fond of worms,' and it was a delicious worm too. Badger thought the rabbits ought to know what else he liked. 'The occasional beetle or slug would be very welcome,' he added, 'and fruit and berries too, when they are in season.'

And that is how it all began. There were so many rabbits that it was really no bother supplying one solitary badger.

Badger grew fatter and his unused claws grew longer. He protected the rabbits with the occasional display of fierceness. He even chased the deer from clearings where the rabbits had never normally been allowed to graze. But in general his life was one of ease.

Badger lived down the rabbit burrows with the rabbits, but he couldn't really get used to their smell, or to being squashed by dozens of baby rabbits who scratched and kicked out with their back legs as they slept.

When he visited the sleek badger he loved and told her of his easy life and the wonderful food provided for him, she just sniffed the air and said that he smelled like a rabbit.

'You are turning into a Babbit or a Radger,' one of her friends said to Badger with a laugh. Badger felt dreadfully hurt.

'I don't suppose you would dig me a burrow of my own?' Badger asked the rabbits eventually. They agreed, but one or two of them were a bit grumpy at having to excavate such a large hole. It took them several days and Badger found he was losing patience. 'If you don't dig a little harder,' he whispered to the rabbit who had complained the most, 'then I shall come down your burrow one night and give you a jolly good bite.'

Badger's hole was quickly finished. But he wasn't very comfortable. With no mate or brothers and sisters to groom him, Badger soon became plagued by fleas. As he lay awake itching and scratching he blamed the rabbits. After only a few days, Badger left his new hole for good.

'I'm going to sleep above ground from now on,' he informed the rabbits. 'I want you to build me a canopy to keep the rain and the sun off, and I also want you to bring me enough dried grass so that I can have a fresh bed every day.' There's nothing like good hygiene to get rid of fleas, thought Badger.

The rabbits were fed up. 'If, as well as gathering a badgerful of worms, we have to spend all our day nipping off blades of grass and drying it in the sun and fluffing it up into a nice bed for Badger, then we're going to starve. We need some help.'

And because they had been ill-used by Badger, they very quickly thought of a way to get what they needed by ill-treating somebody else. Some of the tougher rabbits set off through the forest in gangs searching for partridges. The partridges nested on the ground and they were easy for rabbits to find.

'You're very good at building nests,' said the rabbits, 'we need lots of dry grass to make Badger a bed, and we hope that you will collect some for us.'

'And if we don't?' said the partridges, surprised.

'If you don't,' said the rabbits darkly, 'Badger will give us a bite and we in turn will come and stamp on your eggs.'

The partridges drew in their breath with a quivering sound.

'And there's another thing that Badger wants,' said the rabbits, 'something that we have neither the skill nor the time to arrange.'

'What's that?' asked the partridges.

'A nice canopy to shield Badger from the hot sun and the rain.'

'But we can't build canopies,' protested the partridges.

'That,' smirked the rabbits, 'is your problem.' And they hopped away back to their burrows.

So the partridges, bullied by the rabbits, soon hatched a plan that involved bullying someone else. 'We can't tie poles together with creeper and build Badger a tent,' they agreed, 'but we do know someone who can.'

And the partridges, in a great whirring of wings, went to visit the monkeys. Flying together in one large flock made them feel quite brave.

'We need your help,' they explained to the monkeys. 'We can do the grass collecting, and carry it to the rabbits, but we can't do the building work.'

'And why should we do it?' shouted the monkeys, laughing rudely. 'We don't owe Badger anything.'

There was quite a long silence before one of the partridges swallowed hard and hopped to a branch nearer the monkeys. 'If you don't build the shelter for Badger,' said the partridge, 'we will peck a little hole in each and every young piece of fruit in the forest and they will rot before they ever have a chance to ripen.'

'But we would starve if all the fruit went bad!' cried the monkeys. 'This is a joke, isn't it? Is it to pay us back for some harmless trick we played on you in the past and have long since forgotten? If that's so, then we're sorry. You know we never mean anyone any harm.'

'We're sorry too,' said the partridge, 'but it's no joke; we have no choice. And neither have you.'

So the monkeys built Badger his beautiful tent. They tied branches together and wove wall panels out of rushes. They lashed thick leaves to the roof, all in neat rows, so that water would run off the edges when it rained. Each day the partridges collected beaksful of dry grass for Badger's bed, and the rabbits dug deep holes in their search for the juicy roots and fine fat worms that Badger demanded for his breakfast.

On sunny days, even under the shade of his canopy, Badger said he felt too hot. He asked the monkeys to fan him with large water lily leaves, and, though the monkeys took it in turns, their thin arms soon ached with all the flapping. It wasn't long before they, with some threat or other, bullied the finches and hummingbirds into fanning Badger for them with their little wings.

'My house still smells of rabbits,' complained Badger, so the monkeys decorated it daily with the brightest and sweetest smelling flowers they could find. Badger was very comfortable, but the other animals were miserable. His power had spread across the island like a disease. Fear was making the animals mean. It was easier now to be on Badger's side than not to be. It was better to accept the tasks forced on one than to refuse.

One day Badger decided he wanted to move house. 'There is a place I like by the drinking pool,' said Badger. 'It has good shade and a nice cool wind blows off the sea. And best of all, the Rizzleberry tree will be growing right outside my door.'

So the monkeys had to build Badger a bigger and better home on his chosen patch of grass; and when they had finished decorating it with jasmine and honeysuckle – and the partridges had heaped up a bed of fluffy grasses and the rabbits had fetched him leaves heaped with grubs and worms – then, Badger was almost satisfied. But not quite.

'Bring me that glossy badger from the other side of the forest,' he ordered, 'so that she can see just how much I have improved. Once I was nothing and now I am king!'

The finches groomed him, the rabbits polished his hideously long claws, the hummingbirds fanned him and the monkeys brought rare blue flowers to carpet his doorway.

But when the beautiful badger was brought unwillingly before him, she had nothing encouraging to say. 'I am sorry for you,' she whispered, 'you have everything you want and yet you are further now from being a true badger than ever you were.'

Badger shrugged his shoulders when she had gone. 'Who cares,' he grunted. But deep down he did care.

To be fair, Badger didn't really see how much his luxury was based on the misery of others. He didn't see all the whispering and suspicion, the bullying and threats. He didn't realise what a monster he had become. For him life was good. In the heat of the day he could swim in the drinking pool; and what if it tasted ever so slightly of Badger – it didn't matter breaking the rules: *he* made the rules now.

Honeycomb, thought Badger, as he lay on his back one day listening to the distant waves breaking on the sand, a nice dripping honeycomb would make life better than good – it would make life perfect.

So Badger demanded that the rabbits bring him honeycomb for his tea. The rabbits asked the partridges, the partridges asked the monkeys and the monkeys decided that scooping honeycomb out of hollow tree trunks and getting stung was something they really did not want to do.

'We'll get Coati to do it,' they agreed. So they found Coati blissfully asleep under a moonberry bush, and they woke him up rudely and told him to bring a honeycomb to Badger's palace by tea time, without fail.

'And if I don't?' asked Coati.

'If you don't, we will make life unbearable for you,' said the monkeys. 'Whenever you go to sleep we will drop nuts on you and wake you up; and on the odd occasion when we *do* allow you to sleep, we'll dribble juice from the sticky-fruit all over your fur so that the wasps and bees come and pester you.'

'Why have you become so horrible all of a sudden?' Coati asked.

The monkeys had no answer; they could not look Coati in the face. 'Don't forget,' their voices echoed, as they swung away through the branches. 'Tea time, Badger's palace — or else!'

And so it was that a miserable Coati came to see Tortoise. Coati's nose and eyelids were all bumpy with bee stings.

'Something has to be done,' nodded Tortoise when he'd listened to Coati's story. Tortoise went to visit Badger in his beautiful palace. The flowering Rizzleberry tree was heavy with finches and hummingbirds waiting their turn to cool King Badger.

'This has got to stop,' said Tortoise gruffly when

he reached Badger's dazzling doorway, 'this is not the way things are meant to be.'

'What you really mean,' snorted Badger, 'is that you don't like being an ordinary tortoise again. You would have liked to have stayed in charge for ever.'

'It doesn't matter who's in charge,' said Tortoise. 'What matters is that everybody is unhappy. If Big Bottlenose were to visit our island today, he wouldn't recognise it — it's a changed place and changed for the worse.'

'Nobody else is complaining,' said Badger rudely.

'No one else dares complain,' snapped Tortoise.

'It looks as though you are intent on spoiling things,' sighed Badger. 'Roll Tortoise over!' he shouted suddenly to the monkeys, 'and take him away and leave him on the beach on his back.'

The monkeys hesitated. Birdsong in the forest died away. There was a long, long pause. The only sound was the sea breaking on the rocks in the lagoon. It was as if the whole island held its breath. Was Badger's power terrible enough to do even this?

'It won't take long,' said Badger encouragingly, 'we'll soon be able to forget all about him.'

And so the monkeys swarmed over Tortoise shouting and jeering to give themselves courage. They rocked him onto the back of his shell and slid him away between the thin trees and out onto the baking sand.

If Tortoise had lain upside down in the sun very long he would have died. But he was lucky. Great boulders of purple cloud had been gathering out over the sea and a cold wind now heaved in the trees. The sun was swallowed up by the clouds and the wind grew stronger still. Drops of rain as big as frog's eyes drummed on Tortoise's underside. The rain beat on the roof of Badger's palace too.

'Hold on to the corner posts,' Badger shrieked at the monkeys, 'you haven't built it strong enough, you idiots; the whole thing is going to take off!'

The little birds from the Rizzleberry tree scattered into low-lying bushes. The sky was split by a jagged flash of lightning; the crash and rumble of it followed a second later. The monkeys let go of Badger's palace and fled into the trees. The rabbits dived for their burrows and the partridges scuttled away to protect their nests. Badger was left all alone in the storm.

The next blinding finger of lightning cracked out of the black sky and stabbed right through the roof of Badger's palace into the earth. Badger had been so close to the lightning-bolt that every hair on his body was singed clean away. He ran from under the collapsing canopy of poles and leaves and out through the doorway of spoiled flowers. Deafened by the thunder, and pink and smooth as a newborn piglet, galloped poor ridiculous Badger. Behind him, his bed of dried grass had caught alight and the whole of his palace was ablaze – his power, and his life, in ruins.

'Who turned you back over?' asked the animals when Tortoise finished his story about Badger.

'The monkeys did; with many apologies,' smiled

Tortoise. 'There was much forgiving to be done on our island that night.'

'And what about Badger?' asked Pig, looking anxiously up at the dark clouds.

'He grew a new coat after a while,' said Tortoise, 'an especially fine one as luck would have it. And he was glad to enjoy the ordinary pleasures of being an ordinary badger. As for the sleek and beautiful badger: well, eventually she agreed to be his mate and they dug themselves a really deep burrow on the edge of the clearing. You won't see old Badger much, he keeps himself to himself, especially on a night like this.'

Spots of rain began to darken the sand and the animals drifted back into the forest one by one. There was another flash and growl from far over the sea. Tortoise secretly hated thunderstorms – they were beyond his understanding – but he didn't want the other animals to know that he, their leader, was afraid.

I shall tuck in my head and legs and pretend I am a boulder on the beach, he thought, and then the thunder will not notice me.

But in the end the storm passed harmlessly by, at a great distance. And Tortoise fell deeply asleep and woke the next morning, brave and refreshed.

VII

THE RIZZLEBERRY WAR

'Why do the goats live high up the mountain?' asked one of the young deer as Tortoise sat on the beach telling them stories. 'It is so dry and steep up there and bare of anything to eat except thorn bushes.'

'The goats are different to us,' said Tortoise, 'they don't think the same way as we do; they live their lives by different rules.'

'Do they ever come down?' asked the deer.

'No,' said Tortoise, 'they have been up there ever since the Rizzleberry War.'

'The Rizzleberry War?' said the deer. 'What was that?'

'Give me a moment to gather my memories,' said Tortoise, 'and I will tell you . . .' And he tried to remember exactly what had happened.

The famous Rizzleberry tree stood on the small strip of grass that grew between the edge of the drinking pool and the steep cliffs of Firefly Mountain. Its twisted trunk threw out many branches: a few of these touched the water and one or two brushed

172

against the rock face. In the blossom season the tree was covered in a dense speckling of small pink flowers. The bees and moths came then, hungry for the nectar in the flowers. And while they were busy in and out the sweet blossom, they carried on their furry backs – without knowing it – the pollen from the male flowers to the female flowers. And where the pollen mingled, there the fruit of the Rizzleberry tree had its first tiny beginnings.

And what a fruit it was! Wonderfully cool even on the hottest day, it burst on your tongue, fizzy, fruity, slightly sweet. There was no taste so fantastic as a ripe Rizzleberry.

But there was a long time to wait between the blossoming and the fruiting, and each year the Rizzleberry tree carried only one harvest of berries. You would think that with so many fruit-eating creatures on Firefly Island, the Rizzleberry tree would be stripped of its berries before they had a chance to ripen. But of all the trees this tree was considered above any ordinary sort of greed. It was a rule, the most important rule on Firefly Island, that the berries were left on the branches until the longest day of the year when the shadow of Eagle Rock lay at its shortest. On that day the animals held a race from one side of the island to the other: and the winner had the first glorious picking of the Rizzleberries.

While the fruit ripened, the animals and birds disciplined themselves not even to look up at the Rizzleberry tree; the temptation to steal might be too great to resist. The animals came to the drinking pool with their eyes lowered, they drank and then they left. That anyone would ever steal the Rizzleberries was quite unthinkable – the Rizzleberry tree was a symbol of the animals' trust of one another.

One year, around the time of the longest day, the monkeys went as usual to measure the length of the shadow on the cliff face. Today the shadow was very short; the day of the race was very near.

In their excitement the monkeys couldn't help glancing down at the drinking pool and at the green haze of the Rizzleberry tree. But wait a moment: it shouldn't be green at all! It should be *red*. Red with ripe berries.

The monkeys sounded the alarm. Somebody had stripped the Rizzleberry tree of its fruit. It wasn't long before all the animals had gathered under the tree to try and work out what had happened. The berries were gone and somebody was to blame.

'It wasn't us,' cried the rabbits. 'Whoever saw a rabbit climb a tree! You know we need someone to shake the tree for us so that the fruit drops to the ground.'

'It wasn't us,' said the deer. 'We've been over the far side of the island for two days.'

'Maybe,' said Pig suspiciously, 'but how do we know exactly when the fruit was stolen: it might have been several days ago.'

'It wasn't us,' protested the finches. 'You'd know if we'd stolen the berries by the colour of our droppings.'

'Well, it certainly wasn't me,' said Pig indignantly, 'you'd see my hoof marks on the bark.'

'Hush, all of you,' said Tortoise. 'Now think carefully. Does anyone remember the last time they saw berries on the tree?'

There was a long silence. Nobody seemed able to remember. The truth was there had never *been* any berries on the Rizzleberry tree that year – and for a very good reason. In the blossom season, Badger's palace had stood right beside the tree; the finches had crowded onto the branches while they waited to fan Badger, and whenever a bee or a moth had come anywhere near the blossom they had pecked at it or gobbled it up.

The pollen had not been carried from flower to flower; the fruit had never even begun to grow. And when the finches left the tree during the thunderstorm, heavy raindrops had knocked the blossom to the ground.

The great race that summer was a dull event; nobody tried very hard and – without a prize waiting at the finish – who could blame them. But the next year when the tree was once again heavy with blossom, all their old suspicions returned.

'We are not going to allow the thief to strike again,' said Pig one day. 'From now on I am going to keep guard right under the tree until the day of the great race itself.'

'Don't be silly,' said Tortoise, 'you've got to sleep and eat; you can't manage on your own.'

'Anyway, how do we know Pig won't steal the berries?' said the deer. 'We've as much right to guard the tree as he has.'

Tortoise sighed. 'Pig can guard the tree during the day,' he said, 'and you can guard the tree at night. If anything happens to the berries we will know who's responsible.'

While the tree was still in blossom, the other animals were content to leave it up to Pig and the deer to keep guard – after all, it wasn't a very satisfying job – but as the first hard green beginnings of fruit appeared, all the animals began to take a closer interest.

'Perhaps we wouldn't know if Pig or the deer were stealing the fruit,' said Porcupine. 'If they just took small amounts each time they were on guard nobody would notice; the tree would look the same.'

'Quite so,' said Lizard. 'I'm going to guard the deer to make sure they keep their noses out of the branches at night.'

'And I am going to guard Pig,' said Porcupine, 'to make sure he isn't tempted into the occasional nibble.'

For a while the other animals considered the Rizzleberry tree to be safe. They didn't envy the guards their long hours of duty. But after the rains, when the green berries began to swell and turn pink, the animals' mistrust of each other grew fast.

'How do we know that the deer and Lizard might not come to an agreement to enjoy a little bit of fruit in secret and then promise not to give each other away? Pig and Porcupine might do the same.'

'In that case we are going to guard Lizard and the deer,' said the dormice.

'And we are going to keep a careful eye on Pig and Porcupine,' said the squirrels.

'This is ridiculous,' said Tortoise, 'no good can come of it all. Let's go home peacefully.'

But the animals ignored him: they were too busy expecting the very worst of each other. They quickly divided into two sides; the daytime guards and the night-time guards.

The riper the fruit became, the more tense and suspicious each side grew of the other.

'What if Pig's army suddenly agree to share out the fruit among themselves,' whispered the deer, 'they could strip the tree bare in less than a day.'

'Don't worry,' said Lizard, 'we will make sure there are enough of us to stop them.'

Pig's followers were saying much the same thing about the deer's army.

'If they really stuffed themselves,' warned Porcupine, 'they could eat all the berries in one night.'

'Maybe,' said Pig, 'but our side will be strong enough to recapture the tree at the first sign of any trouble.'

Each army was eager to get the support of as many animals as possible. Soon there were very few creatures on Firefly Island who had not joined one side or the other.

Pig even went and asked the goats to join his army – though they were usually considered too stupid to be of any help over anything. But the goats wouldn't answer Pig, they just stared at him with their indignant faraway eyes.

★

The tree grew riper each day. One evening, Tortoise went to the drinking pool and called the animals together.

'I'm very worried,' he said. 'No good can come of us getting ready to fight each other. Something terrible will happen if we don't sort this out soon.'

'What do you suggest then,' said Pig crossly, 'that we all go back to our ordinary lives and trust to luck that the berries will stay on the tree? Be realistic!'

'I wish we could go back to the old ways,' said Tortoise, 'I don't see how we have come to be in such an awful muddle.'

'It's not a muddle,' said the deer solemnly. 'It's a war.'

Tortoise shivered: some sort of ugliness had seeped into their lives; it grew amongst them like a patch of poisonous toadstools pushing up through sweet grass. 'Perhaps there is a solution,' he said at last. 'There are only a few days until the fruit is fully ripe: if neither side can trust the other side to be left alone to guard it, then maybe we should all guard the tree together.'

'That's stupid,' said the rabbits.

'Yes, it is,' Tortoise agreed, 'but it's better than having a war.'

So that night all the animals settled down under the Rizzleberry tree to keep guard as one big group. They were all determined to stay wideawake but it wasn't long before their eyelids began to droop. They lay so close together around the trunk of their precious tree that not one of them could have made a move to steal the fruit without waking someone else. Tortoise did wake once in the night and thought he heard a noise like pebbles sliding down the rock. But he soon drifted off to sleep again.

In the morning, the animals woke up and yawned and stretched and looked up at the Rizzleberry tree to make sure everything was all right.

'Somebody has been stealing berries!' sang the finches furiously.

'Nonsense,' said Tortoise, with a feeling of dread, 'it looks all right to me.'

But sure enough, near the top, a few branches stood out completely bare of fruit.

'It must have been the bats,' snorted Pig.

'One of those monkeys climbed the tree in the dark,' said the deer.

'I expect it was the finches themselves,' said Lizard, 'they just pretended to be surprised and cross when we woke up.'

'Perhaps Tortoise has got a longer neck than we thought,' said Mole.

'Nobody would have felt Grass Snake slithering between us while we slept,' clucked the partridges.

'Maybe Bear came back specially to steal the berries,' said Rabbit.

So there *was* a war at the foot of the Rizzleberry tree after all: but at least it was a war of words. Everyone accused everyone else, and nobody admitted anything. Tortoise looked for claw marks on the tree trunk or tufts of hair caught in the bark but there were no clues. 'The thief must be invisible,' he decided, 'and weightless too – if he can walk all over us while we sleep and not wake us up.'

That afternoon, Tortoise went to see his friends the fireflies to ask them a small favour. It was almost dark by the time he arrived back to take his place under the tree. He had made up his mind to stay awake right the way through until morning.

Tortoise felt tired and sad. The night stretched ahead of him, black and endless. Sometimes he would begin to slip into sleep and then wake with a sudden jolt: as if he had slid off the edge of the goats' track that led to Bear's cave. It was a hot and sticky night and Tortoise longed to be down by the cool sea. He could hear the leaves of the Rizzleberry tree trembling in the breeze . . .

What breeze! There was no wind – and yet the leaves were trembling. Tortoise was wide awake now. Something was happening in the tree.

'Wake up everybody!' shouted Tortoise. 'Wake up!'

His friends the fireflies hovered above the tree in a great cloud; they gave out only a dim light, but enough for the animals to see who was in the tree.

There, with their hindlegs on the cliff face and their front legs making a bridge into the branches, were two goats.

They sprang back from the tree in alarm and clattered up the steep rock face and away.

The goats had never even thought of stealing from the Rizzleberry tree until Pig first planted the idea in their heads by asking them to be guards in his army.

'We must forgive the goats,' said Tortoise when morning came and the indignant growls and snorts and twittering had died down.

But nobody could ever get close enough to the goats to tell them they were forgiven. They would just climb higher and higher up the mountainside, stopping to look back now and again, their defiant, distant eyes seeming to say: well, what *is* there to forgive anyway?

'Even today I still feel a bit sorry for the goats,' sighed Tortoise when he had finished the story of the Rizzleberry War. 'It must be a lonely life on top of the mountain.'

'If they ever did come down,' asked the young deer, 'do you think they would steal from the Rizzleberry tree again?'

'I think they probably would,' nodded Tortoise.

'In that case we must keep a guard on duty underneath the tree, night and day,' said Pig, very seriously.

'No,' said Tortoise with a smile, 'I don't think that would be a very good idea.'

The other animals laughed at Pig's foolishness. And in the end, so did Pig.

VIII

TURTLE'S MEDICINE

Tortoise settled down to sleep but he couldn't stop thinking about the goats. Like Eagle in his empty sky and the coloured fish in their deep lagoon, the goats inhabited a separate, lonely world. Since the Rizzleberry War there had only been one occasion when the goats had touched the lives of the other animals.

'Tell us about it, Tortoise,' begged the young deer, 'please, tell us.'

So though it was late and the first stars already winked in the dark roof of the sky, Tortoise told them.

The goats were very agile and sure-footed on steep rock but they did sometimes have accidents. One day a young and inexperienced goat was tiptoeing along a narrow path when the loose rock under his hooves suddenly collapsed and down he slid in a tumble of dust and pebbles. He would certainly have been killed had he not landed on a ledge only a little way below. On the ledge lay a large circle of dry twigs and leaves. It was an eagle's nest. The goat's fall was cushioned by the nest; he didn't even notice the bundle of squawking feathers he had sent spinning over the edge and into the tree tops far below. The goat scrambled back onto the path above, a little bruised, to look for his friends.

The eagle returned later and found her nest empty. What had happened? Where had her baby gone? She was in a panic. The eagle dived to where the cliffs met the tree tops; but the branches spread out so thick and so close against the rock face that, with her broad wings, she could not find a way through to the forest floor below. Her shadow put fear into the other birds nesting there and their calls of alarm drowned the squeaks of the baby eagle.

A little monkey happened to be exploring that part of the forest and he found the eagle chick crying in the undergrowth.

'Where do you come from, little fellow?' said the monkey, and the eagle chick told Monkey how he had been knocked out of his nest by a falling goat. 'Never mind,' said Monkey, 'I'll put you back in your nest,' and tucking the eaglet under one arm he went to the foot of the cliffs and began to climb.

Climbing was what this monkey loved best: rocks or tree trunks, it didn't really matter which. He had already climbed all the tallest trees in the forest – except the Snake Tree – and he had been wandering around that day just in case there was a really special challenge he might have overlooked.

It wasn't long before Monkey was high above the

trees and putting the baby eagle back into its rather flattened nest.

'Goodbye then,' he said cheerfully. He was just lowering himself back over the ledge when something hit him so hard it knocked all the breath out of him; letting go with his arms and legs, he rolled down the cliff and into the trees below. The eagle had asked no questions; she had seen Monkey with his hand in the nest and had decided he was to blame.

Monkey lay where he had fallen and was glad to be alive. But his tail hurt terribly and his legs felt very strange. 'That's all the thanks I get for helping out,' he cried, and pulling himself up he headed painfully for home.

The further he went, the more his tail hurt and the more tingly his legs felt. By the time he reached his home tree on the edge of the forest he felt very strange indeed. His mother was furious with him: 'You are very foolish to have gone anywhere near Eagle's nest,' she said, 'we've always told you to keep well away from the eagles.' Monkey felt too ill to argue.

Then his mother comforted him and gave him a big monkey-hug.

'I'm only cross because I'm worried,' she said. 'The best cure for you is a good night's sleep.'

And Monkey did sleep, but his dreams were full of huge shadowy wings and cruel curved beaks that pecked at his tail. And in the morning when he woke, Monkey couldn't feel his legs at all.

'Don't be unhappy,' said his mother when he burst into tears, 'I'm sure you'll be all right soon, you are probably just a bit stiff and bruised.' She brought him some juicy fruit to eat and made him a comfortable bed of leaves on the forest floor. As the days went by, Monkey did begin to feel a bit better: except in his legs – he still couldn't move them or even feel that they were there. His friends came to see him and tried to cheer him up.

'Don't worry,' they said. 'You'll soon be the monkey you used to be. Just give your legs a chance to recover.'

But Monkey was miserable; how would he ever climb again without the use of his legs?

'Things will improve, I'm sure they will,' said Pig confidently.

'You will get better,' clucked the partridges, 'you wait and see.'

'Everything takes time to heal,' said his special friend, Coati, 'be patient and hopeful.'

But Monkey lay on his bed of leaves and watched the others sliding down the waterfalls and swinging in the trees and he was filled not with any hope, but with envy.

The other monkeys saw his longing and made an effort to include him in their games. They carried him through the branches and swung him by his arms, but never very high or very fast because it would have been dangerous. Monkey was glad to be up amongst the leaves again and to feel the wind in his ears but somehow it wasn't at all the same.

'The trouble is,' he said to Coati, 'they are very kind, but all the time I know that they are aching to leave me and get back to their own games. And who can blame them? I am just a burden to everybody.'

'Nonsense,' said Coati, 'nothing has changed, you are still our good friend.'

Every day, after his games, Monkey asked to be carried down to a shady spot on the edge of the beach. Then he would tell his friends to leave him. He would sit under the trees staring out to sea, watching the waves rolling in over the reef.

Coati was worried by Monkey's sad sea-watching, and he made up his mind to go and find some medicine for Monkey's useless legs.

'Ask Pig,' suggested Monkey's mother, 'he knows all about strange roots and fungi.'

But Pig laughed and said he only knew which plants made him sick.

'Ask Badger,' Pig said, 'he's always saying how he knows everything.'

But although Badger knew which leaves to rub on a nose stung by bees, he had heard of no plant to mend a broken monkey.

The squirrels had a store of berries that put fire in your tummy and helped you to sleep when it was very cold, but nothing that might bring back life to tingly legs.

Even the deer knew of no herb or flower which might cure Monkey's legs. 'You could ask Turtle, I suppose,' they said. 'This is the season to find her.

She comes to the beach at the end of the island where the sun rises, and there she lays her eggs.'

Coati thanked the deer and set off at once to find Turtle. He travelled through the night, following the fringe of sea as it washed in and out over the moonlit sand. By morning he'd reached the far end of the huge curving beach and there he found the female turtle digging a hole for her eggs.

'The deer say that you are very wise,' said Coati, 'and coming from the sea you know things that we can never know.' And then Coati told Turtle about Monkey's accident and how even though Monkey's friends now did everything for him, he was still miserable and sat watching the waves and wishing he was dead.

'We keep telling him he'll wake up one morning and everything will be fine again,' said Coati, 'but he's just empty of hope.'

'Did you say you want him to walk again,' said Turtle carefully, 'or to get better?'

Coati was surprised, 'Aren't they one and the same thing?'

'Not necessarily,' said Turtle.

Coati didn't understand.

'Do you really want Monkey to get better?' asked Turtle.

'Of course I do,' replied Coati.

'Will you do exactly what I say?' said Turtle.

Coati nodded. 'I think so.'

Turtle now looked Coati in the eyes with a strange ocean-deep stare. 'You must tell Monkey that he will

187

never get better; that there is no medicine for his useless legs, and that he will never again be the monkey he was.'

Coati was horrified. 'Do you call that good advice?' he cried. 'I call it a death sentence. You are nothing but a mean ugly old sea monster!'

But the turtle ignored him and returned to her digging.

'What a wasted journey,' muttered Coati to himself as he headed back along the beach. He was very tired and the noise of the waves booming on the sand made it difficult for him to think. All the way home, Coati tried to work out *why* Turtle had behaved in such a heartless way.

Towards the end of day he drew near the beach where Monkey usually sat on his own in the shade. But today Monkey was not alone. A whole crowd of excited animals was with him, waiting for Coati's return.

'What have you brought Monkey?' they called out.

'What did Turtle say?'

'Where's the medicine then?'

Coati looked at their hopeful faces, he felt ashamed to have come back empty-handed.

'Turtle has this advice for Monkey,' he said at last. A hush came over the animals. 'Monkey will never walk or climb like he used to. There is no cure or medicine for his useless legs, and they will never get any better.'

The animals drew in their breath; they were

shocked, and embarrassed too, because Coati had said out loud what each of them had secretly been thinking for quite some while. They muttered excuses and drifted away into the forest to get on with their lives.

Only Coati remained.

Monkey was astonished. Turtle's cure wasn't at all what he'd expected. He stared out to sea and had a long think.

'Who cares,' he said at last, shrugging his shoulders, 'I'd climbed every tree on the island anyway.'

He turned to his friend. 'Thank you, Coati,' he said, 'I needed to be told the truth, otherwise I would have been sitting around until the end of my life just waiting for my legs to get better.'

Monkey suddenly felt more hopeful: maybe there were still exciting things to do in life. Perhaps I could try and climb the easiest trees again, he thought, using just my arms and tail.

By the time he and Coati had found the other animals, Monkey was full of new ideas. 'I'll need your help to begin with,' he said, 'but after that I won't want any special treatment.'

Every day Monkey did exercises to make his arms and tail stronger. He practised by holding on to a loop of creeper and pulling himself up and letting himself down many times in a row. He balanced heavy stones in his hands and pushed them up and down above his head until his shoulders ached. Soon he had bigger and better muscles than any of the other monkeys.

Coati organised the building of a sleeping platform high in the branches of a twisted starleaf tree. The platform had a fence around the sides to stop Monkey rolling over the edge in his sleep and a lovely woven roof to keep him dry. Hanging from the edge of the platform and reaching to the ground was a ladder made from strong sticks and twisted ivy. Tied to a branch above the roof were many lengths of creeper; these had been stretched and tied to other trees in the clearing so that it was easy for Monkey to travel from tree to tree.

'It's fantastic,' said Monkey when Coati showed him over his new home, 'thank you all for making it.'

Monkey was much more cheerful now. It wasn't long before he had climbed some of the easier trees in the forest without the help of any ladders or ropes. It didn't matter that he had climbed them before as a baby monkey.

'What an adventure,' said his friend, Coati, 'to start a new and different life.'

'Yes,' said Monkey. 'If it hadn't been for Turtle's medicine, I'd still be staring out to sea.'

Tortoise had come to the end of his story.

'Did anyone ever thank the turtle?' asked one of the young deer.

'I don't think she expected any thanks,' said Tortoise, 'she knew how hard it would be for Coati to follow her advice.'

'I would love to see a turtle,' said the young deer.

'Turtle is only here for a very short time,' said Tortoise. 'Her young hatch in the sand and then they too slip into the sea and are gone. Her underwater world is a very different place to ours.'

Tortoise left the animals then and went down to the very edge of the lagoon. Sometimes he was able to see right into the beautiful clear rockpools, with their gardens of coloured weeds and rainbow shells. But it was night now and the surface of the water was dark and wind-ruffled and hid everything beneath it.

How strange it must be, thought Tortoise looking out to sea, to have no edge to one's world. We have a beach; we know the shape of our island and just how far we can go. But Turtle can swim away in any direction and keep going – her world has no limits, no ending. She can, if she chooses, swim on for ever and ever and ever.

IX

THE SNAKE TREE

'Why are we not allowed to climb the Snake Tree?' asked one of the little monkeys when Tortoise had settled down for an evening of stories and memories. 'It looks such an easy tree to climb,' the monkey went on, 'it's the biggest and tallest tree on the whole island; it would be such fun to reach the top.'

Tortoise put on his most serious face. 'You know very well it is absolutely, completely, and utterly forbidden to even think of climbing the Snake Tree; to even touch its lowest branches.'

'But why?' the little monkey persisted.

Tortoise was just about to get very cross when he realised that the monkey needed something more than a rule and a threat – he was old enough for an explanation.

'Settle down around me then,' said Tortoise with a sigh, 'and I will tell you the story of Porcupine. It's a frightening story and when I've finished you won't have any more questions about the Snake Tree.'

*

Porcupines are good climbers. By day they sleep in caves or hollows, but at night they climb trees and eat bark, which they find nourishing and delicious. When Porcupine was young he loved climbing; it was the only thing he was any good at. He had many noisy young friends: tiny mischievous monkeys; boisterous badgers; naughty little wild pigs. They were always in trouble, daring each other to do sillier and yet sillier things. The piglets came home again and again with scratched and bleeding snouts; the monkeys suffered bruised bottoms and sprained tails; the badgers ended up stung all over by angry bees. But Porcupine was usually lucky – until the day his friends dared him to climb to the top of the Snake Tree.

Porcupine had an awful cold sick feeling when his friends first suggested it. Everybody knew how important it was to keep well away from the Snake Tree. But the more he thought about it, the less terrible the idea became. If there was anything really bad about it, thought Porcupine, then surely somebody would have told us exactly what the danger was. It's probably just because we'll get dirty, or too tired, or because there's something really delicious at the top. The adult animals were like that: rules often seemed to be for their own convenience or simply to be obeyed because they themselves had obeyed the same rule when they were young.

My mother is Porcupine the famous conjuror, he thought, but I will be known as Porcupine 'the nothing', unless I do something special in my life.

The idea of climbing to the top of the Snake Tree, the highest and only unconquered tree on the island, became more and more attractive to him.

One night, when he and his mother were moving from tree to tree, chewing bark, Porcupine slipped away. I'll just have a look at the Snake Tree, he thought, to see how difficult a task it's going to be.

The undergrowth became thinner and thinner as Porcupine neared the clearing where the Snake Tree stood: it was as if the grass and weeds had grown sick. Soon there was only dry earth beneath his paws. The moon threw a criss-cross of shadows over the forest floor. Porcupine could hear no rasping or clicking of insects, no gurgling streams, no comforting song from the night finches.

The clearing was still and dead.

There stood the tree. The base of its trunk was enormous, as solid and dark as rock. The lower branches were themselves as thick as tree trunks, they spread out sideways in every direction before bending upwards and disappearing into the canopy of leaves above.

Porcupine trod gently across the clearing. He touched the bark. From a distance he had thought it was smooth, but in fact it was covered in large scales like a snake's skin. The scales pointed downwards. Every now and again there was a ring of loose scales which stuck out slightly. If you put your paw up underneath these loose scales, there you found a useful ridge to hold onto. It would be as easy to climb the Snake Tree as climbing Monkey's stick and ivy ladder.

Porcupine felt a fluttering in his chest as if he had breathed in a large dragonfly. The bark of the Snake Tree gave out a lovely perfume, an exciting smell that made Porcupine feel eager to begin; a smell that made him feel everything would be all right and that at the top there would be something especially nice waiting for him.

I will just go a little way up tonight, he thought, to see what it's like.

He chose one of the side branches that almost brushed the ground before it turned skywards. He pushed one paw under a loose ring of scales and there his claws found a ridge to hook onto. His other paw he slipped under the next loose row of scales slightly higher up and there he found another ridge – see, it was easy!

In no time at all he had pulled himself to a giddy height above the clearing. I will carry on until I reach a good turning-around point, he thought. And he climbed a bit higher. Soon I will reach a good place to rest, he thought. And he climbed a bit higher. I will wait until I get a chance to cross over to another tree, he thought, and then I'll be able to get down. And he climbed a bit higher still.

Porcupine soon realised that there were no good turning-around points; no convenient places to rest; and no chance of crossing to another tree. A sick, cheated feeling began to spread to his arms and legs. He was suddenly very afraid.

Climbing upwards, it was simple to see which rows of scales were loose and hid the easy handholds; but looking downwards the scales appeared to be all the same. Like snakeskin — which is rough to the touch if you stroke it one way, yet streamlined and smooth when you stroke it the other — the bark of this tree made it easy to go up and impossibly slippery to go down. And worse still, though it was dry when Porcupine climbed up, the pressure of his feet and body on the bark produced a thin oily juice which ran out from under each scale and down the branches of the tree.

Porcupine kept climbing. He knew now that the tree had tricked him. It no longer had an exciting perfume — it smelled of rotting fish and toadstools. He shouted out for his mother, but the spiked leaves of the Snake Tree muffled his cries.

'I am too tired,' he said, 'I shall fall, I know I will.'

But there was no stopping now, the trunk and its thick branches pointed on and upwards. Hearing the wind rattling the leaves and seeing flecks of moonlight on the branches, Porcupine knew he had already climbed clear of all the other trees in the forest.

'I am Porcupine, the first climber of the Snake Tree,' he whispered to himself, 'and I am surely going to die because of it.'

It wasn't long before Porcupine reached the very top of the tree. On the tip of each branch grew a huge flower. The fleshy petals of each flower formed a cup big enough to have held even Pig. Porcupine pulled himself up between the rubbery petals and lay panting inside the flower.

The sky over Turtle beach was already turning pink. The sun would soon be up. Porcupine was too frightened to appreciate the view he had of the island. In the centre of the flower, rainwater had gathered. It lay there forming a pool and the slippery petals of the flower led down to the sweet-smelling water. Porcupine was thirsty. Digging his claws into the petals he crouched and touched the water with just the tip of his nose: 'Ouch!' A terrible pain like a wasp sting burned on the part of his nose that had touched the liquid. Porcupine jerked back – it wasn't just his sore nose that worried him. Under the surface of the stinging juice he could see a brown sludge of drowned flies and moths and there, in the very deepest part of the flower pool, a scattering of little white bones. So, he was not the first creature to reach the top of the Snake Tree. Porcupine now understood how the tree trapped and digested its food. It had led him here and now it waited. Porcupine wouldn't be able to stay awake for ever. Eventually he would fall asleep and roll down the smooth petals into the pool at the heart of the flower.

Porcupine's mother was very worried. She had spent all night searching for her youngster, calling for him through the forest.

'I know the mud in the frog's swamp has sucked him under,' she cried to the deer, 'or else he has gone to the beach to play and been pulled out to sea by a freak wave.'

But nobody had seen young Porcupine near the swamp or down by the sea, so his mother kept imagining other and more awful things that might have happened to him. The finches said they would fly up and down the island and see if they could spot Porcupine: perhaps he had fallen from a tree and banged his head, or got his foot tangled up in a creeper. The finches searched beneath and above every tree on the island, except the Snake Tree – they avoided it. The tree was always empty of birds. It was a bad place. Porcupine would not be there.

But Porcupine *was* there. He poked his head out between the petals of the hideous flower that had captured him and cried for his mother. Far below lay the forest, the tree tops bunched like cushions of moss on a boulder. Flocks of searching finches skimmed over the trees like shoals of tiny fish and he could see the lines of white waves curling onto the shore, but too slow and silent they moved, like in a bad dream.

At last the pelicans joined the search, flying higher and more steadily than the finches. They checked the steep cliffs of Firefly Mountain and the isolated rocks far out on the reef. And last of all they flew low over the top of the Snake Tree. There was Porcupine.

'We'll never get him down,' said Pig, when the pelicans reported back to him. 'Nobody else is going to climb the tree and no bird can land up there safely.'

'And even if we did,' said the pelicans, 'we couldn't

fly Porcupine out of the flower. He's too prickly to touch and he weighs as much as a fat rabbit.'

'We could ask Beaver to chop the tree down,' said Pig. But the pelicans shook their heads, it seemed there was no sensible solution. 'We'll go and ask Monkey if he has an idea,' said the pelicans, 'but we won't tell anyone else: Porcupine's mother would be just *too* upset if she knew what had happened.'

Monkey was in his house high in the starleaf tree. 'In the old days I might have climbed the Snake Tree with a length of creeper and rescued him myself,' said Monkey; but he couldn't think of a plan.

When the pelicans flew back to Pig, Monkey sat looking at the humming-birds hovering over the forest flowers and at the weaver finches busy building their basket nests. And as he sat, an idea blossomed in Monkey's mind in the same way as tightly furled petals in a bud open out into a big and colourful flower. But the idea frightened Monkey too; and a coldness, like the shadow of an eagle's wings, came over him.

To begin with, Monkey asked the weaver finches to weave him one of their basket nests, but a much bigger basket than usual, big enough to hold a piglet or a baby monkey. 'It must be very light and very strong,' said Monkey. He told the finches to build the basket right on top of the starleaf tree.

While the weaver finches were busy, Monkey set out for Firefly Mountain, swinging by his arms from the spider's web of creepers that the other monkeys had built for him. He was very afraid of what he had to do, but at the same time he was filled with a terrible determination to do it. 'You fool, you idiot,' he kept muttering, 'turn back, let someone else think of a way to rescue Porcupine.'

Soon the net of overhead creepers came to an end and Monkey was forced to swing to the ground and make his way through the undergrowth as best he could. It was easier when he got to the foot of the mountain; Monkey's arms were strong and his hands clever at finding cracks and ledges. It wasn't long before the last branches had brushed against his back and he was out on the bare cliff face.

'What are you doing here,' cried Eagle when Monkey reached her nesting ledge, 'you, of all the animals!'

'I came to ask you a favour,' said Monkey. 'I helped you once – though you never even knew it – and now you are the only one who can help me.'

'You helped me?' said Eagle with a mocking laugh. 'You came to steal my baby!'

'No, I found your chick at the bottom of the cliff,' said Monkey indignantly, 'it was the goats who knocked him out of the nest. I was putting him back when you attacked me.'

The eagle was silent. The mountain wind ruffled her golden feathers. She cocked her head and stared at Monkey with first one orange eye and then the other. Was this the truth or was it a lie? the piercing eyes asked. Eagle decided that Monkey was telling the truth: but she didn't apologise for the injury she had caused him. She only asked where she could find the starleaf tree and the weaver finches' basket. Then she spread her wings and flew from the ledge, leaving Monkey alone in the sun.

Eagle found the Starleaf tree, and the basket waiting in its topmost branches. She gripped the basket in her black talons and flew off towards the Snake Tree, its horrible purple flowers easily visible way above the tops of the other trees.

When she got there, the down-draught of Eagle's wing beats rattled the flower petals together. She hovered above each one like a giant searching bumblebee, and then she found Porcupine. With perfect control, Eagle lowered her yellow legs down into Porcupine's flower until the basket swung just above the surface of the stinging juice. 'Climb in!' Eagle ordered Porcupine. And Porcupine did as he was told. The basket was made of dry grasses and reeds that had been perfectly woven together. The finches had left a large round hole in the side as a doorway, and through this hole Porcupine scrambled.

At once, Eagle's powerful flapping quickened and she lifted the basket up and sideways, out of the flower and away. As Eagle flew higher and higher over the forest the wind whistled through all the tiny gaps in the woven walls of the basket. Porcupine put his head out of the round doorway and looked down on the whole of Firefly Island as no four-footed creature had ever done before. 'I am Porcupine the Flyer,' he sang in delight, 'higher even than the Snake Tree. The first and last and only flying Porcupine!'

Porcupine knew that he could see everything now: there was the tiny drinking pool and the beach where they sat for their stories. There was Firefly Mountain, small as a pointed boulder, and, on the other side of it, the dark shaded woods that not even Tortoise had seen. Bear must be down there somewhere, fishing in the powerful rivers; berry-picking on the frosted mountainside. And the sea! How far and blue it reached on every side, curving away beneath the sky so that Porcupine could not see where, or even how, it ended.

Eagle folded her wings then and dropped like a boulder. The rushing air screamed and tore at Porcupine's basket. 'Stop fooling about,' cried Porcupine, 'I shall be sick.' The waves and the beach and the tree tops flew upwards to meet him. At the last moment, Eagle opened her wings and glided low and level just above the soft sand. She let go of the basket and flew off at once towards her mountain.

Porcupine climbed giddily out onto the hot sand. Eagle had gone without waiting for any thanks. And when the next wave came in and picked up the basket and carried it out to sea and sank it, Porcupine began to wonder whether any of it had ever really happened. His friends didn't believe his story and he could prove nothing. He never found out who had arranged his rescue. Pig, the pelicans and Monkey told no one what had happened: they wanted no special praise or thanks. It was enough for them to see young Porcupine grow up strong and prickly instead of being a little underwater pile of bones in a flower at the top of the Snake Tree.

'And that,' said Tortoise, 'is the end of Porcupine's story.' Porcupine never became known as Porcupine the High Flyer or Porcupine the Great Climber: he just became Porcupine the Teller of Tall Tales – and he was happy enough to leave it at that. But his story was just frightening enough to keep any other youngster from ever daring to try and climb the Snake Tree.'

'Why doesn't Beaver chop it down?' the little monkey asked Tortoise. 'Then the last bad thing on Firefly Island would be gone.'

'Beaver says the bark tastes of dead crabs,' said Tortoise. 'He can't bring himself to take even one decent bite out of it.'

Tortoise looked at the animals around him. 'We all want to be happy,' he said. 'Badness seems to sprout up here and there in our lives, and I don't understand why. Sore throats, broken legs, filthy tempers – we can't escape these things; we have to carry on regardless and live our lives around the edge of them. In the same way we must simply avoid the Snake Tree. Just because it grows here we mustn't let it spoil our enjoyment of the rest of our beautiful island home.'

X

THE DAY OF THE SHORTEST SHADOWS

Every hot season, when the midday shadow cast by Eagle Rock lay at its shortest, Tortoise would announce that the following day they would have their feast. Everyone looked forward to the feast; there was always good food and lots of games and, on the second day, a great race.

The monkeys prepared the food. It was something they had always done for the other animals since the beginning of memory, and they did it well. The fruit in the forest was now at its ripest, the flowers and leaves at their fullest.

The monkeys worked hard and spread out the feast in a clearing at the far edge of the island. What colour, what noise, when, towards evening time, the feasting at last began! Tortoise was happy: didn't this party show how all the different animals of Firefly Island were really one – they were friends, they feared no-one. Suddenly Tortoise felt a great love for all of them, large or small, ugly or beautiful.

Porcupine's mother who was a conjuror had a magic log to show them. It was hollow. She rested the log on a small pile of stones she had built. The log is empty, see! But Grass-snake goes in one end and disappears!

The animals cheered.

See! The log is empty, but suddenly, here is Dormouse! Closing each end with a large leaf, Porcupine muttered the magic words and held up the log again: Dormouse has gone!

The feasting animals held their breath. Porcupine closed the ends of the log again, rested it on the pile of stones, lifted her eyes to the stars, mumbled a spell and . . . a mist of moths and fireflies billowed out from each end of the log and hung like a dancing cloud above Porcupine! It was beautiful, it *was* magic; the animals applauded. Porcupine's conjuring went on and on.

Then one of the monkeys stood up and began juggling. Porcupine's show was over. She went and hid her magic log in the bushes; she didn't want anyone to spot the secret trap-door Woodpecker had drilled for her in its floor. There had been a lot of comings and goings through that hole during Porcupine's display. When at last no-one was looking, Grass-snake and Dormouse were glad to slip out of the hidden hollow in Porcupine's table of piled-up stones. The moths and fireflies had made Dormouse sneeze.

The moon rose from the ocean, huge and round. It was time to play hide-and-seek. 'Remember, don't go far,' called the monkeys as the other animals and birds spread out into the surrounding forest. The monkeys stayed in the clearing and shut their eyes, chanting together:

'Hop or tip-toe
Away you go,
Are we looking?
The answer's NO.

Creep and crawl
Slither or slide,
Choose the cleverest
Place to hide.

Too late to climb,
Too late to run,
We've hidden our eyes
But here we come!'

The monkeys found Lizard straightaway; he was easy to find for he had hiccups. Lizard was very upset; usually his camouflage was so good he did well at this game. 'If I can't even win hide-and-seek, what *can* I win?' Lizard went off to sulk, he hated the great race, there was never any Rizzleberry fruit left by the time he reached the finishing line. 'I'm just an ugly old fool,' he muttered.

'Don't be unhappy, Lizard,' said the monkeys, 'you'll spoil everything.'

Dormouse was the next to be found: she was still sneezing, so the monkeys knew exactly where she was. 'Bother!' said Dormouse.

'Ouch!' cried one of the monkeys, who had

brushed against Porcupine hiding under a thick bush. 'If you'd kept your quills down, I would never have found you,' he said.

The deer stretched their necks upwards and tried to look as much like tree trunks as possible. Pig lay on his back and pretended to be a rotten log. Tortoise was not difficult to find, even though Lizard was resting on his back – thinking Tortoise's bony shell was a large warm stone. The monkeys were not so easily fooled.

Nobody ever found Mole; every time he cheated and dug deep underground.

Grass-snake was the winner: he had wrapped himself around a tree like a length of creeper.

Everyone was tired out. 'It's time to rest,' said Tortoise, 'but don't forget tomorrow is the day of the great race. Since it's impossible for anything as slow and ponderous as a tortoise to win, I shall travel overnight to the finish by the drinking pool. There I will wait and judge who is first across the line.'

'When do we start?' chattered the chipmunks.

'As soon as the rising sun strikes the top of Firefly Mountain,' replied Tortoise, 'and remember, first one to the pool gets first picking from the Rizzleberry tree.'

And leaving the rest of the animals, he set off into the dark forest so as to cross the island and be ready at the finishing line by morning. Tortoise wasn't aware he had a passenger, and Lizard lay so deeply asleep in the coolness of the night that he didn't realise he was getting a free ride. It was only when

Tortoise had nearly reached the drinking pool that Lizard slipped off his back into a patch of deliciously soft grass; so smoothly did he slide from Tortoise's shell that he didn't even wake up.

Tortoise positioned himself at the finishing line and then he too fell asleep.

As soon as the far horizon began to brighten, the animals woke one by one and stretched and yawned and rolled in the dew. They lined up in the clearing where the feast had been held. They waited in silence, watching the peak of Firefly Mountain for that first orange light of the rising sun which meant the race should begin.

'There it is!' screeched the finches. At once the animals set off on their chosen routes into the forest.

'I'm as slow as Lizard,' grumbled Porcupine as he waddled off into the trees, 'I really don't know why I bother.'

'It'll take all day,' complained the rabbits, who might easily have won if only they didn't stop to nibble grass in the clearings.

The squirrels set off towards the mountain; they had a special plan all their own.

Dormouse had decided to cheat. 'Otherwise I haven't got a chance,' she reassured herself. A friendly pelican had agreed to help her, and not to tell anyone either. 'Whatever you do, just keep your mouth shut,' said Dormouse.

The frogs did quite well to begin with, but their legs got awfully tired.

Pig knew exactly which of his usual forest trails

he'd follow – but so did the monkeys. Just as he'd got up speed, something always seemed to stop him in his tracks. The monkeys had dug a pit and disguised it with branches and leaves. Quail and Pheasant were so light on their feet that they scuttled over the top, but when Pig arrived, he crashed down into the pit. 'It isn't fair!' he snorted, knowing who was to blame.

The monkeys built a delicate floating bridge of twigs and large leaves across a muddy pool. Pig thought it was a path and kept going. 'What a fool I am!' spluttered Pig when he splashed hoof over snout into the ooze. There was a lot of laughter from the tree tops. The monkeys could well have been the first to reach Tortoise, but they were more interested in the outcome of their tricks than in winning anything.

Mole was deep in the earth and moving in the right direction, but he'd gone only a few feet when underground boulders put an end to his race.

The deer would easily have won, but as usual they kept stopping and flapping their ears and twitching their noses and sniffing the air, so they were always being overtaken.

Hedgehog was rather slow, except when going downhill: then he curled up in a ball and rolled.

As for Grass-snake, he usually went so smoothly and quietly that nobody ever knew where he was. But the monkeys had stopped him from going anywhere at all this time: they'd tied his tail in a knot around a tree root while he slept.

After a steep climb the squirrels reached the stream that cascaded all the way down Firefly Mountain to the drinking pool at the far end of the island. There they had hidden something rather special: a hollowed-out canoe that Woodpecker had helped them to build. 'The second half of the race is going to be easy for us,' they said with a laugh. But it wasn't quite as easy as they'd hoped!

Each animal dreamed of the solitary Rizzleberry tree that grew over the drinking pool and of how heavy its branches would be with the delicious red fruit which ripened only at this season of the longest day. The winner of the race was allowed to take his fill first; and the others – in order of finishing – to eat what was left. If Pig won there would be nothing left for the others! There was no taste as good as the Rizzleberry fruit; just the thought of it made your paws weak and fluttery.

Tortoise could tell, by the ripple of excitement spreading through the forest, that the leaders of the race were near. In fact, what with one thing and another, they were all very close together: anybody could win.

'Put me down!' called Dormouse to the pelican as they came in to land.

The squirrels had got a soaking in the mountain stream, they were wet and miserable.

'Come on! Come on!' cried Tortoise and the finches, as the noise of the race grew nearer: 'Come on, not far, not far, hurrah, hurrah, you're winning, you're winning!'

Lizard woke up under his tent of grass; he was not yet fully warmed by the morning sun and therefore not very alert. But he heard Tortoise's cheering and encouragement.

'Winning?' said Lizard to himself. 'Winning? Do they mean me?' And at that he pushed himself out into the sunlight and scuttled jerkily towards Tortoise's enthusiastic shouts.

'Really winning?' he panted. It hadn't seemed so difficult after all.

At the same time a line of assorted animals broke through the undergrowth into the clearing. It really was a race to see who would reach Tortoise first. 'Come on, come on!' yelled Tortoise. 'You can do it, Lizard, you CAN do it!'

And he did. Lizard was there first. What a smile spread across his face: 'Me, a winner?' said Lizard with disbelief. 'Really? It was nothing, easy, a pleasure in fact.'

He was as surprised at his victory as anyone else, though he couldn't quite remember how he'd done it – he wasn't out of breath, his legs didn't ache, it had been effortless. I am a true athlete, thought Lizard to himself.

Now for the prize! Lizard ate as much of the Rizzleberry fruit as he could. He stood on Tortoise's back to reach it. He'd often tried to imagine what it would be like, but it was better than any of the tastes he'd invented – red and fizzy, cool and fruity.

It was a good crop and the tree was heavily laden. There was plenty left for the others when Lizard lay burping and tight-bellied in the shade.

'And now to cool off,' said Tortoise, for it was a very hot day. They made their way down to the little beach where the stream ran out into the sea. Here in the dappled shade they rested. Some of the animals went down to the waves to play. Pig lay in the stream. The deer drank and flicked the flies away with their long ears. The wind trembled in the leaves and flowers above them.

Tortoise was happy, he wanted this day to last forever, and in a way he knew it would. Even when, finally, his scaly skin fed the roots of the trees; when the finches bathed and drank in his hollow upturned shell – this day, this happiness he felt, would not have gone; nothing could destroy it. It would still be there in the forest like breathed-out air, like mist hanging as brightly as a cloud of stars or fireflies in the dark.

FARTHING WOOD, THE ADVENTURE BEGINS

Colin Dann

PREFACE

The air was quite still. Starlight bathed the frosty ground with silver. The woodland seemed to be drowsing in the silence of a winter's night. A lean fox trotted noiselessly beneath the trees, seeking shelter before sunrise. A vixen's cry – one he recognized – caused him to halt suddenly, then change direction. He answered the cry with three short yaps.

The vixen was standing under a huge beech tree, her body pressed against its smooth grey trunk. She too was lean; leaner than the fox. She called again. The fox ran towards her.

'I need your help,' said the lean vixen. 'Just as before.'

'Good,' the lean fox replied. 'I'm glad you thought of me.'

'It's for a different reason this time,' the vixen said. 'Come and see.' She led him through the Wood to a clearing. In the clearing several animals were darting about, chasing one another playfully. These were otters. The foxes stood and watched them for a while.

'What's the problem?' Lean Fox asked.

'They are,' came the answer. 'The otters. This is

my hunting territory. I've told them to leave, but they only mock me.'

Lean Fox turned to look at his companion. She was regarding him steadily; expectantly. He turned away again. 'They don't appear to be doing any harm,' he murmured.

'Of course they're doing harm,' Lean Vixen corrected him irritably. 'They're snapping up all the voles. What am *I* to eat?'

Lean Fox's eyes widened. 'Otters? Killing voles?' he queried in surprise. 'Why would they do that? They're fishing animals.'

'How do I know why?' the vixen barked. 'Because they're hungry, I suppose. I thought you'd be some help,' she added disappointedly.

'Well, I . . .' Lean Fox began awkwardly. 'You know, otters are special creatures, aren't they?'

'Oh, not that old story again,' the vixen sighed. 'That's all we ever hear. Well, what am I to do then? Starve?'

'Isn't there anywhere else you can go? I mean, there are voles and mice throughout the Wood. Plenty for everyone.'

'It's difficult poaching another fox's territory,' Lean Vixen replied. 'Besides, what's to stop these precious otters scouring other areas once they've laid this one waste. They're lethal hunters. I've seen them in action.'

Lean Fox felt he had to do something. The vixen was relying on him. He trotted forward. As he approached, the otters stopped gambolling for a moment and looked at him. They showed no fear.

'Why must you take our prey?' Lean Fox yapped boldly, aware the vixen's eyes were on him. 'Don't you have enough of your own?'

The largest otter, a mature adult and a sleek, healthy-looking animal replied airily, 'No, we don't, although what business it is of yours I fail to see.'

Lean Fox's hackles rose. 'It's my business because voles are a fox's staple diet,' he growled.

'Really? How interesting,' the sleek otter answered sarcastically. 'Perhaps you'd better improve your hunting technique.'

The younger otters giggled in a kind of high-pitched whistle. Lean Fox tried to chase them away. They began to show off, tumbling and somersaulting and leaping around, but always keeping well out of his reach. The otters had a wonderfully fluid kind of agility. Lean Fox returned to the vixen's side.

'I don't think there's much I can do at present,' he muttered. 'They simply make me look foolish.'

'Something *will* have to be done,' Lean Vixen declared. 'Why should foxes give way to these . . . these . . . animal clowns?'

1

OTTERS ABROAD

There had always been otters in Farthing Wood. They lived on the fringe of the woodland along the banks of the stream. There they made their homes and dived for fish and frogs and mussels. Over the years their numbers had steadily declined as the resources of the stream – and indeed the pond – had dwindled almost to exhaustion. But as long as there were otters, however few, Farthing Wood was safe and the site protected from development.

These otters enjoyed a special status because they were the only ones to be found over a wide area. Local wildlife groups had campaigned hard, and successfully, for their preservation. The otters knew they were special and they made sure all their neighbours knew it too. They were far from being the most popular of creatures. When they turned to hunting on land because of the shortage of aquatic prey, there was bound to be resentment.

The crucial decision had been taken by one of the most experienced females. She was a mother of three cubs, none of whom was getting enough to eat. One evening, instead of leading her youngsters out of their holt to the stream, she headed for the woodland. The cubs were puzzled.

'The water! Where's the water?' they chattered to each other.

'Hush,' their mother quietened them. 'Aren't you hungry? Of course you are. Well, we must try our luck elsewhere.'

The cubs began to treat the outing as an adventure. They bounced along behind their sleek mother, whistling excitedly. The darkness of the Wood, however, affected their high spirits. The cries of unfamiliar night creatures reached their ears. They fell silent. There was a rustle of dead leaves and Sleek Otter, the mother, pounced suddenly. The youngsters surrounded her. A vole dangled lifeless from her jaws. Sleek Otter dropped it amongst her cubs.

'The first of many,' she said. 'This wood's alive with prey.' She watched the cubs sniffing at the unusual food, unsure of its taste. 'You'll soon get used to it. You'll *have* to,' she added. Her rippling body bounded forward again.

The cubs juggled with the dead animal, tossing it from one to another. Finally one of them ate it, chewing the vole on one side of the mouth as with a fish.

'Good,' the cub whispered and smacked her lips. The three cubs rejoined the hunt.

Sleek Otter's expertise proved to be deadly to any mice, shrews or voles who were scurrying through the leaf litter that night. These little animals had accustomed themselves to the threat of foxes or stoats. But the swiftness and acrobatics of the otter party were something new to them. They didn't know how to escape these new hunters. All four of the otter family caught prey and their appetites were more than satisfied.

'Fish or no fish, we shan't starve,' cried Sleek Otter.

The cubs took up the chant. They felt pleased with themselves.

And this was when Lean Vixen, who was hunting that night too, first encountered them. Her astonishment at seeing her territory invaded by otters made her lose her own quarry and she went hungry.

'Clumsy fox,' shrilled the cubs. They had witnessed her bungled attack on a young rabbit which had managed to reach the safety of its burrow. Lean Vixen growled and she bared her teeth.

'Pay no attention to her,' scoffed Sleek Otter. 'She wouldn't dare to meddle with us.' The otters ran on, under the nose of the vixen who gaped after them. Moments later Sleek Otter killed a shrew without apparent effort, as if to emphasize her superiority. The cubs giggled with delight.

'We shan't starve,' they squealed. 'We shan't starve.'

Lean Vixen watched angrily as Sleek Otter's antics produced four more voles for her cubs to enjoy. The sight of the otter family gobbling up prey from her own preserve made the vixen very angry.

'Haven't you space enough to hunt around your den without stealing from me?' she barked.

As if by way of an answer Sleek Otter snapped up a fieldmouse and ate it herself with elaborate pleasure. 'We're not stealing anything,' the mother otter retorted. 'The mice are here for any hunter to catch. It's not my fault you weren't skilful enough to catch them first.' She turned and called to her cubs. 'Come, youngsters. Let's go for a swim.' The otter family went on their way, chattering and laughing merrily.

Lean Vixen shivered in the cold night air. 'They'll be back,' she told herself. 'I need some support.'

Other otters joined the hunters in Farthing Wood as the winter progressed. They really had no choice. Fish large enough to satisfy their appetites were increasingly difficult to find. Frogs, their other mainstay, were in hibernation and would mostly be hidden until the spring. So the competing foxes, stoats and weasels began to suffer. They couldn't keep any part of the Wood for themselves. There seemed to be otters all over the place, seizing their quarry before their very eyes.

'You and me,' said Sly Stoat to Quick Weasel, 'are fools. Look at the way we're being cheated. And what do we do about it? Nothing. No wonder those otters are so scornful.'

'Don't you have a sneaking admiration for their ability?' Quick Weasel asked. 'Otters have such style.

But you'd better talk to the foxes. *They're* in a very ugly mood.'

'Maybe,' Sly Stoat grunted, 'although they appear to me to be as hypnotized as you are by the whole display. If there's going to be trouble I'll be on the side of the foxes. We ought to drive those slippery customers right back into the water where they came from.'

'You creatures are so envious, aren't you?' a voice said behind them. Smooth Otter, a big male, had heard every word. 'You ought to be grateful to us, all of you. We otters are the protectors of Farthing Wood. Why is the Wood untouched? Because of us. We're very special animals. Humans daren't meddle here. We're the only otter colony for miles around. So as long as we choose to live here with you, you're safe. Remember that!'

'How can we ever forget?' Sly Stoat complained. 'You never cease to ram it down our throats!'

'Stoat has a hasty temper,' Quick Weasel chipped in. She was a little scared of the dog otter who towered over them. 'He didn't mean everything he said.'

Smooth Otter laughed hollowly. 'I imagine not,' he grunted, staring fiercely at the stoat. Then typically, his mood changed and he began to dance around them playfully. 'Try and catch me,' he cried.

Sly Stoat turned away in disgust. 'I'd rather catch myself a meal if you've no objection,' he answered sourly.

★

The foxes were certainly planning to act. 'They over-look how vulnerable their young ones are,' Lean Vixen said. 'Just let me get hold of an otter cub! It'd be worth a whole clutch of voles. *I'm* not going to stand idle any longer,' she vowed.

A badger, an acquaintance, was party to the foxes' discussion. 'We shouldn't take that attitude,' he cautioned. 'There must be a fairer solution. We all have to get along somehow.'

'Tell that to the otters,' yapped Lean Vixen.

'Yes, it's easy for you to talk,' said Lean Fox. 'You badgers aren't affected by this . . . this . . .'

'Theft,' Lean Vixen finished impatiently.

Kindly Badger looked from one fox to another. 'I'm surprised at you all,' he said mildly. 'You're clever animals, you foxes. You live by cunning. How is it one of you at least hasn't managed to outwit mere otters?'

There was silence. It seemed the badger had touched a sensitive spot. Then Lean Vixen said, 'I'll use my wits on them all right. I'll think of some way that'll halt them in their tracks. They won't be so full of themselves – you'll see!'

2

TORMENT

For a while nothing changed. The otters continued
to lord it over the other animals in Farthing Wood.
They even treated the conflict over food as a sort of
game. The other hunters were made to look
awkward and second-rate. A group of otters would
work a patch of the woodland, taking everything
that came their way – mice, shrews and voles – then
move on to another area. Although they hunted
independently, the effect was the same. Stoats, foxes
or weasels struggled to gain a mouthful or two. And
then the otters began to taunt them.

'You're not in the same league,' Sleek Otter
laughed as Lean Fox lost a fieldmouse he had been
trailing to the otter's superior agility. 'You've no flair,
you see. No wonder humans pay you no attention.'

'What do you mean?' snapped Lean Fox.

'Ask yourself. Why haven't the humans moved in
here? They've done so everywhere else.' She paused
to eat the mouse. 'You foxes,' she went on with her
mouth irritatingly full, 'are common creatures like
the weasels and stoats. Humans disregard you. They

ruin your homes and habitats and build over the top of them. But not here. Why? Because of us. How fortunate you are to have us in your midst.'

'You can go *too* far,' Lean Fox snarled. 'I've heard threats. Watch out for your youngsters!'

'Pooh. You'd never catch us,' scoffed Sleek Otter. 'Just you try!' And the otter family raced away through the darkness in a looping sort of movement, the mother at the front and the cubs in a line behind, for all the world like a kind of serpent's tail.

Lean Vixen was plotting revenge. She knew roughly where the otters had their lairs and she wanted to teach them a lesson. She intended to strike at the cubs. When she knew the otter population was absorbed with its hunting she slipped along to the stream-side and, in the evening shadows, followed Sleek Otter's scent to a hollow tree that stood by the bank. Lean Vixen sniffed all around. A cold wind blew, ruffling her fur. She could see no entrance to the otter family's holt, but their scent was so strong she knew their den must be somewhere inside the hollow tree. Growling low in her throat she decided to hide herself nearby and lie in wait for their return.

'You're in for a little surprise, my slick friends,' she muttered and chuckled at the thought, lying down amidst a tangle of dry rushes. Water lapped at the edges of the dead vegetation as the stream glided past. Lean Vixen waited patiently, ears cocked for the slightest sound of movement along the bank.

Nothing. Only the wind sighing in the leafless

boughs of the Wood and the dry rasp of reed–stems around her. Lean Vixen yawned and shivered slightly. Suddenly upstream there was a series of splashes. The vixen turned her head. There was no sign on the dark water.

'A fish jumping,' she grunted.

But, beneath the surface of the stream, Sleek Otter and her three cubs were swimming silently to their holt entrance underwater. They pulled themselves, dripping, into their den inside the hollow willow and shook themselves vigorously. Lean Vixen heard the chatter of the cubs and sprang up in amazement. She ran to the tree. The otters' voices were unmistakable. They were safe inside their den and she had been outwitted. She snarled. The chattering ceased abruptly, then broke out again.

'Mother, I heard a fox!'

'So did I, so did I. It's outside.'

'Take no notice,' Sleek Otter answered them. 'Let it snoop. It'll gain nothing,' she added in a raised voice for the vixen's benefit.

Lean Vixen knew she was powerless and she spun round angrily. She looked at the stream, then back at the willow, and all at once she realized how the otters had bypassed her. She crept down the bank and peered closely at the icy water, leaning far over as she tried in vain to locate the otters' secret entrance. Moments later something bumped hard against her from behind and she was tipped forwards, plunging helplessly into the stream.

A whistling screech of laughter followed her fall.

Lean Vixen recovered herself and, as she struggled to keep afloat, she recognized Smooth Otter who was prancing gleefully on the bank. The dog otter had returned from hunting, had seen the prowler and had deliberately run into her, pitching Lean Vixen into the water. Now, as the vixen began to yap angrily, other otters arrived to taunt her.

'Fox in the water!' one cried. 'Can't seem to swim, can it?'

'Stiff as a piece of wood,' another answered. 'Doesn't move its body at all.'

'Isn't it slow, its legs hardly move,' commented a third.

'Small wonder it can't catch anything,' Smooth Otter laughed. 'It'd take all night to cross a field!'

Lean Vixen was seething. While she had no pretensions to being a skilful swimmer she prided herself, like all foxes, on being speedy overland.

'You – you smarmy, conceited pu-pup-puppies!' she roared, kicking out furiously for the bank. She wanted to tear into them, bite them, snap at them, anything to vent her anger.

'Let's teach her to swim,' suggested Sleek Otter who had left her holt again to join in the fun. Her cubs dived and splashed around the vixen, spraying her with water and goading her all the more. The other otters hustled into the stream and Lean Vixen was surrounded by bobbing, dipping bodies that seemed to appear and disappear again in a bewildering variety of places. They jostled and pushed her away from the bank. Then they grasped her legs with their horribly sharp teeth and pulled her underwater, only releasing her when her lungs seemed about to burst.

'Get . . . away,' Lean Vixen gasped helplessly. 'Leave . . . me alone. Cowards, all . . . of you. Can't fight . . . fairly!' She battled to the bank but, just as she thought she was free, they surrounded her again and, shrieking with delight, butted her over on to her back. Lean Vixen was almost too tired to resist. With a supreme effort she righted herself, scrabbled for a foothold on the bank and heaved herself clear. There was nothing to do now but run for it. Yet running was out of the question. She was exhausted, freezing cold and humiliated. Her legs smarted painfully where the otters' teeth had bitten. Blood flowed from the wounds. She drew several shuddering breaths whilst her tormentors leapt around her like demons.

'We don't like snoopers,' Sleek Otter shrilled. 'Tell that to the other foxes, in case they have any bright ideas.'

'Wasn't worth it, was it?' chanted another. 'You do look a mess!'

'You can't put one over on an otter!' cried Smooth Otter. 'We're supreme. Haven't I said so before? Now you've only made yourself look silly.'

'Run on home and dry off, I should,' Sleek Otter taunted.

'Dry off, dry off and clear off,' one of the cubs cried and shrieked with laughter at the cleverness of his joke.

Lean Vixen slunk homewards, her pride and self-esteem battered. She avoided any of the other foxes and crept into her earth. Luckily Lean Fox was absent. For a long time she shivered miserably.

Gradually anger rekindled in her heart. Certainly the otters had bested her this time. She realized she had made an error of judgement. They were clever animals all right and she knew she should have used a more subtle approach.

'Conceited, vain buffoons,' she growled. 'I'm not finished yet. They won't be jeering next time. A bit of old-fashioned fox cunning is what's needed: the badger was right. There's more than one smart animal in Farthing Wood.'

3

NO PLAYFELLOW

During the following days Lean Vixen racked her brains for a means of retaliation. She didn't mention her humbling experience with the otters to the other foxes. She hoped that none of the animals in Farthing Wood would learn how she had suffered, passing off her injuries as bramble scratches. And now the otters showed another side of their nature.

Snow had been falling intermittently for a day or two. The ground was covered throughout the Wood to a depth of a couple of centimetres. It was an open invitation to the otters' playfulness. They made slides on the stream's banks and, one after another, the cubs tobogganed down them in the greatest glee, then returned for another go. Their mother didn't hesitate to join in. Up and down the length of the stream the otter community was playing, from the youngest to the oldest. They loved the snow and couldn't understand why the other Farthing Wood inhabitants appeared to be ignoring its possibilities for fun.

'Dreary lot, aren't they?' Smooth Otter remarked

to a lone female. 'They need cheering up. Ought to be enjoying themselves on a lovely crisp day like this. Life can't be serious all the time.'

'What are you going to do?' asked the bitch otter. 'Most creatures are asleep in the daytime.'

'Seek some of them out,' he replied as he ran off. 'Why,' he cried, 'they don't know what they're missing.'

Under the trees Smooth Otter sought playmates amongst those who were, in other respects, rivals. This contradiction in roles didn't strike him. He was bent on a round of pleasure and he wanted others to be the same. Fresh prints in the snow led him to Sly Stoat's den. He bounded along boisterously, slipping and sliding on purpose in the powdery snow, calling all the while for others to join him.

A jay screeched at him from a lofty bough. 'Mad creature! Lost your wits?'

The otter skidded to a stop, somersaulted over and looked up, his head caked with lumps of snow. 'Wits? You don't need wits on a day such as this,' he cried. 'All you need is high spirits!'

The jay screeched again and flew off in alarm. Sly Stoat's head popped out of a burrow. 'Oh, it's you,' he said as he saw Smooth Otter. 'I might have guessed an otter would be causing the commotion.'

'Where's your sense of fun?' was the answer. 'Come on, I'll chase you through the snow.'

Sly Stoat's head disappeared at once.

'There's nothing to fear,' Smooth Otter assured him. 'It's only a bit of sport. Tell you what, you chase me. Set your blood tingling!' He raced away, expecting the smaller animal to follow. After a while he turned, but there was no sign of the stoat. 'Oh, what's the matter with them all?' Smooth Otter muttered. 'Where are – ' He broke off as he saw a familiar figure padding softly, cautiously, across a glade. It was Stout Fox. 'Hallo, let's see how the land lies here,' the otter said to himself. 'All foxes aren't the same. Perhaps this fellow would enjoy a run.'

He gambolled across. Stout Fox was at once on his guard. His hackles rose and he bared his teeth.

'No call for that, Foxy,' Smooth Otter told him glibly. 'What's the problem?'

'What a question,' the fox growled. 'You otters are always a problem.'

'Let bygones be bygones,' the otter offered. 'I want your company.'

'Company? Whatever for?' Stout Fox asked suspiciously.

Smooth Otter explained.

'Snow? Play?' the fox repeated dully. 'I don't know what you're talking about. You otters are all crazy, but I've more sense than to listen to you. And I'll give you a spot of advice. Keep away from Farthing Wood if you value your safety.' He turned his back and continued on his way.

'Please yourself,' Smooth Otter called after him. 'You're the loser.' Setting his face once more in the direction of the stream he mumbled, 'Better stick to my own kind. What's the use of courting others' friendship?'

Of course there were plenty of playfellows amongst the otters. But the antics of the otters that early morning had attracted interest, after all, outside their own group. Two delighted human onlookers were trying hard to keep still behind a thin screen of vegetation as they watched the animal gymnastics. Wildlife enthusiasts were not a rare sight in Farthing Wood. They came hoping chiefly for a glimpse of the otters whose existence was well-known in the area. Usually these clever animals confined their activities to those times when people were absent from the Wood – during the night and around dawn – and so they were only occasionally spotted. Now their enjoyment of the snow drove caution to the winds. The two amateur naturalists couldn't believe their luck. It was as though the otters had put on a special display for them. And the humans were not the only witnesses.

'Just look at those show-offs,' Lean Vixen grumbled to Lean Fox as they stood together on the threshold of their new den. 'Running and sliding about like that, don't they ever grow up? They have no dignity.'

'I'm more concerned about the way they draw humans into our home,' Lean Fox answered. 'They're always bragging about the fascination they hold for humankind. And look, there are two of them now on the other side of the stream.'

Lean Vixen instinctively dropped to her belly. 'I never feel safe when they're about,' she murmured, half to herself. 'They can never be trusted. Come inside the den; let's get out of sight.'

Lean Fox followed her through the entrance to the dark interior.

'We ought to protest,' Lean Vixen complained to her mate. 'We don't want human intruders around when our cubs are born.'

'That's a long way off,' Lean Fox answered. 'But I agree. Otters are a constant nuisance these days. I'm concerned about the problem of food when we're bringing up our litter. We shall have to come to a sort of agreement with them before then.'

'Don't kid yourself,' Lean Vixen said sarcastically. 'The only kind of agreement they'd want is one on their own terms.'

The competition for prey heightened after some heavier snowfalls. Food became particularly difficult to find for every creature. There were thick layers of snow throughout the Wood. When prey did occasionally surface, there were tussles, not only between fox and otter, but fox and stoat, stoat and weasel. Every hunting animal was ravenous and they scuffled continuously. The foxes sometimes caught a rabbit unawares. Otters never attempted to hunt rabbits and so, except for the stoats, the foxes had a clear field. But rabbits were always quick to recognize danger and it was generally only old or sick ones that the foxes could reach.

As tension between the different groups reached

its height, the otters stopped visiting the woodland. The foxes were first to notice.

'They've seen sense,' Stout Fox remarked, recalling his warning.

Lean Fox wasn't convinced. 'No,' he replied cautiously. 'It's not as simple as that. There's another explanation.'

It was Kindly Badger who provided it. He was digging holes in the snow nearby to get at acorns and roots. The foxes stopped to pass the news.

'Oh, hadn't you heard?' was the badger's reaction. 'The otters have fallen sick – at least, many of them have. Voles, mice – wrong diet, you see. Doesn't suit them. They should have kept to what they like – fish.'

'There you are,' Lean Fox said to his larger friend, 'it's not as simple as you thought.'

Stout Fox was irritated. 'Does it matter? As long as they leave the Wood alone . . .'

Kindly Badger looked from one to the other. 'It'll be of benefit to all of us, won't it? I mean, if they revert to fishing. Yet there was some question of a dearth of fish, so it's anyone's guess what the otters will try next.'

Quick Weasel was about to cross their path, but she saw the bigger animals in time and altered her route. 'She's a cunning one, isn't she, your mate?' she cried to Lean Fox from a safe distance.

He was puzzled. 'What do you mean?'

'She planned this. With the sly stoat. The otters are sick because the voles are sick. The vixen and stoat knew of a vole colony where most of the adults were ailing – some sort of infection, I believe – perhaps from a parasite. So they rounded up as many as they could and left them in the path of the otters, where they come from the stream.'

Stout Fox was impressed. 'Well, there's cunning for you,' he remarked. 'To think that she planned all that without your knowledge,' he added with a glance at Lean Fox.

Lean Fox looked uncomfortable. He had nothing to say. But Kindly Badger had.

'Cunning, maybe, but rash,' he commented. 'We can't afford any danger to the otter population. We depend on their thriving.'

'They'll survive; you can count on it,' was Stout Fox's opinion. 'At least they won't be so keen in future to raid our woodland larder.'

4

CHANGES

Some of the otters looked unlikely to survive. Indeed the cubs were failing visibly. Sleek Otter was at her wits' end.

'What can I do?' she implored other adults. 'They can't move, they can't eat. They won't leave the holt. Their sad little cries haunt me day and night and they're growing weaker all the time. I can't bear to see the looks of anguish in their big weeping eyes.'

'Have you brought them a fish?' another female enquired. 'Healthy food is their only chance now.'

'I swam half the length of the stream yesterday to catch them something wholesome,' Sleek Otter replied. 'There wasn't enough for all of them. I brought some large mussels to the den, but the youngsters ignored them.'

'Have you consulted the smooth one?' asked the other female. 'He's been trying to help some of the sick adults.'

'No, but I'll do so,' Sleek Otter mumbled despairingly. 'I really don't think I've much time left.'

She knew where to find the big male, and trotted

purposefully through the snow towards his holt. The otter slides were still visible on the banks of the stream but no animal played now. How things had changed, the otter mother thought to herself. It hardly seemed possible that her cubs had galloped up and down in such high spirits only a few days earlier.

'It's my fault,' she blamed herself. 'I didn't take sufficient care of what they ate. *I* wasn't raised on furry mice. How could I expect my young ones to benefit from them?' A little later she wailed shrilly, 'But they have to eat *something*. What was I to do?'

Smooth Otter greeted her gravely. Then he said, 'I can guess why you're here. I've told others and I'll tell you. We're all guilty of neglecting to take precautions.'

'Precautions? What precautions?' Sleek Otter muttered hopelessly.

'The water plants are what we've neglected,' Smooth Otter explained. 'Small quantities taken with our usual fare – fish – kept us healthy. We ate strands here and there almost without noticing. The plants have beneficial qualities. That's what our bodies are lacking now.'

Sleek Otter's mouth dropped open. 'You really think . . . I mean, it's that simple?'

'I'm sure of it,' Smooth Otter said with conviction.

'Then which plants – which plants must I gather?' the mother otter cried pitifully. 'My cubs are so weak; they can't walk as far as the holt entrance.'

'The plants in the stream,' Smooth Otter told her. 'The cressy plants that grow where the water runs swift and clear.'

'I know!' Sleek Otter whistled. 'I know the ones.' And she raced away as fast as she could go. She dived into the stream and paddled against the current. She knew exactly where she was heading. A bed of watercress where she had often fished for small fry was her destination. The plant was her cubs' only hope now. She swam intently. Other otters, who had listened to the big male's advice, were ahead of her. All the animals in the water converged on the thick tangle of cress. Without pausing for a word, Sleek Otter tore off mouthfuls of the deep green leaves with her sharp teeth. In a few moments she was swimming downstream again.

'I'm coming, my babies. I'm coming,' she murmured as her body rippled through the water, her fur glistening with silver where it had trapped pockets of air bubbles below the surface. She swooped up from the stream into her dry holt entrance and scattered the plant stems by the still bodies of her cubs. 'Eat this,' she commanded sharply. 'You must eat this. Please, please, eat!'

The young otters didn't stir. Their sufferings were over. Lean Vixen had wrought her revenge.

Sleek Otter was not the only one to mourn. Other youngsters succumbed as a result of eating the diseased voles. They hadn't the fortitude of the adult otters who had fallen sick. Those animals managed to recover after taking the measures advised by the big dog otter. They were suitably grateful and Smooth Otter began to be looked upon as a kind of leader. Now he believed more than ever in his own superiority.

After this scare, the otters tried to rely once more on their normal diet. The entire length of the stream and its surroundings were scoured for a viable food supply. There were small numbers of crayfish and mussels and some tench and roach, but the otters were only too aware that these prey could soon be exhausted. At the same time they knew they must steer clear of voles.

'We must return to the woods,' Smooth Otter said.

'The woods are dangerous,' another male argued. 'Do we want to poison ourselves again?'

Smooth Otter's whiskers twitched. 'We shall know better this time,' he said. 'We have no alternative but to hunt once more where the foxes, stoats and weasels catch their prey. We can learn from them. *They're* not sick. They must know which prey to avoid. So we watch them closely. We watch where they go, we watch what they catch and then – ' he whistled assertively – 'we take it from them.'

'How do we take food from a fox?' the other male queried. 'An otter could never win a fight with a fox.'

'That's debatable,' was Smooth Otter's opinion, 'as it hasn't been proved one way or the other. And it probably never will be because, you see, we're not going to fight them.'

'Oh, so they'll just pass over their food to us when we ask for it?'

'Sarcasm is lost on me. Look – don't you remember how we showed the other predators how much quicker, how much more agile we are? Well, we can do so again, only this time we'll let them catch the prey first. When they've made a kill, we'll rush in and whisk it away before they know we're around.'

The smaller dog otter wasn't convinced. 'I'll come with you on your next hunting trip, then,' he remarked, 'and you can show me how it's done.'

Smooth Otter's confidence was unbounded. 'Nothing simpler,' he assured the other.

The Farthing Wood hunters had been lulled into a false sense of security. Lean Vixen and Sly Stoat had congratulated themselves on their clever plan and had reverted to being rivals. As the weather grew milder, prey was easier to find. The snow gradually melted and fox, stoat and weasel had their minds on other things. They followed the lean foxes' example and began to pair off.

Stout Fox's image of a suitable vixen was of a female with health and strength similar to his own. So when he found a stout-looking vixen tracking an old rabbit which he had singled out himself, he surrendered his interest in it and lay down to watch her tactics. The vixen was big for a female and appeared to have eaten well throughout the winter. This impressed Stout Fox at once. Here was a female who would have definite advantages as a mate. Under the eye of the old rabbit buck, she began to chase her tail. Stout Fox grinned as he saw the rabbit's puzzlement. The vixen twirled around as if she had nothing else on her mind except play. Every so often the rabbit nibbled at some herbage but it never lost sight of the vixen's antics. The animal was, if anything, rather curious about the female predator. It certainly didn't take fright. Stout Fox's tongue hung loose and he panted as he watched the vixen's dance take her closer and closer still to the rabbit without its least suspicion.

'You've had it, chum,' Stout Fox whispered prophetically.

The vixen began a final mad spin, ending with a beautifully timed pounce. The rabbit knew nothing about it. It was dead before it knew it was under threat.

Now Stout Fox rushed forward. 'Bravo,' he barked. 'A fine example of skill. Where have you been hiding yourself? I don't recall seeing you before.'

The vixen regarded him coolly. She guarded her kill in case Stout Fox's approach was some kind of ploy. Her face wore a very worldly expression as if she had seen everything before at least once. 'I don't hide,' she replied, 'but I cover a lot of ground.'

'You must do,' the fox acknowledged. 'Have you – er – ever encountered the otters?'

'Now and then. But not recently.'

Stout Fox was eyeing the rabbit.

'I suppose you're hoping to share my kill?' the vixen asked baldly.

'No. No. I merely watched you from interest and – and – admired what I saw.'

The stout vixen softened. 'Well, after all,' she resumed, 'there's more than enough for one. Do you have a permanent den? Mine's a long way off.'

'Yes.' Stout Fox was encouraged. 'My earth is in the side of a badger set. We get along.'

'Just as well,' the vixen commented. 'Show me the way then. We can share my catch in comfort.'

The fox wondered at her abrupt change of attitude but assumed she had seen something in him, at any rate, that she liked. He led her across a glade to a clearing in the Wood where the set was situated. The badgers were absent except for a young male who was rooting up worms near one of the entrances. Stout Fox and the badger recognized each other and paid no attention to one another's activities.

The stout vixen dropped the rabbit carcass on the sandy floor of the den. 'Hm. Comfortable looking place,' she observed appreciatively, looking around and then sniffing the air.

'It suits me,' Stout Fox said.

'Might suit me too,' the vixen remarked.

Stout Fox wagged his tail. 'Sure to,' he replied, 'Look upon it as your own.'

★

Shortly after this episode the otters were once again seen in the Wood. Sly Stoat, who had recently acquired a mate also, was the first to fall victim to their new determination. Smooth Otter provided the demonstration the other otter required. He followed the stoat on its hunting run, allowed him to fell a shrew and then snatched it from his grip.

'Easy come, easy go,' he sneered at the stoat who was too stunned to react.

'You said to make use of the foxes; there was nothing about stoats,' the other otter said critically. 'I want to see how you tackle foxes.'

Smooth Otter glared. 'Stoat; fox; what does it matter?' he growled.

'There's a deal of difference between the two,' his companion insisted. 'Any of us can get the better of an animal the size of a stoat.'

Smooth Otter was stung into action. 'All right. You eat this shrew while I go for a bigger prize.' He dropped the stoat's kill. 'I can cope with foxes, don't you worry.'

'Mine, I think,' Sly Stoat muttered, snapping up the shrew and running for his den.

'Oh-ho, you're so slow you *need* lessons,' Smooth Otter derided the other male. 'Come on!'

There weren't any foxes in the neighbourhood just then. 'Look, forget what I said,' the slow male called to Smooth Otter after a while. 'I'm ravenous. Can't we just find our own food?'

The big leader otter ran on regardless. He was resolved, now his ability had been challenged, to demonstrate his prowess. Slow Otter, grumbling constantly, dropped farther and farther behind. Eventually he lost sight of the big male.

'Oh, to blazes with *him*,' he said to himself. 'I've had enough.' He stopped running. He had no idea where he was. He hadn't explored much of the woodland before. 'Now where on earth am I going to get something to eat?' As he looked around, wondering what to do next, he heard a tremendous commotion break out elsewhere in the Wood. Barking, shrieking, whistling, yapping – it sounded as though a really serious fight was taking place. Slow Otter this time was quick on his feet. With the inquisitiveness of all his kind he ran under the trees towards the din. Secretly he longed to find Smooth Otter in difficulties with a fiercer animal. He didn't take kindly to his boastful manner at all.

When he arrived on the scene the noise had ceased and there was a tug-of-war being enacted between Smooth Otter on the one hand and a very angry and determined Lean Vixen on the other. In the middle, with its legs in the jaws of the fox and its head clamped in the sharp teeth of the otter, was an unfortunate and very dead pheasant. Both animals had braced themselves, digging their feet into the damp soil and pulling hard. The vixen's greater strength began to tell. But with the arrival of Slow Otter her antagonist was spurred on to new efforts.

'Whatever is he doing?' Slow Otter muttered. 'This is a struggle he can't possibly win.'

Sure enough the carcass began to come apart.

With a final wrench the vixen tore the body loose and Smooth Otter was left with only the pheasant's head in his mouth.

Lean Vixen dropped the bird. 'You stupid animal,' she snarled at Smooth Otter. 'Do you plan to wrest our food from our very jaws? What kind of madness will you get up to next? Be warned.' She turned to look at Slow Otter. 'You too,' she growled. 'Try those sort of tricks again and we foxes will drive you from the Wood!'

'You and who else?' muttered Smooth Otter. But it was his turn to feel humiliated and he turned to go.

Slow Otter followed. 'Just lead us back to the stream,' he urged his companion. 'There's nothing for us here.'

'There will be,' Smooth Otter vowed grimly. 'You don't think I give up that easily, do you?'

5

OMENS

In March Farthing Wood was carpeted with banks of celandine and wood anemone. Primroses gleamed in the sunny glades and marsh plants sprouted along the stream's edges. Frogs, toads, newts and reptiles emerged from hibernation and, in the mammal world, hedgehogs woke and went about their business again.

One old creature, who had lived in the Wood for many seasons, was known as Sage Hedgehog because of his wisdom. During his long winter sleep he had experienced strange and striking dreams which he believed were some kind of premonition. He related them to those animals willing to listen.

'I saw a strange place with many animals. Animals such as us; such as those who live here. It was like Farthing Wood, yet it was not Farthing Wood. A beautiful antlered beast with the grace and carriage of a deer, but ghostly white, stood on its edge. On the one side was a poor broken piece of ground, barren of creatures and full of the noise and danger of humans and their works. On the other, rolling grassland and woodland. The white beast looked from one place, the one with nothing, to the place with the animals. Then it grew dark and the deer's white coat shimmered like a pale beacon in the gloom. All at once the beast disappeared and there was nothing but darkness. Over and over I have dreamed this dream. I believe there is a message in it; that it foretells the end of Farthing Wood.'

A group of hedgehogs who were listening stirred uneasily. They were puzzled and a little shaken. One of them said, 'Dreams are dreams. This could mean anything – or nothing.'

Sage Hedgehog looked at the animal steadily. 'There is a different air in Farthing Wood now,' he said. 'The Wood is threatened. I feel it in my bones. It's a new sensation. Before the winter I felt nothing and was content.'

'There's no evidence of a threat,' a young hedgehog said. 'Everything is just the same as when we began our sleep.'

Another hedgehog was more cautious. 'There have been other times when the sage one has spoken strange words. And I recollect when once he foretold a great storm and urged us to take shelter and we – '

'Yes, yes,' cut in another. 'We didn't take any notice of him and then there *was* a storm and some hedgehogs were drowned when the stream burst its banks. So what? Simply a coincidence, *I'd* say.'

'Well, I wouldn't,' the first hedgehog returned. 'He's something of a prophet in my view.'

'We shall see,' the second remarked. 'Do you detect any sign of change?'

There was no answer. Sage Hedgehog said, 'I sense disaster. I beg you, all of you, to be on your guard.' He went on his way, and left his fellows to make of his dreams what they would.

Other animals in Farthing Wood were to learn of the vision of the white deer. Some of them were impressed and felt concern, others were openly scornful. It didn't take much to unsettle the squirrels and rabbits who were always jumpy, whereas the weasels and stoats laughed at Sage Hedgehog behind his back.

'There's no fool like an old fool,' Quick Weasel chortled. 'That we should be taken in by his tales!'

Sly Stoat's wily mate commented, 'Time will tell. If his warnings prove correct we shall remember them ruefully. In any case, what provision could any of us make?'

'He's ancient and his mind wanders and makes up pictures,' Quick Weasel chattered. 'There's always been a Farthing Wood and there always will be. We have the otters to thank for that,' she added explanatorily.

'Yes. That's their habitual refrain, isn't it?' Wily Stoat said. 'My mate and I are sick of hearing it. And what if one day there were no otters? Have you thought of that?'

'Of course,' Quick Weasel answered. 'But I don't worry myself. Otters don't suddenly disappear and they'll be around for as long as we are.'

★

The dispute over food and prey continued to occupy the foxes and otters. They had no time to take account of dreams or predictions. Smooth Otter hunted alone now. He had realized it was as well not to have witnesses to his success or failure. He steered clear of the mature, canny foxes, and concentrated on filching titbits from younger or weaker animals. His skill and dexterity usually paid dividends. The other otters were capitalizing on the spring gathering of frogs and newts in the water courses. For a while there was plenty for all, then abruptly the amphibians' brief mating season was over and the survivors dispersed throughout the Wood and surrounding grassland.

Smooth Otter ignored the frogs. He loved to pit his wits against rivals and whenever he bested them he never failed to crow about it.

A young badger, a male cub a few seasons old from the set where Stout Fox and his vixen lodged, fell victim to the dog otter's gibes. The badger had been about to eat a pigeon fledgling which had fallen from its nest. The otter had been shadowing the bulkier animal for a while without arousing suspicion, waiting to see what food the badger might turn up. The feeble fluttering of the injured fledgling had attracted the young badger's curiosity and, just as he was about to seize it, Smooth Otter dashed in, flicked the bird to one side with his paw and made off with it.

'Oh, how you woodland animals suffer when we otters are on your heels,' Smooth Otter boasted.

'You're a cumbersome lot, heavy-footed and ponderous.' He trotted to a distance of a few metres in case the badger was inclined to react.

Young Badger, however, was nonplussed. 'Why do you do this?' he asked with genuine bewilderment. 'Why do you make a game of everything? Eating isn't a game; it's how all of us keep the threads of life together.'

'Except when there's an otter on your tail!' the other animal laughed.

Young Badger looked sulky. 'It's no laughing matter,' he said. 'There's a time for play and – and –'

'And why didn't you join in our games, then, in the snow?' Smooth Otter interrupted. 'You wouldn't come, any of you. I came looking for high-spirited animals like you!'

'Oh yes, mock all you like,' Young Badger remarked, aware of the sarcasm. 'We can't all be athletes and swimmers, can we? We are as we're made. But you know, you're really rather silly. You seem set on annoying everyone. What for? It might rebound on you. My father, the kindly badger, always taught us youngsters we should get along with everyone as best we can, because in that way Farthing Wood thrives. But it seems *you're* set on disruption.'

'Disruption? No,' Smooth Otter chuckled. 'We just enjoy life whichever way we can. So catching prey can be as much fun for us as anything else. Too bad most of you are such a dull lot!' He bounded away, jigging this way and that around some chestnut saplings.

Young Badger watched and shook his head. 'I'm afraid otters and woodlanders simply don't blend,' he murmured.

When the glut of frogs was over for that spring, other otters had no alternative but to return to hunting small mammals. The badgers were not the only inhabitants of Farthing Wood who felt a crisis was looming. The squirrels and hedgehogs and many of the woodland birds, who were not among the hunted, watched the behaviour of the otters with alarm.

'Someone should t-try to c-calm them down,' Nervous Squirrel stammered. He sat on a high branch watching a pair of otters chasing Quick Weasel beneath the trees. 'They're so un*settling*.'

'Madness!' screeched Jay who couldn't keep still when there was any disturbance. He flew to another tree. 'Madness! The foxes are gathering, I've seen them. When they're not being robbed, they're being goaded and irritated.'

'Hunting calls for silence and perseverance,' an owl fluted from a hollow oak. 'I should know. There's just no peace and quiet any more.'

'W-why don't we t-tell them?' Nervous Squirrel chattered. 'Tell them to p-pipe down. And – and – '

'And respect the ways of others?' the owl suggested.

'Yes. Ex-exactly.'

'Some of us have tried, but the otters won't

compromise. They're the jokers of the animal world. They have no seriousness.'

The foxes were indeed planning to take action. The youngsters had been tested to the limit and were looking for some support from their seniors. Groups of foxes began to debate their grievances and it was these gatherings that Jay had watched from the tree-tops. Lean Vixen backed up the young foxes.

'I warned the big otter about the consequences if he and his kind continued with their tricks,' she told a large group of all ages. 'My mate and I are ready to do whatever's necessary. It's time we struck a blow.'

Lean Fox hadn't been consulted about whether he was in agreement with this. He said nothing therefore, hoping the others wouldn't realize the vixen was dominant.

The young foxes related their experiences. Time and time again otters had interfered with their hunting techniques, sneaking prey from them and deriding them afterwards.

'It's intolerable,' said one. 'We can never hold our heads up again if we let them get away with it.'

'Otters or foxes,' Lean Vixen growled, 'one group has to come out on top.' She looked around the gathering and her eyes rested on Lean Fox. 'And it won't be the otters!'

'No. No, it won't be,' he concurred hastily. 'Tomorrow night we'll muster. All of us who care for our way of life – our fox ways – must take part. We'll chase those slippery pests from the Wood!'

Lean Vixen grinned a foxy grin. These were strong words; rousing words. The young foxes were satisfied. They ran off to carry the message to as many others of their kind in Farthing Wood as could be found.

The next evening the foxes rallied. With Stout Fox and Lean Vixen at their head, they trotted quietly through the depths of the Wood, intent on forestalling the otters close by the stream. Little light filtered through the budding branches but, at the edge of the woodland, the setting sun shone on the glistening water, turning it blood red. The foxes stood silently.

'It's an omen,' whispered a youngster. 'Blood will be shed.'

Stout Fox murmured grimly, 'Yes. I fear blood will flow if the otters persist in their ways.'

'You can count on it,' Lean Vixen snarled. 'Before the Wood is in leaf.'

6

ONE TRICK TOO MANY

There was something about that evening that seemed to affect the entire population of Farthing Wood. The atmosphere was remarkably quiet. A spring breeze, a cool breeze, blew across the grassland. Nothing stirred. Not a single otter appeared. Were they suspicious? Lean Fox broke the silence.

'It doesn't look as if there's anything to chase after all,' he said.

'Give them time,' said Lean Vixen.

The sun sank below the horizon. Darkness cloaked the foxes and the stream ran black. At last there was movement. Something approached, then turned and set off in another direction.

'Follow it,' Lean Vixen yapped. The foxes ran forward. The creature, which was indeed an otter, turned at the sound of running feet. Far from taking fright, it stood its ground. The foxes' rush slowed, then halted.

'Rather unfair odds, isn't it?' Sleek Otter asked, for it was she.

'Are you alone?' Stout Fox growled.

'You have eyes.'

'Then where are the others?' a young fox piped up.

'How should I know? In the Wood perhaps.'

'In the Wood?' Stout Fox barked. 'Nothing passed us as we came. How can that be?'

'Hardly likely they'd want to come face to face with a force of foxes,' Sleek Otter observed, 'if they *are* in the Wood.'

'What game is this?' Lean Vixen snarled.

'There is more than one way to enter a Wood,' was the reply and Sleek Otter tittered.

Lean Vixen was infuriated. Had the otters outmanoeuvred them again? While the foxes were standing idle, were they plundering the woodland in their absence?

'Back to the Wood!' she roared. 'They've gone behind our backs!'

The foxes, in one mass, turned and galloped towards the trees. Sleek Otter could hardly contain herself. She rolled over in her delight, whistling and giggling. Her cool-headedness had tricked the other animals into retreat. For she knew quite well not one otter, apart from herself, had yet left its holt.

Try as they might, and they searched high and low in twos and threes, the foxes couldn't find anything to chase. But their activity flushed some other creatures into the open. Amongst these were hedgehogs. The hedgehogs were very frightened, but soon realized the foxes were after different game. Sage

Hedgehog unrolled himself and called to the others, 'We're safe for the moment. We're of no interest to them.'

Stout Fox paused to grunt, 'Not unless you can tell me if you've seen otters tonight.'

'No. None. Why do you seek them?'

'We're at loggerheads. Foxes and otters need to settle their differences and now there's one way . . .'

'You wish to fight them?'

Stout Fox growled, 'If necessary. But certainly to frighten them.'

'Then we hedgehogs shall remain silent,' said the sage one bravely. 'Were we to see otters, we couldn't expose them to danger.'

'Very well. But we foxes will find them one way or another,' Stout Fox replied determinedly.

'We take no sides in your dispute,' the hedgehog continued. 'But we wish the otters no harm. Indeed their presence here must be preserved.'

'Not in Farthing Wood!' Stout Fox snapped. 'We have our own ideas about that!'

'Don't do anything we shall all regret,' Sage Hedgehog pleaded. 'If the otters go, I dread the consequences. You're more sensible than most. I appeal to you to avert a disaster.'

'Stuff and nonsense,' Stout Fox remarked dismissively. He knew all about Sage Hedgehog. 'You and your crackpot notions! Now listen to me. We foxes mean to keep the otters out of our territory. There's no two ways about that. And we'll use any means necessary.'

'No, no,' wailed Sage Hedgehog. 'We shall all be losers. Don't let the humans in!'

'Humans? They've been coming and going here ever since I can remember,' Stout Fox said and went on his way.

Sage Hedgehog's head sank on to his paws. More to himself than to any other creature he murmured sorrowfully, 'I fear the time will arrive when the humans come, but don't go.'

There was no discovery and no fighting that night. Sleek Otter made haste to give the news of the foxes' massing to her kind. The otters saw sense and decided to avoid confrontation. Smooth Otter, however, couldn't resist a retort.

'How we've impressed them all,' he quipped glibly. 'We've really ruffled their pride.'

'Well, we can't match them in strength,' Sleek Otter cautioned. 'You should have seen them. They looked an ugly lot.'

'Oh, they'll disband soon enough,' the big male assured her lightly. 'What can they do? They know they can't touch us.'

This was not at all how the foxes saw the situation. They had reached the end of their tether. Stout Vixen, who had stayed behind in the den, greeted her mate's return with the words, 'I don't see any signs of a scrap. Your coat's as clean as a cat's.'

'There was no scrap,' Stout Fox admitted, 'because there were no otters.'

'I told you so,' said the vixen. 'You need to use more subtle methods with that bunch.'

'Perhaps we've frightened them off?'

'No. They'll slip back to the woodland unnoticed when things have quietened down.'

'What do you suggest then?'

'As the otters seem to bother you so much there's only one course of action. Get rid of them altogether.'

'You mean – kill them?' Stout Fox muttered as though he hardly dared pronounce the words.

'Not all of them. When they see their lives are at stake they'll get the message soon enough and move out.'

Stout Fox baulked at the idea of wholesale slaughter. 'Let's hope they won't provoke us any further,' he said without much conviction.

Of course it wasn't in the nature of the otters to lie low. It was quite out of the question for them to be quiet or still for long. And, in any case, hunger asserted itself. They had to hunt whether they liked it or not. Some of them explored the grassland which surrounded the Wood and found a mouse or two. But this was a poor alternative to the rich fare offered by the Wood itself.

With the confidence born of their belief in their special status, the main bulk of the otters once more penetrated the woodland. They hunted singly and thoroughly. It was not long before they once more found themselves competing with the habitual woodland dwellers.

Smooth Otter, predictably, was the spark that lit the fatal fuse. His vanity made him incapable of heeding any warning signals. He forgot Sleek Otter's experience and set about stalking Lean Fox with the idea of relieving him of his catch. Lean Fox had set his sights on a young hare that was less watchful than it needed to be. Luckily for the young animal, it was able to make its escape. For, as Lean Fox closed, freezing every time the hare turned to look, Smooth Otter tried to circumvent his ploy. The otter's final dash, in front of the patient, painstaking fox, alarmed the hare who scooted away as swift as the wind.

Lean Fox, who had spent many long minutes carefully positioning himself, hurled himself on the culprit. He bowled the otter over and a vicious fight began. They were a match for each other.

The noise attracted onlookers. 'F-fox in a fight! Otter on the f-floor,' Nervous Squirrel skittered, leaping from branch to branch.

Sly Stoat hid behind a tree-trunk, peering round every now and then to watch the contest. As a predator, both animals were his rivals, but as a woodlander he was on the side of the fox. Smooth Otter gave a good account of himself. He was strong and supple and quick-footed. Lean Fox found it impossible to get a grip on him. Equally, the otter's smaller stature didn't allow him to gain advantage.

'It's l-level pegging,' Nervous Squirrel squeaked to anyone who cared to listen.

'Keep quiet,' said Owl. 'Let them sort it out.'

Smooth Otter, jigging to right and left, and nipping the fox's tail or leg whenever he got the chance, resorted to taunts. 'Catch me if you can, Fox. Whoops! Missed me! Where am I now? No, not there. Here! Clumsy fox!'

The bigger animal was panting heavily and beginning to look confused. Then Lean Vixen rushed up and the scales were tilted. The two foxes together were too much for the athletic otter. If he avoided one's attack, he stepped right into the other's. He received a succession of deep bites and suddenly wilted. The Wood was quiet. The onlookers held their breath, expecting a kill. The foxes lunged on both sides. Smooth Otter rolled over, bleeding from a dozen gashes.

'He's done for,' Lean Vixen panted. 'Leave him.'

Lean Fox stepped back and looked at the stricken animal. His sides heaved from his exertions.

'D-death, death of an otter!' shrilled Nervous Squirrel.

The cry was taken up by a host of other small animals and the news spread through the Wood like wildfire. Other creatures came running; badgers, weasels, rabbits, hedgehogs. Elsewhere the foxes heard the cry and responded. Their blood was up. Four other otters were cornered in the Wood and pulled down by their long-suffering adversaries. Another was caught and savaged as she raced for safety to the stream. Stout Fox took no part in the killing. He restricted himself to running along the

Wood's perimeter and driving others on who were trying to escape. The otters were vanquished. Those who survived abandoned their holts and ran for their lives, believing the foxes would massacre them all if they stayed.

By dawn not a single otter was left in Farthing Wood.

The foxes came together in the centre of the Wood, grimly satisfied with their work. They were not yet aware that the surviving otters had disappeared for good and indeed were at that moment still running across country under cover of darkness.

'It had to be done,' Lean Vixen spoke for all of her kind. She panted deeply. Many of the foxes still simmered from the heat of battle. They had not escaped unscathed. The otters' sharp teeth and claws had left their mark. Blood lust still glinted in some eyes. The foxes were ready for more killing if any creature dared to cross them. For the moment none did and, gradually, their fighting ardour cooled.

'The Wood's ours again,' Stout Fox said. 'But surely we could have achieved that without such extreme savagery?'

The animals returned to their own territories, certain that no otter would ever presume to set foot in them again. They couldn't have known that their action would mean that, in the long run, their lives would change for ever.

7

AFTERMATH

The stoats and weasels were astir soon after the foxes' attack. Sly Stoat found Smooth Otter's carcass and sniffed at it inquisitively.

'Your arrogance put paid to you,' he murmured to the dead animal. 'You wouldn't be told. What's your so-called superiority worth now?' He laughed a stoat laugh. 'A feast for the worms, that's all.' He trotted away, his movements brisker than for a long while.

Quick Weasel had attracted a mate and was oblivious of anything that happened around her. The male weasel was dark and quicker even than she: lightning-fast. He circled her and chased her and they ran through the flower carpet, tumbling and sparring like two kittens. In places the ground was tainted with blood. Where the weasels rolled it flecked their glossy coats with dark spots. They groomed themselves and continued their courtship, forgetful and careless of others' dramas. Life and its continuation was all that mattered to them.

★

In the badgers' ancient set Kindly Badger spoke to his son. 'The foxes reacted as I feared,' he said. 'The otters were too clever for them and they resented it.' He pressed down some fresh bedding and lay on it. 'We had no part in it and yet. . . .'

'Yet what, Father?'

'And yet we *are* part of it,' Kindly Badger seemed to contradict himself. 'We're part of Farthing Wood, just as they are. We can't remain unaffected.'

'Didn't you always believe animals can get along together if they . . . if they . . .' Young Badger groped for the words.

'If they respect each other? Yes,' Kindly Badger mumbled. He was feeling drowsy. 'But it doesn't always work out that way. You can't respect a creature who is' – he yawned widely – 'taking the food from your mouth.'

Farthing Wood warmed itself in the spring sunshine. The night creatures had gone to their rest. Nervous Squirrel called to his family, 'S-strangers in the Wood! Take care!' as he always did when humans approached. The squirrels leapt through the tree-tops, pausing to squint down at the two people who were bending over the remains of Smooth Otter.

'Four,' one man said to his companion. 'What's been happening here?' His distress was unmistakable. The other human shook her head and the two trudged on, systematically searching the Wood bottom.

'Slaughter!' Jay screeched at them but the startled bird was ignored.

By the stream-side the naturalists loitered, vainly waiting for a reassuring appearance of a bobbing head and whiskers in the water or a frisky somersault amongst the reeds. They stared long and hard, never talking and barely shifting their limbs. There was no comfort here. The stream was barren except for a skulking moorhen or two. They walked along its banks, then the woman grabbed the man's arm and pointed at the muddy ground. Fresh tracks, otter tracks, made by several animals led away from the stream and away from Farthing Wood itself. They followed them where they could, but the tracks were soon lost amongst rank grass. Even so the naturalists were left in no doubt that some serious misfortune had overtaken the protected animals. It was now their prime objective to discover their fate.

Seven animals, including Sleek Otter, had fled the foxes' wrath. At first they had run in a blind panic. Then, with distance behind them, they eased up and listened for sounds of pursuit.

'It's quiet,' Sleek Otter whispered.

'Shall we go back?' another female suggested, gazing forlornly across the grassland.

'To certain death,' Slow Otter told her bluntly. 'The big dog otter, the smooth one, brought havoc among us. He courted danger and thought himself invincible. But he put the foxes in a frenzy.'

'Where shall we go then?'

'Why ask me? My world, like yours, was small. I know nothing else.'

'We should head for a waterway,' said Sleek Otter. 'Our stream wasn't isolated. It must empty into another.'

'But where?'

'I don't know.'

'We should search for other otters,' another animal urged.

'There *are* no other otters,' she was told. 'We're the last for miles and miles. We grew up knowing that. How can you have forgotten?'

'I hadn't forgotten. But – but – what else can we do?'

'Go on until we find somewhere bearable,' said Sleek Otter, 'or . . . or . . . die in the attempt.'

They ran on, close-knit, not daring to stray. The grassland gave way to empty fields, then roads, the smell of smoke, moving lights and frightening sounds.

'We're lost,' shrilled a youngster.

'Of course we're lost,' said Slow Otter. 'From now on, we'll always be lost.'

It became apparent eventually to the inhabitants of Farthing Wood that the otters had vanished. There were few regrets but some misgivings.

'What will it mean?' Wily Stoat asked her mate.

'Only that there's more food for everyone,' Sly Stoat answered cynically.

'But they were always full of such tales.'

'Tales of their own importance, yes. Well, we can

get along without them. All in all they were a tiresome bunch.'

The wise hedgehog was troubled by more dreams. Once again the vision of the white deer disturbed his daytime sleep, now with more urgency. The deer had advanced and seemed larger and more distinct. Sage Hedgehog knew then that it fell to him to impress on the other animals that some menace hovered over Farthing Wood; that in some way they must make changes to avert an awful fate.

The other hedgehogs heard him out. 'There are no changes we can make that would make a jot of difference to Farthing Wood one way or the other,' commented one. 'We cause no disturbance. We take what we need and don't interfere with the lives of other creatures.'

Sage Hedgehog said, 'None of us can escape the doom that threatens us, from the smallest to the largest. Unless. . . .'

'Unless what?' an elderly hedgehog asked. 'Unless we sprout wings and fly away? Your riddles are of little help.'

'Unless,' Sage Hedgehog murmured, 'we somehow pull together to – to – ' he screwed up his eyes as he struggled to find words to interpret what seemed to him a message from some mystical source – 'to save ourselves,' he finished in a burst with a long sigh of relief.

'It's the larger animals who can affect what changes take place here, and only they,' another hedgehog said. 'The foxes are the most powerful animals as they've already demonstrated. Take your tale to them. I doubt if they'll listen, but if *they* don't, your breath is wasted on any other creature.'

'I shall speak to the foxes,' Sage Hedgehog confirmed. 'I shall speak to everyone.'

As before, few of the Wood's inhabitants were inclined to listen. Sage Hedgehog persisted. It was his role to warn others and not to be defeated by apathy or scorn.

'You were wrong to make war with the otters,' he told the foxes. 'You will rue the day you drove them out.'

'On the contrary,' Lean Vixen corrected him. 'It's the best thing we ever did. Look how we've benefited.' She and her mate had filled out considerably, and their coats had a healthy sheen. 'We've taken on a new lease of life.'

'A lease that will end abruptly in disease and panic,' Sage Hedgehog predicted.

'You dotty old ball of spikes,' Lean Vixen scoffed, half angrily and half in amusement. 'You come to us with this nonsense and expect us to take you seriously?'

'A threat to the Wood is surely serious?' Lean Fox cautioned.

'What threat? There's no evidence – '

'There have been more humans in the Wood of late,' Lean Fox interrupted.

'Oh, we pay them too much attention,' the vixen

dismissed his remark. 'We always have. But why? They never do anything. They walk, they look . . . what sort of threat is that?'

'Human interest can always be a threat,' Lean Fox muttered sullenly. 'I'd prefer to be ignored.'

Sage Hedgehog said, 'If the human eye is on us, we'd do well to look out for each other.'

Meanwhile the otters, torn between their fear of the unknown and their horror of returning to their homes, made makeshift dens under a hedgerow and ate vegetation, snails and slugs to avoid starvation.

Sleek Otter determined to look for water. She knew that without it their lives were worth nothing.

8

THE OTTERS' PLIGHT

At sunset one dry evening, four days after their flight, Sleek Otter set out. She slipped away while the others made their weary and fruitless search for nourishment. She had eaten almost nothing since abandoning her holt. She knew that the best way to find food was to find water. The memory of her cubs' deaths after eating unsuitable prey remained with her.

The air was balmy and still. She loped across a field. On the far side a road loomed – for the moment quiet. Sleek Otter sprinted across without pausing. Her heart beat fast. She sniffed the aroma of human food and human bodies hanging thickly in a cottage garden. Her nostrils twitched. Her whiskers brushed a wall as she ran along its length, then she slipped through a gate into the garden and trotted noiselessly to a garden pond. Her eyes widened. The scent of water lured her like a magnet. Noises from the house – a televised voice, the laughter of a viewer – made her hesitate. Then silence resumed.

Sleek Otter dived joyfully into the pond. It was

tiny and clogged with weed, but the feel of water over her back and head was exhilarating. A terrified frog leapt for safety on to a water-plant. In a flash Sleek Otter seized it and her teeth crunched on her first real prey for days. The frog tasted delicious. The otter's eyes closed in sheer enjoyment, but her hunger was merely irritated by this mouthful and seemed greater than ever.

And then she found them. Nestling nervously amongst the weed and trying to stay hidden: goldfish. Sleek Otter whistled with excitement. One, two, three fish about the size of carrots and with no escape route.

'There's only one place you can go,' Sleek Otter told the luckless goldfish as she savoured the moment. 'And that's' – crunch – 'in here!' She gulped them down and then searched the entire pond for anything else that was edible. There was nothing more.

Reluctantly she pulled herself out and shook a fountain of spray from her coat. She thought of the six other otters scratching for morsels along the hedge bottom. The goldfish had put new heart into her. Perhaps there were more fish to be found nearby?

Slow Otter had hardly bothered to look for food at all. He was the most pessimistic of the seven and already believed that death for all of them could only be a matter of days away. He watched the only other male grimly chewing an earthworm with an expression of distaste on his face.

'You can't put off the inevitable,' he told him. 'Bird food won't keep us alive.'

The other male limped from a wound sustained in a fight with a young fox. 'Maybe,' he grunted. 'But we can't simply curl up and die.'

'Might as well,' was Slow Otter's opinion. 'Oh,' he moaned, 'my stomach's as hollow as a rotten log.'

The four bitch otters had scattered on their own quests. One still had thoughts of returning some day to her deserted holt by Farthing stream. 'I could slip in unnoticed,' she told herself. 'A single otter doesn't make much of a splash. No-one would suspect.' Then she thought about what an endlessly solitary existence would be like and shuddered. 'No. That's not sensible,' she said mournfully. 'I can't go alone. I must have a companion.' She turned to glance back at the two males. There was not much encouragement to be had there. She sighed forlornly and turned again to her foraging.

Sleek Otter left the cottage garden and found herself in a wide muddy expanse planted with vegetables. She threaded her way through these, turning every so often to make sure she wasn't observed. Another field stretched ahead. There was no sign or smell of water in that direction. She paused, reminding herself of the little pond and its situation near a human dwelling. Perhaps that was the key to other stocks of fish. Sleek Otter decided to seek out similar habitations.

There was a collection of buildings comprising a bungalow and various outhouses within easy distance of the vegetable field. Sleek Otter ran determinedly towards it. Desperation made her bold. She pattered cautiously into a yard. Everything was quiet enough. In the darkness the unmistakable sound of swishing water reached her ears. She trotted swiftly forward to investigate. She found six huge, round metal-sided vats spaced around the yard. These were sunk deep into concrete so that the tops were about a metre above ground level. Hosepipes ran to and from each, draining and replenishing water in a continual cycle. Every so often a splash or a plunge could be heard in one of the tanks. There were things moving in them – living things. Sleek Otter was filled with excitement. She ran to the nearest container and leapt up, balancing herself on the tank's rim.

'Fish!' she whistled. 'Hordes of them!' She watched the writhings and weavings of hundreds of plump silver trout. There were so many fish, there scarcely seemed to be a space unfilled. The water was literally alive with them. They were feeding from the remains of a scattering of pellets thrown in earlier by human hand. Sleek Otter's hungry eyes almost popped out of her head. Here at last was real prey – unlimited prey – for the taking. She watched the trout's darting movements as though mesmerized. She knew she must inform the other otters about this miraculous find. First, however, she meant to taste the trout for herself.

She contemplated diving headfirst into the vat, but resisted the temptation. She hooked a good-sized fish from the water which fell with a splat on to the ground where it wriggled furiously. Sleek Otter bounded after it, trapping it with her front paws and killing it with one deep bite to the neck. The flesh was pink and delicious. She ate with the heightened relish of an animal starved of its natural prey for too long.

'This place will be the saving of us,' she told herself afterwards. 'I must get back to the others.'

Cautious as ever, Sleek Otter retraced her journey. Luckily the road was once more deserted and she crossed it again without any alarm. She was soon reunited with the other six fugitives. They showed no particular interest at first in her return. All of them were thoroughly dispirited.

'Cheer up,' Sleek Otter rallied them. 'I've the best news possible. There's a mass of fish just waiting to be eaten.'

'Things are bad enough without your jokes,' Slow Otter grumbled. 'Of course there are fish, plenty of them. We know that. But exactly where they are is what we *don't* know.'

'You don't understand,' Sleek Otter chattered. 'I've found them! Only a short journey from here. There's more than enough for all of us. All we have to do is to take care. Believe me, it couldn't be simpler. We must move from here and find convenient dens nearer the place with the fish where we can hide during daylight. Now, who's ready to join me?'

The others gaped at her, still not entirely convinced by her tale. No-one spoke.

'Well, what's the matter with you all?' Sleek Otter cried in exasperation. 'Aren't you hungry?'

'I'll come with you,' the lame otter said, 'if you promise to go slowly.'

'Can't be too slow,' she replied. 'We must get under cover before dawn.'

'I'll do my best,' he said.

The bitch otters began to look excited. 'And are there really fish . . . like we used to eat in the stream?' one asked longingly.

'Better. Bigger,' Sleek Otter told her triumphantly.

'Have you found a river?' another one breathed, picturing an idyllic watercourse.

'Er – no. Not exactly,' Sleek Otter replied hesitantly, then added, 'but there is water, naturally. And plenty of it.'

The six looked less eager. 'Is it a stream then?' Slow Otter queried.

'No. Not a stream.'

'A pond?' Lame Otter suggested. 'Like in Farthing Wood?'

'A sort of pond, I suppose,' Sleek Otter answered vaguely. 'But stop your questions, do! Come and see for yourselves!'

'Do we have any choice?' Slow Otter muttered. 'If we stay here, we'll certainly perish.'

★

Lame Otter was weak; weaker than the rest. Like most of the others, he hadn't eaten properly for several days. He took his time going across the first field. One of the bitch otters kept pace with him sympathetically. Sleek Otter reached the road together with the three other females. Slow Otter was some distance behind them and the other two brought up the rear.

'Make haste,' Sleek Otter shrilled to the stragglers. Although she was unfamiliar with roads and traffic, she sensed this strip of tarmac posed a threat. It smelt of danger, humans and sour fumes. The bitch otters loped across. Slow Otter reached the verge. They all heard a distant sound of an engine. Something approached. Frightened, Slow Otter accelerated and joined the leaders. The noise increased. Lame Otter and his companion weren't sure whether to go on or turn back.

'Quickly,' urged the safe animals. They knew they must get out of sight.

Lame Otter hesitated, then continued. A motor-bike's headlamp gleamed menacingly, its beam brightening by the second as the machine roared nearer. Lame Otter, terrified, attempted a spurt. In the middle of the road he was caught in the gleam of the powerful lamp. The motor-cyclist braked. Lame Otter limped across, but his female companion stupidly turned to run back. She was too late and the sound of screeching brakes was followed by a dull thud. The rider almost toppled and only brought his machine under control with difficulty. The female straggler was killed instantly. The rest of the otters, panic-stricken, dashed on, not even giving a backward glance to their lost companion. The motor-cyclist bent glumly over the dead animal. He was shaken by the accident. He had never seen otters in that locality before and wondered at the cause of their sudden appearance.

9

THE TROUT FARM

The six surviving otters scattered, unaware that their plight had become the focus of attention. Sleek Otter found that only two females remained with her. The other had dashed blindly to the nearest hiding-place. After a while the lone female found her way back to her friends. The two males lay low in a ditch. Gradually their fright subsided.

'Now what?' Slow Otter grunted.

'Try to find the fish, of course,' Lame Otter answered sharply.

'Only the sleek one knows where they are, and we've lost her,' grumbled the pessimistic dog otter.

'Then we must track her. It's our only hope.'

There was no time to be lost and, despite his painful limp, Lame Otter was the more resolute of the two. He picked up the bitches' scent and began to call. After a while the two males heard a response.

'They're not far away,' the lame animal remarked confidently. 'We may yet taste fish before the night's out.'

The four females arrived in the yard of the trout

farm. Sleek Otter showed the three newcomers how she had found the water. 'Listen! It's unmistakable, isn't it? And you can hear those fat fish moving around. We'll have many a feast to make up for our fast!'

The ravenous females gulped in anticipation. 'Show us how you catch them,' one begged.

Sleek Otter, who was feeling noticeably stronger since her evening haul of goldfish and trout, ran towards the first tank and leapt gracefully to the top. Her balance was perfect. Moments later four large fish had been hooked from the water. The watching females fell upon these voraciously. Sleek Otter rejoined them, contenting herself with a few mouthfuls.

The trout had scarcely been swallowed when the two male otters called from nearby. They were answered at once.

'I can smell that you've eaten,' Slow Otter announced as he came into the yard. He and Lame Otter were drooling. They noticed scraps of fish bone and skin on the ground and snatched them up hastily as though afraid the females might take them.

'Wouldn't you prefer whole prey?' Sleek Otter asked them archly. She was in her element, aware of her supremacy in the group.

'What a stupid question!' Slow Otter rasped. 'Where are the fish? Point me in the direction.'

By way of an answer Sleek Otter repeated her performance. The glistening trout smacked on to the ground where their futile wriggles were swiftly halted. The two males gulped them down – heads, tails and bones. Nothing was left.

'I can get you as many as you like,' Sleek Otter boasted gleefully.

'Huh! The great provider,' Slow Otter mumbled ungraciously with his mouth full. 'Don't worry. What you can do, we can do too.'

'Speak for yourself,' Lame Otter said to him. 'There's no way in which *I* could get to the fish.'

'I'll look after you,' Sleek Otter beamed. She wanted to be appreciated by the males. 'We can make a new start here, all of us. Our old life's finished, but there's no reason why our new life can't be better.'

'If only we'd had such fish in Farthing Wood stream,' sighed the female who still hankered after her old home. 'None of the otters would have lost their lives and all those awful events wouldn't have happened.' She brushed some fragments of food from her whiskers which were exceptionally long.

The others were silent as they digested her words. Each one thought about the fateful lack of food which had caused them to be driven out into a perilous and unknown world. Finally Slow Otter said, 'The sky is paling. We should find shelter quickly: the humans will be astir.'

The six looked around for reliable cover. Sleek Otter had noticed a lake close to the trout farm which was fringed with reeds and other growth. It seemed the obvious place to hide in during the coming day. There would be time later to develop more permanent dens. She led them to it and the otters tunnelled into the vegetation, weary but at least no longer hungry. For a while they talked about the extraordinary bounty of fish. Although they couldn't, of course, understand the concept of a trout farm, they all knew the fish were where they were because of human intent. They knew that the fish must be of value to humans, which meant they – the otters – must exercise extreme care. It was obvious to them that their interference in the humans' plans must not be discovered, otherwise they would be in real danger.

'We need to make sure there's not a trace of our coming,' Sleek Otter summarized. 'It would perhaps be wise to bring the fish to eat here, or wherever we settle eventually.'

'Yes, that's sensible,' Lame Otter agreed. 'We don't want to attract the slightest attention to ourselves.'

Ironically that is exactly what the otters had done. News of the sighting in an area well away from their Farthing Wood habitat reached the local wildlife groups. These were puzzled and concerned. Why had the animals left their usual territory so suddenly? What had caused them to stray into an area of human population? An investigation into this mystery became vital. While the otters were using every ounce of caution, interested parties were combing the area around Farthing Wood for a clue to their present location. It was now generally accepted that there had been some kind of assault upon them by other animals – the dead otters were proof of that –

and that, to escape further slaughter, the remaining otters had fled. It was the business of the conservation groups to secure these animals again, return them to their home territory, and ensure that they were properly protected there.

The inhabitants of Farthing Wood naturally knew none of this. None of them realized the chain of events that had been set in motion by the foxes' attack. Only Sage Hedgehog sensed impending disaster. His words, in the main, fell on deaf ears. Spring broods of young voles, shrews and fieldmice increased the little creatures' numbers dramatically. From owls to weasels, none of the predators went short of food. Rabbits, too, were breeding prolifically, so that the foxes' diet was a particularly good one.

Stout Fox and his vixen were the most skilled rabbit hunters, the vixen especially. 'You have a talent all your own,' Stout Fox told her after he had watched her admiringly for the umpteenth time. 'I can't think why you lay low while the otters made such nuisances of themselves. You could have shown them a thing or two.'

'I didn't lie low,' she corrected him. 'I simply kept apart. All that fuss! You were overawed, all of you, by their antics. Silly beasts, they only deserved to be ignored.'

They trotted home companionably in the moonlight. Ahead of them, they saw Lean Vixen flit like a shadow between two tall trees. The fox pairs didn't encounter one another very often. They preferred not to mingle, now that the fighting was done. But this time Lean Vixen caught the scent of the other two and turned towards them.

'You are well?' Stout Fox asked her, noticing the improvement in her appearance.

'Yes. And you?' Lean Vixen returned, assessing the big male's fitness.

'Well too,' came the reply. 'But some animals seem sickly.'

The lean vixen's ears pricked up. She remembered the trail of disease she had strewn in the path of the otters. 'What's the reason?' she asked.

'Who knows? It could be anything. But sometimes I have a strange feeling that the Wood itself is sickly.'

Lean Vixen's eyes narrowed. 'Has that old windbag of a hedgehog got to you?'

'Nothing to do with him,' Stout Fox declared. 'There *was* disease in the Wood, though, and it may still be around.'

For some days the supply of trout sustained all six otters without interruption. Sleek Otter brought food for the lame male as she had promised. Slow Otter and the other three females were able to catch their own. They soon became proficient at jumping to the edge of the tanks, balancing, and whipping out with their paws as much fish as they needed. Slow Otter became increasingly irritated by the way the lame male was pampered. The six otters were living in unnaturally close proximity to each other and there were bound to be ructions sooner or later.

'Why can't he fetch his own food?' he complained, casting a withering glance at Lame Otter who was accepting the latest catch as though it were his right.

'You know why,' Sleek Otter answered quietly. She was developing a sort of motherly fondness for the lame male.

'We others put ourselves at risk every time we go to the Metal Ponds,' Slow Otter muttered grudgingly. The 'Metal Ponds' was their name for the tanks. 'It's all very well lying around waiting to be fed like some drone.'

'I don't lie around,' Lame Otter defended himself. 'I roam here and there. I try to do for myself what I can, but I can't catch enough in the open water to feed myself properly. You've swum in it. You know there's almost nothing to catch.'

'Oh yes,' Slow Otter sneered, 'but I'm sure you prefer being dependent. It's such an easy life.'

'Easy life? How would you like to have this injury? I'm stuck with it whether I like it or not. It'll never heal.'

Slow Otter's grumbling subsided, only to return on another occasion. There was no doubt that all the females showed a preference for Lame Otter, partly because of his condition with which they sympathized, but also because he had a nicer nature. Slow Otter was jealous. One night his resentment boiled over.

It was the fifth night of the raids on the trout stocks. He and the four bitch otters pattered quietly across the yard, as usual Sleek Otter was first on to the tank. She caught her fish and two of the other females followed. Then Slow Otter and the last female went together. Slow Otter was eager, but the female was faster than he was. She sprang up to the rim, leaving the male on the ground seething with impatience. He trotted up and down, unable to keep still, glaring up balefully every so often at the female who seemed to be taking longer than normal.

'What's keeping you?' he growled. 'I'm famished.'

The bitch otter said, 'I'll be finished in a moment. I just want to find a bigger fish for the lame one. I don't think he's getting enough to eat.'

Slow Otter exploded. '*What*?' he screeched. This was too much. While the other females hastily left the yard with their catches, he scrambled up the tank, determined not to wait any longer. The female at the top overbalanced and fell with a deep splash into the water. The trout thrashed about in terror, making the contents of the tank resemble a whirl-pool. Slow Otter found it almost impossible to target a particular fish in this melee. He raked the surface blindly with his claws and managed to seize one moderately sized trout. He had to be content with this.

Meanwhile the female otter had broken surface and was struggling to free herself. The water level was well below the rim of the vat and she couldn't find the purchase to drag herself out. Moreover the swirling water continually dragged her back so that she had to battle to overcome its force as well. She was in very real danger.

'Help! Help me!' she pleaded in a scared voice.

'Serves you right,' Slow Otter grunted. 'You'll have plenty of opportunity to find the biggest fish now.' And he jumped to the ground feeling rather pleased with his retort. He picked up his one fish and left the yard without experiencing a trace of guilt.

However, he ate alone and avoided his companions afterwards by swimming out to the middle of the lake. There was an islet there where a few ducks were sleeping. The birds awoke and quacked nervously, waddling to the water's edge and paddling away. Later in the night Sleek Otter became aware of the absence of the unfortunate female.

'Where is your sister?' she asked one of her companions. 'You usually stay close together.'

'I don't know. I fear something bad has happened.' She called her sister from the safety of the reeds.

'Perhaps we should go and look for her?' suggested the long-whiskered female.

'I'll go,' Lame Otter volunteered. 'Let me do something for you for a change.'

'No,' the missing bitch's sister replied. 'I'll go. She and I are from the same litter. I can't rest unless I find her. The slow one was with her. He hasn't returned either.'

'He's on the island,' Lame Otter said. 'I saw him swimming.'

'Alone?'

'Yes.'

'Then I'm more afraid than ever.' The female slipped through the reeds.

'Be careful of the humans. They awake as the light returns,' Lame Otter cautioned her, as they watched her hurry away.

10

SICKNESS

Later that day the drowned otter was discovered in the tank. While searching for her, her unfortunate sister had been caught by the farm dog and killed before its owner could intervene. The man at the trout farm knew a bit about wildlife and was aware that no otters had lived in his neck of the woods in living memory. Once again the local conservation bodies were alerted. A search of the area immediately around the trout farm was hastily scheduled. The otters were losing their lives at an alarming rate. If there were any still alive, it was crucial to save them before any further accidents should occur. As for the trout, they had their tanks fitted with wire netting to protect them during the night . . .

Sleek Otter and her two companions had waited in vain for the reappearance of the missing females. They had heard the dog's barks while they cowered amongst the reeds. They had not run, for where else could they go? But as daylight broadened, their fears grew. Slow Otter remained at a distance, sensing that he had been the cause of some misfortune.

'The slow one hasn't shown himself,' Lame Otter said unnecessarily as the three huddled in the vegetation. 'Why is he keeping away?'

They all suspected he was avoiding them deliberately. 'We shall see him tonight when he's hungry,' said Long-Whiskers. 'Then he'll have some explanation.'

The daylight hours crawled by. The otters dreaded to hear the sounds of the dog. At last dusk arrived again and they began to breathe a little more easily. But they didn't move until well into the night hours.

Sleek Otter and Long-Whiskers left the lame male behind and timidly made their way, a few paces at a time, to the yard. They found that the first tank – where the female had been drowned – had been emptied and cleaned. This in itself was a shock. They hesitated. There was no sign of Slow Otter.

'What shall we do now?' Long-Whiskers squeaked.

'There are other fish here,' Smooth Otter replied, trying to sound more confident than she actually was.

When they had checked the remaining tanks only to find the trout safely wired off, they knew there was now no choice for them but to move. 'The humans must have taken our two friends,' Sleek Otter remarked sadly.

This was a heavy blow. They were such a little band of animals that each new loss seemed to presage their own extinction. 'I think we should go home,' Long-Whiskers murmured. 'We don't seem able to survive out here.'

'Neither in Farthing Wood,' Sleek Otter whispered. She turned to her companion. 'We'll see what the lame one thinks,' she said. She didn't mention Slow Otter, although they both wondered where he was.

Lame Otter welcomed them back, but he could see at once that something was wrong.

'What did you find?' he asked.

Sleek Otter described what they had seen.

'No food then?'

'No. But I'm not hungry anyway.'

'Nor I,' Long-Whiskers agreed. 'You see, there are more important things on our minds now than filling our stomachs.'

'She thinks we should go home,' Sleek Otter explained.

'But we don't have a home, do we?' Lame Otter pointed out. 'In Farthing Wood we are at the mercy of the foxes. Unless we prefer to starve to death.'

'I share your sentiments,' Sleek Otter agreed. She looked at Long-Whiskers. 'You must return if you wish,' she told her. 'But you'll be on your own.'

Long-Whiskers sighed. 'Then I'll stay with you,' she answered fatalistically.

'Good. And now we must leave here,' said Sleek Otter. 'It seems our fate forbids us to settle anywhere permanently.'

'Do we wait for the other male?' Lame Otter asked half-heartedly.

'I think the slow one prefers his own company,' was Sleek Otter's opinion.

No more was said on the subject. The three animals set off. Lame Otter was glad. He hoped not to encounter Slow Otter again.

The next day the search for the otters around the trout farm began. By then the three refugees had travelled a considerable distance and were hiding in a hollow log on a railway embankment. They had eaten nothing on the way.

Slow Otter had trailed them, always keeping sufficiently far behind so that his presence wasn't noticed. He followed the three instinctively, unwilling to make one of their party, yet rejecting the alternative of complete isolation.

Meanwhile in Farthing Wood more of the animals had sickened. It was the smaller hunters – the stoats and weasels – who were suffering. The pick of prey always went to the foxes, particularly now there were no otters to compete with them. There was no shortage of food for the smaller predators, but they weren't able to be selective. Some of the voles from the colony affected by disease had survived and managed to breed. They and their offspring were still carriers of a parasite, which meant that those who ate them felt the consequences. And these voles had spread throughout the Wood. Their appearance was different. They looked less plump, less bright-eyed, and were not so nimble in their movements. These signs were evident, yet not always recognized by hungry weasels or stoats.

Quick Weasel was the most noticeable casualty. Her usual darting runs and mercurial movements had deserted her. She appeared strangely lethargic. Her mate, by comparison, seemed lightning-fast.

'Qu-quick Weasel's become Slow W-Weasel,' cried Nervous Squirrel from a tree-stump. 'Her mate c-catches her food for her.'

Lightning Weasel overheard. 'As long as I don't catch anything *from* her,' he muttered through gritted teeth.

Sly Stoat saw his own mate sicken. He knew all about unsavoury voles, since he had been party to the poisoning of the otter cubs. He felt this was a kind of retribution.

'I told you to steer clear of voles,' he reminded Wily Stoat sharply. 'Couldn't you have listened?'

'I did listen,' she replied faintly as she lay groaning in their den. 'But when you make a quick kill you don't always have time − oh! oh!' − to see what you've caught before you − oh! − eat it.'

'Well, eat these mice I've brought you. Perhaps you'll feel better.'

'I − I couldn't. I couldn't eat at all. Oh, I feel so, so poorly. I don't think I'll ever eat again.'

'Don't say that,' Sly Stoat beseeched her. 'That sounds like − '

'I know,' she cut in before he could spell it out.

'I know what it sounds like. I really think . . . I've done for myself.'

'It's the legacy of the otters,' Sly Stoat whispered to himself. 'It's revenge for what we did to them. I must see the old hedgehog. Perhaps he has some advice.'

Sage Hedgehog could often be found near Farthing Pond. There were sedges there whose leaves attracted snails and slugs, his favourite food. Sly Stoat heard the hedgehog smacking his lips over a glutinous morsel before he actually spied him. Sage Hedgehog saw him first.

'Troubled times,' he said. 'You're in trouble, I've no doubt.'

'How did you – ?' Sly Stoat began, then hastily added, 'Of course, you can see my agitation. My mate, the wily stoat, is sick. Her wiles were not enough to save her from the otters' revenge. What can I do?'

'Otters' revenge?' the old hedgehog repeated. He knew nothing about the trail of voles. 'No, the otters are gone. It is not revenge. It is fate. The fate of Farthing Wood and everything in it is sealed. It will not be long before the humans know this.'

Sly Stoat was puzzled and irritated. What sort of advice was this? 'I don't understand your rigmarole,' he muttered. 'All I want is for my mate to be well again.'

'A vain hope, I fear,' Sage Hedgehog replied, 'when the Wood itself is doomed.'

The sly stoat had achieved nothing and was baffled and angry. 'Why, you silly, flea-ridden old thorncoat,' he snarled and made a rush towards him.

Sage Hedgehog instantly turned himself into a pin-cushion and Sly Stoat, more frustrated than ever, had to abandon him.

In the makeshift shelter of their log the three otters shuddered as new, frightening sounds assaulted their ears. The thunder and clatter of passing trains rocked the ground beneath them. It was a noise so terrifying that it made them desperate to escape from that place immediately – even in the daylight. Slow Otter, who hadn't, of course, the benefit of a proper hiding-place, had run at once when the first train approached. He had made the mistake of trying to cross the track and had blundered directly into a live rail. His body was still draped over it when the train passed. There was very little of him to be seen afterwards.

In one of the lulls between trains, Sleek Otter led her companions out of the log. She drew a sharp intake of breath. 'Look,' she gasped. 'We mustn't go across there. Some poor creature has been caught and killed by the monster.'

'Where shall we go? Oh, where *can* we go?' cried Long-Whiskers who was at her wits' end.

Sleek Otter tried to keep calm. 'Away from this dangerous place at least,' she answered. She looked all round for some feature that promised a vestige of safety. There were buildings and other forbidding shapes at every point. She realized they had strayed too far into the alien world of humans.

'We must be quick,' Lame Otter urged. 'We're vulnerable in the daylight.'

'What do you suggest then?' Sleek Otter snapped, overcome by tension.

'I don't know. But we have to find shelter.'

'I know that, I know that,' she hissed. 'All right, let's try this way.' In a nearby overgrown garden, rank plants offered a hiding-place. She set off at a run, leaving the other two to follow at their own pace. Lame Otter was soon trailing behind the females.

'I shall be the next to be separated,' he muttered to himself as he thought of Slow Otter. As he limped along, a crow which had seen the dead meat on the railway track, flew close beside him, carrying part of the severed head of the unfortunate animal. Lame Otter heard the beat of wings and looked up. Slow Otter's disfigured face seemed to stare at him from the bird's coal-black beak. The crow rose higher in the air. Lame Otter squealed in horror as he recognized his old companion. He seemed to feel the full force of the hostile environment pressing in on him. The otters' attempts at survival were futile. Slow Otter had been right. It was only a matter of time before all of them succumbed to the only destiny that awaited them here – extinction. With a terrible regularity, the little party's numbers were being whittled away. Whatever they planned, wherever they went, mattered little. Their defeat, ultimately, in this uneven struggle was inevitable.

'I'm the last dog otter,' the lame male told himself. 'When I die the long history of Farthing Wood otters will be finished.' Mechanically he continued in the wake of the two bitches. But he knew suddenly, beyond any doubt, what he must do. He must choose one of the two remaining females and return with her to the banks of the stream where they were born. For, whatever happened then, the future of the Farthing Wood otter colony wouldn't have been needlessly sacrificed before it had been given a final chance of rebirth.

11

CHOICES

Reports in the local press about strange sightings of otters and their apparent disappearance from their native habitat were not, of course, overlooked by some bodies of people who welcomed the news. While the conservationists were striving to locate and rescue the animals who had fled and endangered themselves further, these other kinds of humans were venturing into Farthing Wood to take stock for themselves.

Almost as if he had been expecting it, Sage Hedgehog saw a group of men pacing the banks of the stream, intent on acquiring the evidence they needed. Safe under a fallen branch on the edge of the Wood, the old creature watched their movements with foreboding. These men were not dressed in the way that humans who entered Farthing Wood were usually dressed. To Sage Hedgehog this implied a different human type altogether.

Later, in the gathering dusk, the men penetrated the Wood itself and passed within a metre of the hedgehog's obscuring branch. He observed them and their furtive glances for as long as they were within sight. Then, as soon as he deemed it safe to move, he scuttled in their footsteps, seeking any fellow woodlanders who would have the sense to stop and listen to him. Luckily he came across Kindly Badger who was busy digging up wild garlic root with his powerful claws.

'I count myself fortunate to have found you first,' Sage Hedgehog began in his usual verbose way, 'because, of all the animals, you are the least likely to discount my intentions.'

'Well now,' Kindly Badger said, chomping on a bulb, 'what's worrying you on this occasion?'

'Did you see them?'

'Them? Who?'

'The humans. They must have come this way only moments since.'

'Probably while I was still in my set,' the badger remarked calmly. 'The youngster thought he detected their smell.'

'They were here,' Sage Hedgehog assured him. 'I watched them for a long while.'

'That in itself is nothing out of the ordinary, is it?' Kindly Badger asked mildly. 'We've been used to humans walking – '

'No,' Sage Hedgehog interrupted sharply. 'Not this sort of human.' He was tired of the same old response.

'What do you mean? How were these different?'

'These humans have the greedy eyes and stony faces of the selfish. My friend, no good will come of their curiosity. These are not tree-gazers like the ones you refer to.'

Kindly Badger was disturbed. 'What does their presence indicate then, do you think?'

'It indicates harm,' the old hedgehog predicted. 'Harm to us and to the Wood.'

'Will you speak to others about this?' the badger asked. 'It does seem, perhaps, that this time we should take note.'

'I shall talk to the foxes,' the determined hedgehog replied. 'I have some hopes that the stout one at least may listen this time. He can help us. I shall tell him the foxes must track the otters and bring them back before it's too late!'

However some of the foxes hastily backtracked, making detours, when they saw Sage Hedgehog approaching. It was spring and they were too pre-occupied with their own needs and duties to wish to bother with him. But the old creature valiantly persisted in calling for their attention. He still hoped by some means to involve them. Stout Fox failed to avoid him and was obliged to stand and listen to his latest message.

'What you say all sounds very plausible, I'm sure,' he told the hedgehog afterwards, impressed by his urgency. 'But I think it must be a long time since you had a mate carrying your young. At times like this there's very little opportunity for the father to think about anything else. I can't deal with your demands just now.' And he carried on his way. He was not yet a father, but he was soon to be so, and in the meantime Stout Vixen needed nourishing and was relying on him to provide for her.

Sage Hedgehog was fatalistic about the animals' reactions. 'They *will* listen to me,' he told himself. 'In time they will. They must. I shall continue to give warnings and try to persuade them to heed them. One day they will understand. I know my role and I shall pursue it.'

Away from the Wood, Lame Otter limped into the thick growth of grass and weeds where the two bitch otters were lying restlessly. He told them what he had seen of the dead male, and let the realization sink in of the otters' mortal vulnerability in this vicious new world. The females were silent and sombre. Lame Otter wondered who would choose to join him on his return journey. He knew it was only in that way that his partner would be decided. He was perfectly aware that, as a prospective mate, neither would choose him in normal circumstances. He waited a while. Then he spoke.

'We shall all die out here,' he said simply. 'And very soon. There is one other option. You must both know what that is.'

Long-Whiskers looked at him longingly, as if begging him to take the decision for her.

'The other option,' said Sleek Otter, 'doesn't exist as far as I'm concerned. For me there's no going back.'

Lame Otter and Long-Whiskers exchanged meaningful glances. They both understood the choice was made.

Sleek Otter understood too. After a period of silence she said quietly, 'Don't persuade me to come with you. I wish you well. But I – I shall be a lone otter with, I think, a better chance of cheating danger.' She was putting a brave face on it. They all knew that and there was nothing more to say.

At dusk the three otters moved. Their first priority was to find food. Whereas before Sleek Otter had taken the lead in exploration, Lame Otter and Long-Whiskers realized now they must rely on themselves. They deliberately took a different direction from Sleek Otter, parting from her without a word and aware, as she was, that they would never see each other again.

'You'll have to do the hunting,' Lame Otter said to his companion. 'I'm useless as a predator.'

'I know,' Long-Whiskers answered. 'I'll do my best.'

Lame Otter limped behind. Suddenly Long-Whiskers turned and said, 'It would be best if you lie low while I'm on a hunt. We need to practise stealth if we're going to eat and – '

'And I'm clumsy? Yes, I've got the foxes to thank for that,' Lame Otter interrupted bitterly. They were both at once reminded of the perils that would have to be faced back in Farthing Wood. 'I'll go back to where we left the sleek one,' he said. 'I don't know where else I can lie hidden.'

Rain began to fall heavily as he returned to the overgrown garden. The evening was cool and the grasses and wet soil smelt sweet. The shower brought frogs and toads out of hiding. The garden, long untended, had provided a perfect refuge for them. Lame Otter was exhilarated. He ignored the foul-tasting toads and pounced on a frog that squatted only a few centimetres away. This success lifted his spirits, but the frogs were able to leap considerable distances and afterwards he never quite managed to get close enough before his prey vaulted beyond reach. He longed for Long-Whiskers to return. He knew that here she could have rounded up a good meal for them in no time. The one frog he had been able to eat had tasted delicious and he was impatient for more.

'Come on, come on,' he fretted as he watched with exasperation while the frogs themselves seized their own prey in the shape of slugs and worms, although he went hungry.

Suddenly, noiselessly, Long-Whiskers was beside him. She had brought no food. 'Quickly, come *now*,' she whispered. 'I ran into some humans and only escaped in the nick of time.' She was quivering with fright. 'One tried to grab me. They're after us — they're carrying traps and bright gleaming lights that shine all around like huge stars.'

'But-but,' Lame Otter stammered, looking at the frogs with regret, 'there's food here. Can't we hide?'

'Not here,' she hissed. Even as she spoke Lame Otter heard human voices, and abruptly the garden was swept by powerful torch-light. Long-Whiskers leapt in alarm and raced away.

'There it is!' a man cried, seeing her movement.

'There's another!' came a second voice as Lame Otter was bathed in light, cowering back amongst the greenery.

The men came crashing into the garden, intent on capturing the animals they had been seeking for days. Fear clawed at Lame Otter's heart and lent speed to his limbs. A net was thrown at him, but he dodged it and scrambled clear, running as he had never run since receiving his wound. He was oblivious of any pain; his injured leg seemed to respond to his desperate need to escape.

'Catch it!', 'Stop it!' human voices cried as the men thrashed about, trying another throw of the net. But Lame Otter had found darkness again and, using its merciful veil, he raced away as though all the foxes in Farthing Wood were after him.

Long-Whiskers had run towards the railway embankment. She could think only of the deep black interior of the hollow log and wanted to wrap herself in its protection again. Her fur streamed with water. She took great gulps of air as she ran, straining every muscle to reach her goal. But, before she could find sanctuary, a train – a monster of speed and light – came rushing, as she thought, towards her out of the gloom. She reared up, changing tack, and ran along the crest of the embankment, parallel to the railway line. The train disappeared. Long-Whiskers continued to run blindly. The embankment dropped down to a road which crossed the line at that point. A few cars were crawling over this level crossing. The barriers had just been raised following the passing of the train. Long-Whiskers slowed and hesitated. She seemed to recognize the road as the way to escape the rushing monsters. She pattered across the line in the wake of the vehicles and then veered away through an orchard that bordered the embankment on the opposite side.

Lame Otter had seen her dark shape illuminated on the crest by the lights from the train windows, and he struggled to keep her in view. He was so fearful of losing her with all that would entail from that, that the shock of the humans' sudden appearance became of secondary consideration. He trailed her to the level crossing and then, on the other side, could find no trace of where she had gone next. He called her urgently.

Long-Whiskers had paused to draw breath. His plaintive cries reached her ears. Joyfully, and with relief, she answered. Lame Otter hobbled towards her. Now that the immediate danger was averted, pain reclaimed his senses and his pace became agonizingly slow. She was waiting for him under an apple tree whose boughs were awash with blossom.

'Brave creature,' she breathed compassionately. 'You saved yourself.'

'At some . . . cost . . . I'm afraid,' Lame Otter gasped.

'We've escaped them for now,' Long-Whiskers

resumed. 'But they won't give us up if they think we're still in the area.'

'Then we . . . must leave it.'

'Tomorrow. You can go no further for the present.'

'No.'

'Rest here while I look for a refuge.'

'Don't go far,' he pleaded.

'Only as far as is necessary,' she assured him.

Lame Otter collapsed against the trunk of the apple-tree. His legs trembled violently from his exertions. He wondered if he would even be able to move as far as the nearest hiding-place. No human sounds were evident and he fell into a sleep of exhaustion.

He was wakened by Long-Whiskers' gentle nudges. It was a while before he could recover himself and recognize what was happening.

'Some luck at last,' she was murmuring. 'I've found a pond in the next field. There's plenty of cover and there are water-fowl and a moorhen's nest. We can take shelter and feed ourselves at the same time. There's nothing like the savour of tender young nestlings.'

Lame Otter looked at her dreamily. 'I have a feeling,' he said, 'things are about to change for us.'

12

ANOTHER VICTIM

The otter pair hid themselves thankfully amongst a thick growth of water-irises. How could they know that the humans they had evaded meant them no harm? That they actually would have delivered them to their old home by a much safer and quicker route? To the animals, these men with their brilliant lamps and their nets seemed terrifying. As for Sleek Otter, she had bolted into a drainage ditch where she lay quaking until the humans had disappeared.

Meanwhile Farthing Wood held its breath. Nervous Squirrel's agitated cries of 'S-strangers in the Wood' were heard more frequently. The tranquillity of the woodland was disturbed regularly by the cold, calculating humans whom Sage Hedgehog had first witnessed. They took a particular interest in the grassland surrounding the Wood, returning to it at intervals, and giving the appearance that they were in their clever way taking its measure.

'Too close for comfort,' Jay screamed as he flew

overhead. And the Wood's inhabitants trod warily and quietly until they were left alone again.

Lean Fox said to his vixen, 'The Wood is uneasy. Every creature is on tenterhooks. Sickness is rife and men come spying. Things were less fraught when the otters were here.'

'How can you say that?' Lean Vixen rounded on him. 'There was constant friction. At least these men don't steal our food. We're of no interest to them at all.'

'I think you're mistaken,' Lean Fox said quietly. 'If we're of no interest, why do they continue to return here?'

'Who knows? Who cares? As long as we can hunt and keep our cubs free from sickness, that's all we need to concern ourselves about.'

The sickness was spreading, claiming more victims. Quick Weasel and Wily Stoat had died and other animals throughout the Wood were now suffering. For some creatures it became increasingly difficult to know where to hunt and what areas to shun.

Stout Vixen, whose cubs would soon be born, saw her mate arrive from his foraging with nothing.

'How can you come into our earth carrying nothing?' she berated him. 'This is the second occasion. Perhaps I should hunt for myself?'

'You certainly have the greater skill,' Stout Fox replied magnanimously. 'Believe me, I've tried everywhere. The rabbits are becoming much more wary and you know I don't like settling for other prey. It's particularly risky with some of them carrying disease.'

'I understand your motives,' the vixen said. 'But what are we to do? If you can no longer catch a rabbit, then you must look elsewhere.'

'I've done so,' he replied. 'Would you want me to bring you beetles and moths?'

'Well, I must eat,' Stout Vixen said. 'Fasting at a time like this is unacceptable.' She stood up. 'Is the Wood quiet?'

'Quiet and still.'

'I'll find something, I've no doubt,' she declared with confidence.

Stout Fox followed her through the exit hole. A shower of rain pattered through the leafy trees.

'I'll go alone,' Stout Vixen told him. 'Perhaps I'll find something.'

Stout Fox said admiringly, 'If anyone can, *you* will do so.'

Stout Vixen trotted beneath the trees towards the stream. She had a feeling that some kind of quarry might be sheltering there, enjoying a period of prosperity in the otters' absence. 'How many have hunted here' she wondered to herself, 'since those animals left?' Almost at once she flushed a water-vole from the bank. It plopped into the water, but the vixen's eager jaws snatched it and crushed it in one swift lunge.

'There are more of you around somewhere,' she said after she had eaten. She paddled into the stream, nosing her way amongst the reeds. A pair of coots scuttled out of her reach, calling in alarm and leaving their neat nest exposed with four unhatched eggs just waiting to be devoured.

'Haven't tasted eggs in an age,' Stout Vixen murmured to herself. She cracked one open with her strong teeth and licked at the succulent contents. She chuckled to herself. 'It doesn't seem right, all this for me while my mate goes hungry.' She smacked her lips and broke another egg. 'They really are delicious.' When there was only one left, her conscience smote her. 'I'll carry this back for the fox,' she murmured. 'He's faithfully tried his best on my behalf.' She picked it up carefully and set off.

On the edge of the woodland she surprised a bank vole. Instinct got the better of her. She dropped the egg, which broke, and pursued the rodent. She was keen to prove to herself she had lost none of her speed. She cornered the vole, killed it, then checked herself.

'Do I eat it?' she wondered. She sniffed at the body. 'Hm. Nothing wrong with *that*. Can't afford to waste anything.' She gobbled it down, then noticed the broken egg. 'Ah well, as I said . . .'

'*Stop!*'

She turned, startled. Stout Fox, who had been searching for her, had seen the kill and was anxious no vole should be eaten in that quarter.

'You?' Stout Vixen said. 'Why did you cry out? It's only an egg.'

'You can eat that and welcome to it. Where's your kill?'

Stout Vixen was puzzled. 'Kill?'

'The vole!'

'You saw me? Was I fast?'

'Yes, as fast as ever. Where *is* it?'

'Well, I've eaten it, of course.'

Stout Fox slumped. 'How could you? After all I've said? I've been so careful, taken such pains . . .'

'All right, all right,' she told him, but now a little worried. 'There was nothing wrong with it. It smelt good.'

'Smelt?' he repeated faintly. 'How on earth did you think it would smell? You can't tell by their odour.'

Stout Vixen gaped. Her stomach lurched. 'It looked healthy.'

'How can we be sure?' Stout Fox demanded. 'Wouldn't it be better to avoid this kind of prey until we know it's safe?'

The vixen felt some relief. 'So you're not sure either,' she retorted. 'Why do you try to scare me?'

'I don't wish to. I'm only concerned for your well-being. And for your litter.'

Stout Vixen softened. 'You're a good partner. I've grown used to you and I like your company. Look – I was carrying this egg for you. Won't you try it?'

'Of course I'll try it,' Stout Fox grunted. 'I've eaten nothing at all!' He quickly demolished the egg's contents. 'Are there more?' He looked at her with hungry eyes.

'Er – no. I don't think so,' the vixen answered evasively. 'Are you going to hunt again?'

'I'll see what I can pick up for myself.'

'Good. I shall return to the den. And I feel perfectly all right, so don't vex yourself about that vole.'

Far away from Farthing Wood, Sleek Otter was feeling very alone. From the drainage ditch she had travelled swiftly and always directly away from the place where she had dived for cover from the humans. She knew that wherever she found to rest at the end of that day, for the first time she would have no company. It was a chilling thought, but she had made her choice and there was no going back.

The dark hours were kind to her. There were no further alarms. When daylight came she looked around in amazement. The entire countryside seemed to have been swallowed up by forbidding patterns of brick, stone, metal and asphalt. These spread before her in a bewildering mosaic which puzzled and frightened her. Behind her was the countryside through which she had just run. She knew she had to go forward, but where? And how?

'This can be no home,' she acknowledged to herself. 'I can't hide in there.' A sudden noise made her jump. An aeroplane droned across the sky, high up, like a monstrous silver bee. A starling flitted over the house-tops and perched on a television aerial. Sleek Otter was impressed by the bird's adaptibility. 'Perhaps there is some shelter somewhere for me after all,' she sighed.

She crossed an empty road and padded along a pavement, looking for an opening between the looming buildings. A cat sitting on a wall arched its back and hissed at the strange beast. The cat was just as strange to the otter and she scampered away. In the distance a milk-float approached with a rattle of milk-crates and clinking of bottles. Sleek Otter was bombarded by new sounds and crushed by an unyielding environment. There were no trees, no streams, no rushes, no reeds. And no food. The town was a nightmare for a vulnerable, solitary and ravenous wild creature.

'I've no chance here,' Sleek Otter told herself. 'I might as well have been taken by the humans.' Then suddenly she saw a gap. As the milkman came nearer she bolted down an alley between two blocks of flats. There was no greenery, no plant growth to hide in. It was a cul de sac, leading to a row of garages. Sleek Otter found she was in a dead end. One garage, however, had been opened. The door had been pushed up and the garage's dark interior seemed her only refuge. She ran inside. It was dusty and dry, but in one corner a clutter of cartons offered some protection. She tried to hide herself amongst them and, thoroughly weary, fell asleep.

Later in the morning there was much activity. Many people were collecting their cars to drive to work or to take children to school. Sleek Otter awoke to the din of revving engines, slamming doors and loud human voices. She dared not move. Yet as car after car rumbled past her place of concealment, she caught the acrid smell of petrol fumes which steadily threatened to choke her. At last she couldn't remain still. She dashed from the garage, almost colliding with some schoolchildren.

'Look, Daddy! What's that? It's . . . it's . . .'

'An otter!' cried the father. 'How on earth . . .?'

The children rushed at the animal, eager to save it from danger. But Sleek Otter slipped past them and, in sheer terror, bolted for the alley. As she neared it a car, reversing from the first garage in the block, hit her and rolled backwards over her. The children screamed out but it was too late. Their father grabbed them as they tried to run forward.

'It's no good, children. We can't do anything,' he told them regretfully. 'Poor creature. Wherever could it have come from? It must have been someone's pet.'

The driver of the vehicle had felt a bump and got out to investigate. It was a young woman who was really distressed by what she found.

'Oh no, not another one,' she wailed. 'They seem to be bent on destroying themselves.'

The father asked her to explain.

'Haven't you heard? There has been a spate of accidents recently involving otters. They've been run over, drowned, killed by dogs. It's all very strange and very upsetting. Such lovely animals too . . .'

'How sad,' the man commented. 'They must be rarities in these parts.'

13

THE LAST OF THE OTTERS

Stout Vixen was certain she had suffered no ill effects from eating the vole. She felt no different.

'You were lucky,' her mate told her.

'No, I don't think so. Probably all the voles with disease have perished or been accounted for by now.'

'Maybe. But don't forget – it only takes one.'

Stout Vixen thought her mate was being over-cautious. She determined that, if he couldn't feed her properly in these last crucial days, she would supplement her diet from the banned area where now no fox nor other predator hunted. 'But I shan't tell him,' she chuckled to herself. 'He gets in such a stew about it.'

Farthing Wood and all it represented was drawing Lame Otter and Long-Whiskers steadily towards it. They had eaten well by the pond and were in good spirits as they continued homewards.

'Do you think we can reach our stream easily?' Long-Whiskers asked her companion who now, also, had become her mate. 'Or will we always be in danger?'

'We must take every precaution,' the dog otter replied. 'And, regretfully, my company will make the journey slower and seem longer than it would be if you were on your own.'

'But I wouldn't be making it on my own,' she assured him gently.

'Well then, we are content.' Lame Otter limped by her side. He tried not to think about what would happen to the other if one of them met with an accident. 'We must aim for the Metal Ponds where we caught all those fish. If we find our way there without trouble, we should be over the worst.'

'Do you ever think about the foxes?' Long-Whiskers asked.

'Sometimes. I have cause enough,' Lame Otter answered, remembering the fight that had disabled him.

'Perhaps if we steal into our holt by the stream quietly, no-one will know we're there.'

'Did you have a den?'

'Yes. Where I was born.'

'Are you attached to it?'

'I suppose so. Did you have a different plan?'

'No. I shall be happy where you're happy. And your comfort must be paramount.'

'Thank you. My holt is a snug home for cubs.'

They fell silent, full of thoughts of a new generation of Farthing Wood otters. They didn't reach the trout farm that night. Lame Otter's leg was painful and Long-Whiskers persuaded him to rest. They took shelter in a rabbit burrow, intending to move on the next night. The rabbits panicked as the otters entered the warren. Most of them took flight, but Long-Whiskers pounced on a youngster who hesitated, and she and her mate enjoyed a feast.

'Will we ever eat fish again?' Long-Whiskers sighed.

The same thought had occurred to Lame Otter. But he said, 'As long as we eat. That's all we can hope for at present.'

They slept during the daylight hours and at dusk the next day, fully refreshed, they set off again. Lame Otter's spirits were buoyant. 'You know, I've had a feeling of confidence since we made our decision,' he told his companion. 'I'm sure everything is going to work out for us. It's as though we have earned our right to survive because we're the last Farthing Wood otters. We *have* to do so for the sake of the rest of them.'

Long-Whiskers was encouraged by his words. Neither of them had spoken of Sleek Otter. Now Long-Whiskers said, 'You really believe we are the last now?'

'There can't be any doubt, can there? There never was any chance of any of us living permanently out here. I have realized that for a long time.'

In the middle of the night they caught sight of the trout lake and the buildings around the trout farm. Lame Otter let out a whistle of delight. 'There!' he cried joyfully. 'That's our landmark. The most dangerous part is over for us. We're almost home. Come on, we can have a swim!'

They loped to the lake and dived in gratefully. Their delight in swimming made them a little reckless, and they were still happily playing in the water when dawn broke. Their antics were spotted by the very dog that had killed one of their old companions. The animal yelped excitedly outside its kennel, fetching its owner, who had then scarcely stepped out of bed, hurrying down to quieten it. It wasn't long before the man discovered the reason for his dog's outburst. He watched the otter pair for a while through binoculars, and then went to telephone a friend who was an enthusiastic member of the local Wildlife Trust. In very little time a party was assembled and on the move to the trout farm. It was hoped that on this occasion, finally, a capture would successfully be made.

The otters' sport came abruptly to an end when they heard the dog bark. They submerged and paddled along the lake bottom. Lame Otter broke the surface briefly to keep a look-out. The dog had disappeared by then. The otters left the lake hurriedly while the coast was clear. All this was noted by the dog's owner. He took care to follow their direction so that he could give the appropriate advice. Naturally the conservationists' plan was to head the animals off.

Lame Otter and Long-Whiskers ran across country. They remembered the hedgerow where they had hidden with their five companions, and hoped to take shelter there again. As they ran a Land-Rover entered a field ahead of them, stopped suddenly and disgorged a handful of eager people. The people came quickly towards them, pointing and gesticulating. The otters knew only too well what this meant. This time there were no brilliant lights but the animals hadn't forgotten the terrifying experience near the railway line. They turned instinctively and ran back towards the lake, the only place now where they knew they could hide themselves. Lame Otter lagged behind. He gasped, 'Save yourself! Don't wait for me.'

Long-Whiskers looked back. The men were closer. With extreme anguish she forced herself to abandon him. She knew she must survive now at all costs if the Farthing Wood race of otters was not to be extinguished forever. All at once her sharp eyes saw a burrow entrance in the corner of the field under a group of trees. She called excitedly. 'Here! Here! We're saved.' She had no idea this was the entrance to a badger set, and not a rabbit burrow.

Lame Otter made a supreme effort as he saw the hole. Long-Whiskers vanished inside as he laboured to make his escape. The humans were almost close enough to grab him. He heard their thudding foot-steps and their quick breathing. A shadow began to envelop him. He remembered the nets. He dived for safety. The darkness of the tunnel enclosed him. He smelt not the smell of rabbit, but of badger. And then, ahead, a violent commotion broke out. Long-Whiskers had run straight into the sow badger's nursery chamber where her new-born young were suckling. The badger reared up angrily to protect her cubs from the intruder. She lashed out at Long-Whiskers with her powerful claws and lunged at the smaller animal with her sharp teeth. At this season the mother badger had a fierce nature, her one imperative being to raise and defend her young. Long-Whiskers backed away. She was wounded, but not severely. The badger sow launched another attack, this time with the purpose of killing the otter who posed such a threat to her litter.

Now Lame Otter came into the fray, in his turn trying to defend his mate. The badger, furious at the sight of a second intruder, called up reinforcements from elsewhere in the set. A tremendous and vicious battle began. The otters were outnumbered and out-matched in power and strength. They had no chance.

Outside the set the group of people heard the furious growlings and roarings of the badgers and the shrieks and yelps of the injured otters. They knew only too well what the outcome of such an uneven contest would be. They waited vainly for the otters to retreat up the tunnel. Retreat was their only hope of avoiding certain death. Gradually the angry snarls subsided into silence. Even then the human onlookers continued to wait. None of them spoke. Each felt that their well-meant plans to save the otters and return them to their rightful home had somehow been blighted. Every one of their attempts to help had backfired. Sadly they had put the animals into greater jeopardy by their good intentions.

One man said, 'Another failure. No otter could come out of there alive. Not from a badger's set in the breeding season.'

A woman said, 'We must wait a bit. Just in case . . .' But she herself knew that the otters had been slain. It was inconceivable that their presence in the set would be tolerated.

'Were these the last two?' another man asked.

'Probably,' said the first man. 'The other female was killed by a car. There have been no other reports.'

'Then we've all lost.'

'It looks like it.'

Wearily and miserably the party trudged back to their vehicle. Each of them were only too aware what might result from the permanent loss of an otter population in Farthing Wood. They didn't voice their thoughts. They were too dejected. They climbed into the Land-Rover quietly, avoiding each other's glances. Soon the field was empty again.

Following this incident the local press printed a report from the Wildlife Trust about its fear that the last of the Farthing Wood otters had perished. A description of their unfortunate demise as a result of entering a badgers' set was given. No further sightings of otters had been made in the area. It was therefore regretfully to be assumed that no other animals still survived.

14

BY THE GREAT BEECH

For a brief period Farthing Wood seemed to breathe more freely. Sickness was on the wane. Nervous Squirrel was quiet. The animals were left to themselves. Then, abruptly, the peaceful atmosphere was shattered. Outside the Wood and beyond the stream, on the surrounding grassland, there was much activity. Men arrived with machines and tools and began to cut a swathe through the tall grasses. In no time they had made a wide, straight path which Jay, from a high perch, could see stretched back from the hinterland towards the area whence they all knew the humans came.

'A trail!' he screeched. 'A human trail in the grass!'

The animals heard and Nervous Squirrel bounded to the top of an ash tree. 'M-many strangers!' he called, flicking his tail in extreme excitement. 'B-busy strangers!'

Sage Hedgehog knew without going to investigate that the moment he had dreaded had come. The humans were too far away for his old eyes to perceive that they were building a road to give them easy access to the centre of their interest. But he shook his head over his fellow woodlanders' refusal to comprehend the perils which he had warned about.

'Such foolhardy blindness,' he muttered. 'Now their eyes will be opened.' He left his roost and went to see how the other animals were coping with the revelation. He expected to see signs that at last Farthing Wood was reacting to the danger now only too evident on its doorstep. Once again the community surprised him. The animals appeared to be continuing with their usual habits and movements, regardless of any new development. He found another hedgehog contentedly munching some grubs dug from a piece of rotten wood.

'Didn't you hear the cry from the tree-tops?' the old creature asked, amazed by the hedgehog's placidity.

'Of course I did. Isn't that silly squirrel forever calling some message or other? Such an irritating animal!'

'Well, he has something to call *about* now, doesn't he?' snapped Sage Hedgehog, annoyed by the other's lack of concern.

'What's so different about this time?'

'Do you need me to explain? The humans have come to stay.'

The younger hedgehog looked less assured suddenly. 'To stay? Where?' he asked faintly.

'Too close to *us*. They're busy in the grassy area.'

'The grassland? Oh, that's too far from here to worry about,' said the younger animal. 'It's hours of travelling.' And of course, to a hedgehog it was. 'Would you like a share of these fat larvae? They're very tasty.'

'Food is of no consequence in the circumstances,' Sage Hedgehog replied sourly and turned his back on the heedless animal.

Sly Stoat watched the approach of the ancient hedgehog prophet and quickly hid behind the trunk of a tall oak. But he wasn't quick enough. Sage Hedgehog saw movement.

'Why try to avoid me? What are you afraid of? That I might speak the truth?'

Sly Stoat muttered out of earshot, 'Afraid of? More bad news, I suppose.' Despite his mate's death, because of the decline in the numbers of sick animals in the Wood Sly Stoat was of the opinion that the otters' revenge had run its course. He slipped into the open. 'Come on, you old doom-carrier, what have you for us this time?'

'Nothing for you,' Sage Hedgehog answered primly. 'I wouldn't waste my breath. I'm on my way to talk with the more intelligent members of the community.'

'The foxes? Ha! They're too wrapped up in fetching and carrying for their mates. Don't you know, families take up a lot of time?'

'I've heard such words from others before,' Sage Hedgehog replied wearily. 'Almost the same words. And I can assure you I know all there is to know about young and their needs and demands. I wasn't always old. But now that I *am* old I have the time to look beyond such immediate concerns where perhaps others haven't. I love this place and I shall continue to do all I can to persuade others that it's vital that we *all* think about ways of saving it.'

Sly Stoat was humbled. 'I'm sorry,' he said. 'We sometimes don't give you the credit you deserve. We should recognize your warnings are driven by the care you have for Farthing Wood. A care we all, of course, share in our own way. Yet is there so very much to concern ourselves with? The sickness has abated and, so far as human presence goes, none of us, I'm sure, will be so foolish as to venture anywhere near the grassland while they're there.'

'So you do know of their presence?'

'The squirrel sees to that, doesn't he?'

Sage Hedgehog was silent for a while and he looked at Sly Stoat pensively. It was evident to him that the stoat, like the young hedgehog, couldn't see beyond the present. Perhaps only he himself had that ability. He sighed. 'Are there none of you far-sighted enough to make plans for the future?' he murmured. But Sly Stoat had already reverted to thinking about his empty stomach. He fidgeted, impatient to be off. Sage Hedgehog left him to his own devices.

The badgers were ready to talk. Kindly Badger realized something needed to be done. 'Human activity is always worrying,' he said. 'I fear for my youngsters. They won't grow up in a Wood free from interference as I and my mate did.'

'I am so thankful to have your attention,' the old hedgehog said. 'The stout fox understands my fears

324

but is too engrossed in domestic affairs to act on them.'

'What can we do?' asked the badger.

'We have to make plans. We can't continue to believe our lives will remain unaffected.'

'We're powerless to alter the course of any human plans,' said Kindly Badger, shaking his head. 'What plans can we make?'

'You're a thoughtful animal and your size makes you more likely to be respected than I,' Sage Hedgehog told him. 'You can perhaps make the others understand they have to think about the future, even if our generation will complete its cycle without tragedy. They *must* do this for the sake of their youngsters and those still to come.'

'I think I follow your reasoning,' Kindly Badger remarked. Sage Hedgehog's words were, as always, difficult to interpret for ordinary beasts such as himself who hadn't the gift of prophecy. The old hedgehog seemed often to be on a kind of higher plane. 'I'll discuss everything with my mate,' the badger resumed. 'The sow badger is such a comfort to me. We'll try to find a way of involving all the woodlanders.'

Sage Hedgehog nodded. He thought there was very little more he could hope to achieve for the moment. 'I'm grateful to you,' he said. 'And I trust that others, too, will have cause to be so before long.'

Over the next few days the lives of the Farthing Wood animals were punctuated at regular intervals by cries from Jay or Nervous Squirrel reporting human developments.

'A wide path with machines!' shrieked Jay.

'More and m-more humans,' chattered Nervous Squirrel.

'Grass going bit by bit,' Jay called.

'B-busy humans making m-mud,' Nervous Squirrel cried.

The animals paused and tensed each time they heard a cry. Those in their daytime dens huddled closer for a while. The distant hum of human endeavour – engines, voices – droned constantly in daylight hours. For most of the animals, it was too faint to bother them unduly. Kindly Badger began to wonder what would happen if the grassland disappeared.

'The rabbits will move closer to the Wood,' the sow badger remarked. 'As the hares have done.'

'Which means the humans will have done so too,' Young Badger pointed out shrewdly.

'Quite right, my son,' the kindly old boar said. 'And then we shall all feel as if they're spying on us. Life won't be very comfortable for the birds and beasts who are around in the daytime.'

'Let them worry about that,' his mate suggested.

'I don't know. We're all together in this in a way. It's our Wood we're talking about. We all live here. I'd like to get the opinions of some other animals. We ought to do *something*.'

'What? What can we do?'

'Well, think about protecting ourselves as best we

can. You know, keeping our secrecy as wild animals, and simply maintaining our natural behaviour. Humans can be very inquisitive and disruptive.'

'What shall we do, Father?' asked Young Badger.

'I think we need to get together with the other senior animals – as many as we can persuade – and talk things over. We could meet any night in the centre of the Wood – somewhere that's a good gathering place.'

'Everyone knows where the middle of the Wood is,' the sow badger said. 'By the Great Beech.'

'It'll be difficult to get the smaller animals to come along,' Kindly Badger reflected. 'They won't feel safe unless they're given a kind of promise.'

'Well then, give them one.'

Kindly Badger fell to thinking. 'It'll need the foxes' co-operation,' he murmured, 'and that's not an easy thing to arrange.'

So it was to prove. Lean Vixen scoffed at the notion of a promise. 'An absurd idea,' she said. 'To think that foxes would commit themselves in any such way. If you want to have a meeting; fine. But let everyone come at his or her own risk.'

'The badger's not so silly,' Lean Fox disagreed as he often did. 'We should have as many wise heads as we can get. Some of the smaller animals, such as the weasels and stoats, have a kind of cunning all their own. I, for one, would be willing to listen to them. They may have ideas that would be useful for all of us. I would promise to leave them unmolested.'

'And the squirrels and rabbits?' Lean Vixen mocked him. 'You'd give them a promise of safety?' She gave a hollow laugh.

'Why not?' Kindly Badger asked. 'For just the duration of our meeting?'

'They wouldn't come!' Lean Vixen protested.

'That's up to them. The squirrels might well do so. They could sit in the branches.'

'When do you propose to meet?' Lean Fox asked.

'The sooner the better. There will soon be a new moon. The darkest night is our best security. We should choose then, I think.'

'By the Great Beech?'

'Exactly. I shall invite as many woodlanders as I can find.'

'I'll speak to the stout fox,' his lean counterpart offered. 'I think he'll attend. He has been going around with a very worried look recently.'

'Oh, that's nothing to do with any human presence,' the vixen informed him glibly. 'His mate's ill and she's almost reached her time. No wonder he's worried.'

'Nevertheless . . .'

'The old hedgehog will join you,' said Lean Vixen. 'You can be sure of that. He wouldn't miss any opportunity to regale everyone with his weird fantasies.'

Stout Fox had begun to view the humans' incursions with misgiving. His own cubs would soon enter the world in the shadow of their presence, and who could say how things would develop? But his concern for his unborn cubs was overridden by a much more profound concern for his mate. Stout Vixen was very sick indeed and the big fox ran in and out of their den, unable to rest for a moment. He was at his wits' end.

'There must be something I can do,' he would mutter. 'I can't just let her suffer.' Inside the earth he looked longingly at her. 'Poor vixen! Are you in great pain?'

'Pretty much,' she whispered.

'If only I could help,' Stout Fox moaned.

'But you can't . . . we both know that.'

'Perhaps there is a creature somewhere . . .' he murmured and broke off as he heard a voice outside.

Lean Fox had come to give news of the meeting. Stout Fox scarcely listened, his mind was so taken up with his mate's illness.

'The Great Beech, you say? All right, I'll come.' Then a thought struck him. Maybe one of the animals at the meeting could offer some hope. He called after Lean Fox as he left. 'I'll certainly attend. As long as it's safe to leave my vixen . . .'

The night of the new moon arrived. Kindly Badger and his mate, along with various hedgehogs, Lean Fox and Lean Vixen, sat waiting beneath the Great Beech. Sly Stoat, Lightning Weasel, and others of their kind, came cautiously. In the branches of the beech Nervous Squirrel and others perched restlessly. A pair of hares, who trusted the badger's word, had come to listen to the discussion from a safe distance. Other smaller animals peeped from holes nearby. And various birds clustered in the tree-tops, alert to every movement.

Jay spied Stout Fox loping through the Wood to its centre. 'The stout fox is coming!' the bird screeched, putting several timid beasts to flight at once.

'Come back, come back,' Kindly Badger called. 'There's no danger. Everyone assembled here must take the Oath of Common Safety, so that none can be harmed. Otherwise there will be no exchange of views and no opinions heard.'

Stout Fox appeared out of the gloom. He was the largest animal present. 'I swear,' he growled, looking around the gathering, 'to respect the safety of all creatures assembled for this meeting.'

Others followed suit. It was a solemn moment.

Stout Fox mumbled in a low voice, 'My vixen is sick. She must have found the last diseased vole. There has been no other sickness for days. Does anyone know of a creature who has survived the sickness?'

No-one answered.

'I must save her if I can,' the fox continued. It was strange to see the powerful hunter wearing a look of helplessness. 'She will bear our cubs very soon. She mustn't die. Not yet.' It was as though he were talking to himself.

'Some of the otters cured themselves,' Sage Hedgehog said when the fox fell quiet. 'They had the knowledge. But you drove them away. They are not here to help you now.'

Stout Fox hung his head in misery.

'I thought this assembly was all about protecting ourselves from human interference,' Sly Stoat interposed drily. 'Much as the stout vixen has everyone's sympathy, we really have to think of what concerns us all.' His sarcasm was evident, but none of the smaller animals dared to acknowledge it.

'Well, it doesn't concern *me*,' Lean Vixen announced, 'if you're referring to the humans' activities. I don't hunt in the grassy area any more. I don't need to. There are plenty of other places to find all the game *I* want. And I can't believe anyone here is so stupid as to go nosing around that quarter these days. Let the humans attend to their interests, whatever they are, and leave me to attend to mine.'

'A more shortsighted remark would be difficult to utter,' Kindly Badger retorted, angry for once. 'I wonder you came along.'

'She's fully occupied with our cubs, you see,' Lean Fox tried to excuse her. 'She can't think of anything else.'

'Perhaps she'd better return to them, then, and leave us to the serious discussion.'

'An argument!' Jay shrieked. 'Not a good start!'

'But the vixen's right,' Lightning Weasel gave his opinion. 'We don't have to watch the humans' every move. We can forget them, at any rate for the forseeable future. They're too far away to cause us any concern.'

'M-moving nearer, I think,' Nervous Squirrel said. 'I w-watch them. They s-seem to creep closer each time I l-look.'

'You're imagining it,' the weasel replied. 'How can you tell?'

'Why don't you look for yourself?' Sly Stoat sneered. 'Then you'll know!'

'I can't climb into tree-tops,' Lightning Weasel snapped.

'I think we're losing sight of why we're here,' Kindly Badger interrupted.

'Why are we here?' Lightning, Weasel chortled, glancing around.

Kindly Badger sighed. 'In your case – and in some others – it would be difficult to say. But I called this assembly so that all of us can air our views as to how to proceed in these difficult times.'

'What's he talking about?' one hare muttered to the other.

'I don't know. Waste of time coming, if you ask me.'

Lean Vixen cut across the mutterings. 'There is nothing anyone here can do to put things right.' She looked serious for once. 'That's if you believe things have gone wrong in the first place. We drove the otters out. We have more to eat, but the humans seem to have replaced the otters. That's the story in as few words as it takes to tell.'

'And what of your cubs' future?' Sage Hedgehog asked her. 'How do you propose to protect them?'

'The same way my parents protected me,' she

answered. 'Nothing has altered that. And when they no longer need me, well . . . they're on their own.'

These words seemed to summarize the situation for every creature present. Beyond usual parental duties, there *was* nothing more in their power to do. The meeting began to break up without reaching any agreement. The smaller animals left first. And gradually all of the beasts and birds returned to their homes or their normal occupations in the night hours. Kindly Badger and Sage Hedgehog were left alone under the Great Beech.

'They are beyond redemption,' the hedgehog said with finality.

15

STOUT FOX'S QUEST

Far away from Farthing Wood another group of badgers were tidying their set after their fight with the intruding otters. It had been a short and savage fight. The mother badger watched her mate take the lifeless form of Lame Otter by the scruff of the neck and carry it along the entrance tunnel to the outside air. Lame Otter had borne the brunt of the attack as he had tried to shield Long-Whiskers. His wounds were ghastly. The badger dropped him far enough from the set so that no taint could foul the air of the nesting chamber. Then he returned for Long-Whiskers.

The badgers believed both otters were dead, and indeed Lame Otter was at his last gasp. But, severe though Long-Whiskers' injuries were, she had some chance of making a recovery. She was dropped by the side of Lame Otter. The badger returned to his set, satisfied that the intruders had been properly dealt with.

Long-Whiskers opened her eyes. It was still light. She knew she must somehow crawl away from that place before dusk, because then the badgers would leave the set to forage. If they should discover she was still alive they would quickly finish her off. She sniffed at the still body of the lame male.

'Are you lost to me?' she whispered. The horrible ache of loneliness had not yet made itself felt. Pain and fear dominated her senses. She detected the tiniest flicker of movement in her companion as he struggled to draw a breath.

'You're still living!' she whistled softly, though aware life was ebbing from him.

Barely audibly Lame Otter gasped, 'Leave here. Go on. You . . . must get back.' The effort exhausted him, but he tried to speak again. 'You . . . the last. For the cubs . . .' These were his last words. He shuddered and was then quite still.

For a while Long-Whiskers remained loyally by his side. Then, for his sake as well as for her own, she began to crawl away. She had lost a lot of blood and she felt weak and sick. Her gashes were extremely painful. Amazingly, though, her limbs were still sound. The badgers' attack had been directed against her chest and head. She paused after dragging herself a metre or two; then continued. She knew she couldn't rest just yet. Little by little she removed herself from the scene of that horrible encounter, so that by dusk she was able to haul herself under a hedgerow, secure in the knowledge that she had escaped the badgers. She slept the deep sleep of exhaustion; helpless, injured and totally alone.

★

The grassland around Farthing Wood shrank steadily as the human construction site began to take shape. The Farthing Wood animals, for the most part, tried to ignore the fact. But some of them recalled the otters' boasts. They remembered how there had, in truth, been no human activity when the otters lived by the stream. And they remembered how the foxes and others had plotted to rid themselves of the clever animals, and, in particular, that the foxes had joined together to drive the otters out. Rabbits and hares had already lost their chosen homes in the grassy areas they loved best. Some of the more thoughtful animals wondered now if that was only the start.

'Do you think that our set will always be here?' Young Badger asked his father one day.

'Of course it will,' Kindly Badger replied at once. 'Why, generation after generation of badgers have been born and raised here. It's – it's – *unthinkable* that that could ever change.' He glanced at his mate for corroboration, as though perhaps needing reassurance himself.

'Don't worry,' she said softly to the youngster. 'You'll grow old here, of that I'm quite sure.'

The young male couldn't think beyond that point and was happy.

The foxes didn't worry themselves about past events. The otters had gone and they thought that was a good thing. Yet Stout Fox would have been prepared to humble himself and ask an otter's advice about the sickness of his vixen if an otter had been around for him to do so.

Stout Vixen lay listlessly in their earth. She regretted her failure to be guided by her mate and to shun any voles as food. She hadn't cared for his over-protection. But he had been right. The sickness had taken hold of her and wouldn't go away. Each day she felt a little worse. She tried to eat what little Stout Fox brought her, so that at least she would have the strength to bring her cubs into the world when the time came. But gradually she came to realize that the cubs might be infected too, even if disease didn't claim her before they had a chance of life.

Stout Fox was beside himself with worry. There was no creature he could consult who had the secret of the cure. He watched the vixen wilt and sink a little more with every dawn. In desperation he set off through the Wood one evening in quest of Sage Hedgehog. As he went he told himself it was unlikely that the hedgehog could be of real assistance, but even if the old creature should offer one grain of comfort it would be worthwhile.

Sage Hedgehog was even more morose than the fox. The wasted opportunity of the Assembly had depressed him utterly. There was now, it seemed, no hope of alerting the stubborn and feckless Farthing Wood animals to their plight. Then, as he chewed monotonously on a long worm, thinking dire thoughts, Stout Fox appeared to interrupt his reverie.

'Old prophet hedgehog, I beg you to help,' the fox blurted out. 'If you know anything about the otters' methods in curing sickness, tell me.'

Sage Hedgehog paused in his meal. 'Your mate is worse?'

'Day by day.'

'I am sorry for that. Truly. But I fear you are too late to save her. You've brought this misery on yourselves, for there is now no-one who has the secret. The otters kept it to themselves.'

Stout Fox sat on his haunches in despair. 'Is there nothing I can do?' he asked.

'Do you know where the otters went after you foxes drove them from here?'

'No.'

'They're probably widely scattered by this time. But if you could find them – any of them – and persuade them to return, that would be your salvation.' The old hedgehog suddenly perked up, as though there might just be a glimmer of hope. 'Indeed,' he resumed in a stronger voice, 'you *must* find them. For the otters are the salvation of all of us and the Wood itself.'

Stout Fox was encouraged. He looked more resolute. 'You're right! Only they can halt the humans' progress. I realize that now. I'll go and search for them and, if I can, I'll take others to help in the search. I won't rest until I find them!' He turned and ran back towards his earth. He would need to find food enough for his vixen to last her until his return.

Stout Vixen received his news without enthusiasm. 'It's useless,' she muttered. 'You'll never locate the otters. I shall be dead in a few days. Nothing can prevent that.'

But the big fox wouldn't be put off. 'I think you're wrong. And it would be contemptible not to try. I'll fetch food for you before I leave. Promise me you'll try to hold on.'

'Very well,' she whispered. 'You have my word.'

Once he had ensured that the vixen had managed to eat at least some of the titbits he had fetched for her, Stout Fox set off to recruit some helpers. He had no close associates and wondered where to begin. He decided that any swift-footed animal with the keen senses of a hunter would be useful in the search. Lightning Weasel dashed across his path.

'Stop!' the fox cried. 'Wait!'

The weasel turned and looked at the larger animal curiously. 'Well? What is it?' Stout Fox trotted over.

'That's near enough, if you don't want me to run,' Lightning Weasel said sharply. A fox was not a beast he wanted too close to him. 'I don't believe the badger's Oath thing is still in force?'

Stout Fox blinked. 'Oath? What oath?' His mind was on other things. Then he remembered. 'Oh, that. I think not. I want to ask for your help.'

'Help? From me?' the weasel queried in astonishment.

'Yes, I'm going to look for the others. You see, I need their knowledge to save my mate.'

'Oh, the sickness. Yes, we heard all about that at the Assembly. But this is a bit rich. You drove the otters away and now you want me to help you bring them back. That's your problem, I think.'

'I know it sounds odd. I regret now what we foxes did. We all need them here. Without them what future is there for Farthing Wood?'

'Too late for regrets, I'm afraid. No, count me out. I've no time to waste on a fool's errand and, besides, you're no friend to me, so why should I help?'

'But surely, you know how I feel,' Stout Fox said dejectedly. 'Your own mate died of the sickness.'

'That's right. And now I have another mate. If yours dies, you'll soon find another too. That's Nature, isn't it?' Lightning Weasel wasn't prepared to listen any further and bolted into the undergrowth.

Stout Fox sighed and continued on his errand. He began to realize that there wouldn't be much help forthcoming except from other foxes. He did approach Sly Stoat but there was no sympathy from that quarter either.

'*I* don't want the otters back. They took our food from our mouths. When we laid the trail of disease for them, I couldn't have foreseen how I would be repaid in kind. Now you're reaping the same reward. The otters have avenged themselves on us and there's no escaping it.'

Stout Fox accepted that he must look for assistance from his own kind. But he was no luckier with other foxes. These animals, the very ones who had combined to drive out the otter population, scoffed at the notion of inviting them back.

'You're mad,' one said. 'If we'd wanted them here in the first place, they'd still be around.'

'Though *we* might not be,' added another, 'the way our food was being thieved.'

'We're sorry for your mate,' Lean Vixen told him. 'She could have exercised more caution. But you really can't expect us to fight your battles for you.'

'He's only asking for a little help in his search,' Lean Fox reminded her, as usual the more sympathetic listener. 'I could perhaps go with him for a while.'

'And leave me to fend alone for our cubs?' the vixen retorted. 'Don't even consider it!'

'No, no, she's right,' Stout Fox murmured, bowing to the inevitable. 'I shall go alone. I was wrong to try to involve others in my difficulties.'

When he was out of earshot Lean Vixen growled, 'And woe betide any otters he manages to round up. Because they'll find a funny sort of welcome awaiting them in Farthing Wood.'

Long-Whiskers awoke at the end of the night. Rain was falling heavily and she felt cold. She heaved herself further under the hedgerow. Her coat was thoroughly damp but the raindrops helped to revive her. As dawn broke she became aware of the movements of birds. There were nests along that hedgerow and the parent birds, at first light, resumed their quest for food for the nestlings. Long-Whiskers watched them flying to and fro, and she was able to locate the various nests by the twittering of the hungry chicks, and also by the places where the adults entered and left the hedge. Despite her painful wounds, Long-Whiskers felt hungry. She began to raid those nests within reach, one by one. The young birds stood no chance. Their parents cried their distress as they saw the hunter in the hedgerow, knowing they were powerless to intervene.

In the daylight Long-Whiskers licked her chops as she rested again out of sight. She had a full stomach and already she felt stronger.

Under cover of darkness Stout Fox paddled across the stream and skirted the remaining grassland. He knew the otters would have first crossed the grassland to escape the angry foxes' pursuit. The building works loomed ominously in the distance. All was quiet, but the fox smelt human smells and the unfamiliar odours of their machines and materials hanging on the air. Above all there was the stench of mud. He saw a rabbit skip across the fringe of the muddy area and then disappear underground. He was surprised by just how close the rabbits' burrows were to the human presence. The grassland had been inhabited by rabbits and hares for as long as any animal in Farthing Wood could remember. Now some of that area had been destroyed and they had had to move their homes into the Wood. Thus they were more vulnerable to marauding foxes, stoats and weasels.

Stout Fox steered clear of the parts changed by the humans. He discovered that this area extended farther than he and probably any other creature had realized. No animal, save the rabbits, had ventured anywhere near it. He thought it his duty to describe to those who would listen what he had seen.

'But that must come later,' he told himself. 'First I have to sniff out the hiding-place of those clever otters.'

16

A MORASS

The hares and most of the rabbits had indeed migrated into Farthing Wood itself. But, in addition to the added danger of their being within easier reach of their habitual predators, there was pressure for space. A single warren remained in use outside the Wood. It was one of the rabbits from here that Stout Fox had noticed. There were many young – some still suckling – living in the network of tunnels. The rabbits, though fearful of the human din, had almost grown used to the noise and alarms created every day by the builders and their machines. By day they cowered quietly in their burrows. None went above ground until each last sound made by the humans had died away. And even then they waited and waited, finally peeping out to see if it was safe to browse. Usually one of them gave the all-clear signal and then the adults and adolescents would gladly run free and begin to feed.

A period of rain followed Stout Fox's departure. The area around the warren became increasingly muddy. The burrow entrances and the tunnels

344

seeped with mud and the rabbits were very miserable. They wished they had been able to move home. But the babies couldn't yet be moved.

The rain didn't, of course, prevent the humans from proceeding with their affairs. And, to the unfortunate rabbits, it seemed as though the noise and bustle was coming perilously close. They squatted in their slimy tunnels and passages, ears pricked and noses permanently a-quiver. Outside a bulldozer roared and slithered, teetering on one side, then the other, as its angle was dictated by the unstable mud. All at once daylight flooded into the warren. The bulldozer had carved out a huge mass of soil, ripping into one edge of the warren itself. The rabbits fled into the deeper heart of the system. But they were not safe. The bulldozer, having dumped its latest load, reversed and trundled forward again like a juggernaut. Nothing could divert it. Its course was set. The warren was in its path.

As if opening its jaws for another mighty bite, the machine ploughed into the centre of the warren, tearing up the entire labyrinth of runs, nesting burrows with its nursing mothers, babies, and most of the other fugitive rabbits. The load was hoisted high. Rabbits leapt or fell to the ground in terror. Others dangled from the mud, half in and half out of a mangled run. The bulldozer swung round, tipping more animals out as it turned, then depositing the remainder in a pile of soil and sludge where they squirmed like so many worms. They were trapped by the impacted mud and couldn't wriggle clear.

By this time cries from other workers on the site had alerted the earth-mover's driver to what had happened. He quickly turned off his engine as he saw the rabbits struggling and thrashing in the morass, while others twitched helplessly on the ground where they had been flung or had fallen. Only a few animals managed to escape unharmed. A look of consternation passed across the face of the driver who had quite unwittingly caused the destruction of the warren. He jumped from his cab. Other men squelched through the mud to try to free the half-buried animals. When they found the babies, some still beneath their mothers' bodies, they called out to each other in mutual pity and compassion. The driver looked particularly upset. The men did what they could for the animals who had survived, clumsily trying to clean them up and then setting them free. The few rabbits who were unhurt bounded into the Wood.

There was now a kind of bank of mud and grass remaining where the greedy jaws of the earth-mover hadn't yet reached. Inside this bank the last remnants of the rabbits from the warren hid in the few vestiges of holes and passages the machine had missed. They waited, passive victims, for the monster to gobble them up. They were exposed; cut off from any further retreat. There was nowhere to run. Yet somehow they seemed to be forgotten. They didn't hear the roar of the machine that they expected to hear. And they were left, to their amazement, undisturbed. The humans, strangely affected by what had recently happened, left that part of the site alone for the rest of the day and began working elsewhere.

Rain continued to fall. The treacherous mud absorbed more and more water until it was saturated. Puddles formed on its surface. The bank, too, was saturated through and gouts of mud broke away from it and slid down its side. The ground there was very unstable. Cold, wet and frightened, the rabbits inside the bank shivered through the day in a huddle. When darkness brought a cessation of human activity, one danger was replaced by another. The exposed holes in the bank were an open invitation to any hunter who picked up the rabbits' scent.

The foxes, of course, did so. There were more rabbits in the Wood, trying to enter other families' burrows and dens after fleeing the humans. Some were accepted, but in other places there was overcrowding already. The foxes went on a killing spree. Stoats and weasels joined in. A number of rabbits, driven from one side to the other in their efforts to escape, even began to run back to the muddy building site which had recently been their home. A few predators pursued them. Amongst these were Lean Fox and Lean Vixen.

'The cubs must do without their mother for a while,' the vixen had told her mate. 'I shall eat rabbit tonight, and I don't mean to be left out of the chase.'

Lean Fox knew better than to gainsay her. The

two ran together. They started an adult rabbit on the fringe of the Wood and raced in pursuit. Another rabbit ran from their approach. Lean Fox chose this one, the vixen the other. It was soon apparent that these rabbits had no bolt-holes. They dashed out of the Wood and on to the top of the bank.

'Catch it, catch it,' Lean Vixen called to her mate as she hurtled after her own quarry.

The rabbits hesitated. The foxes' hot breath ruffled their fur. They leapt and landed in the sticky morass of mud where so many of their own kind had already met their fate. Lean Fox had no time to draw back. He crashed after them, the weight of his body embedding him in the ooze. He saw Lean Vixen falter on the brink.

'Don't jump!' he cried. 'It's a trap!'

Lean Vixen watched her mate thrashing about in his attempts to free himself from the quagmire. She saw the rabbits – their prey – beginning to pull their lighter bodies out of the mud. The rain beat down on them all mercilessly.

'They're getting away!' Lean Vixen shrilled, her one concern above all else being the loss of her prize. Lean Fox struggled harder, but the cloying mud seemed to engulf his body. Lean Vixen teetered indecisively. Suddenly beneath her feet she spied another rabbit trembling in its inadequate hole. Instinctively she began to dig, more and more furiously as the urge to kill enveloped her. The hole gaped and crumbled and, as she lunged, the entire bank collapsed, burying her mate and the fleeing rabbits, while she was brought crashing down with it. Where the bank broke, a rush of water from the swollen stream flooded through the breach, and Lean Vixen was swamped by more mud, carried by the spate. The water poured over her head and the few rabbits who had been sheltering in the unstable bank were drowned with her. Some small trees, whose roots were ripped out of the soil by the subsidence, fell on their sides. The breach, blocked by tree-trunks, vegetation and gathering silt, was sealed. But a new muddy pond had formed on the edge of the building site. On its surface two dead foxes and a number of rabbits floated: a testimony to the human menace. The first animals had been killed, the first trees had been felled. Moreover a small, but ominous, gap had appeared like an open wound in Farthing Wood.

Beyond this place of drama Long-Whiskers was ready to continue her return journey. It was dark. The rain beat against the hedgerow with a relentless rhythm. She shook her coat vigorously and set off. Recognizable features that she passed on her way cheered her and strengthened her determination. Traffic noise reminded her of the road she must cross eventually. 'It won't be so formidable now I'm alone,' she said to herself, thinking of Lame Otter's vulnerability. But at once her thoughts were full of her own solitariness and she felt forlorn.

'You are my companions,' she whispered to her unborn cubs. 'Though I travel alone, we travel together.'

She stopped just short of the road, hiding in a

leafy garden. Her sores were healing and she was almost able to put them out of her mind.

From the opposite direction Stout Fox set his face against the lash of the rain. The taint of otter tracks was still strong enough for his sensitive nose to detect. He was pleased with his progress. His ailing vixen was constantly on his mind. He knew time was not on her side. He pictured her, head on paws, lying morosely in their den.

'I must save her. I *will* save her.' Stout Fox kept up this chant as he went, urging himself on to a greater effort and pace. 'The otters have the secret, and I have their scent.'

In the morning Nervous Squirrel saw the devastation. 'A hole! A hole in Farthing Wood!'

And Jay screamed, 'Dead foxes! Dead rabbits! Who's next? Who's next?'

17

FEAR AND REGRET

The deaths of Lean Fox and Lean Vixen, as well as the way Farthing Wood had been penetrated, soon became common knowledge. While the humans busied themselves with cleaning up operations, news of their advance, slight though it was, spread through the Wood like a flame.

'I told you, I warned you,' Sage Hedgehog cried bitterly to anyone who would listen. And now most did. 'They intend to destroy us. Little by little, Farthing Wood will fall. We're in their grasp and they won't let go. Only the otters held the key to our preservation. And where are they now?'

'Stout Fox is searching for them,' Sly Stoat said. 'Oh, how I regret I didn't go with him!'

'It's never too late,' Kindly Badger said. 'He needs help. He asked for it and was rejected. And the Wood is at the mercy of the humans if he fails. We have a duty to go. We can't depend on one creature alone for our salvation.'

'Were I young I'd be with the fox now,' Sage Hedgehog said sadly. 'But, as I'm constantly reminded, I'm old and forgetful of the ways of the young.'

'You have more than played your part already,' Kindly Badger assured him. 'If we had listened more to you at the beginning, things might have been very different.' He turned to Sly Stoat. 'There's no time left for talking. We should bring all the animals together who want to help save Farthing Wood, and leave this very night. If the otters are still around, one of us should be able to discover them.'

There was quite a gathering that crept carefully from the Wood in the dead of night and dispersed beyond the humans' workings in the all-important search. Stout Vixen had tottered to the earth entrance to watch the departure. It was impossible for her not to know what was afoot. Murmurs, rumours and chatter had been audible above ground for hours. She wondered how far her mate had travelled and whether he had met with any success. She was battling to fight off the sinister clutches of the disease – forcing herself to eat, lapping at raindrops, and determined to 'hold on' for Stout Fox's return as she had promised him.

Long-Whiskers awoke in the garden. A loud clatter outside the house disturbed her. At once she tensed, her muscles taut and ready to power her into flight. There was nothing to be seen, but she sensed a presence. Whatever it was, it wasn't human and she relaxed a fraction. A feeling of weariness overcame her. She had over-exerted herself the previous night and was reminded now of her weak state. She must lie low and conserve her strength for a while. She thought of her abandoned holt. How long ago it seemed when she and the other otters had played so freely and carelessly in the snow! And how ill-deserved was their fate at the hands of the foxes. She thought of them with hatred. The misery she and the others had suffered, the futility of their escape from Farthing Wood, the accidents, the deaths – all as a result of the foxes' jealousy and persecution.

Long-Whiskers lay down again amongst the drenched plants in the garden. She didn't feel ready to eat yet and wanted only to rest. Then all at once she saw the creature who had caused the clatter. It was a fox.

The fox was a well-built animal. It had smelt meat outside the house and had overturned a dustbin to get at it. It was making a meal from human left-overs. Long-Whiskers' heart beat fast. She recognized the animal at once as Stout Fox, the most powerful of the foxes from Farthing Wood. She shrank back, unsure whether to remain or run. What was the fox doing there? Why had it left the Wood? The conclusion she reached was one that made her shudder. It was hunting for her!

Naturally Long-Whiskers knew nothing of the change of heart regarding the otters in Farthing Wood. She remembered only the animosity and the savagery of the foxes. She believed now that Stout Fox had come to seek out every otter; to ensure that the last of them was killed so that there could never be any recurrence of the rivalry over food. And she suspected also that there were others of his kind around, bent on the same task. She was in terrible danger. She thought of her cubs. She must preserve their chance of survival at all costs. She knew all about the foxes' powerful senses of smell and hearing. She didn't think she could avoid discovery in the garden.

Slowly, painfully slowly, Long-Whiskers pulled herself from the vegetation and began to move off. A flicker of movement might have given her away, but the fox's head was turned towards the house. Long-Whiskers increased her speed. Now the rustle of her body made Stout Fox look round. He sniffed the air. He saw where the plants waved and parted. He ran forward. Long-Whiskers could think only of escape. She broke into a run and headed for the road. It was not late and there was traffic passing at intervals. With the fox behind her, the otter had to gamble. To be caught by the fox she believed would mean certain death. As for the human machines, there was just a possibility she could dodge them.

Stout Fox saw her intention. 'Don't run from me!' he barked. 'You don't understand: I haven't come to harm you. I've come for your help.'

Long-Whiskers was oblivious to his cries. She was concentrating as hard as she could on choosing her moment. She saw that the swift machines had separate movements. There were spaces between their passing. But she had no idea of their speed. To an animal it was unimaginable.

'Stop!' the fox barked. He could see her desperation. 'You'll be killed! The machines. They – ' His last bark was muffled by the roar of a huge lorry. When it had passed Long-Whiskers had disappeared. She was neither on his side of the road, nor across on the other. He sniffed the air for her scent. It was there. He looked down the road. And then he saw her. One of the giant wheels of the lorry had struck Long-Whiskers a glancing blow, sending her spinning through the air. She had landed some metres away, farther up the road, and was trying to drag herself from its surface.

'She's injured,' Stout Fox muttered. 'Her legs are crushed. I must try to pull her free.'

Traffic continued to pass. No vehicle stopped, but each one went around the struggling otter. Stout Fox trotted forward. Selfishly, he had no thought at that moment of the otter's vital importance to Farthing Wood. His one idea was to obtain the information he needed for his vixen's survival. As soon as it was safe, he crossed the road.

Long-Whiskers saw him approaching. She knew she had no defences. 'So you've come to finish me off?' she gasped. The fox ignored her. He grasped her by the nape of the neck and lifted her in his jaws. She was heavy. He laid her in soft grass in the nearest field. She stared up at him with glassy eyes.

'The machine has done the job you came to do,' she panted.

Stout Fox blinked uncomprehendingly. 'Where are the others?' he asked.

Long-Whiskers sighed a long sigh. 'There *are* no others. I'm the last. And in me die the last of the Farthing Wood otters.'

'But you mustn't die. Not yet,' Stout Fox pleaded. 'You saved yourself from the sickness. Give me the knowledge, I beg you, to save my mate.'

A realization seemed to dawn in Long-Whiskers' eyes. 'So that's why you came?' she whispered.

Much distressed, Stout Fox recalled his other motivation. 'No, not that alone. I came to find you and to bring you home. Our home. The home we all share.'

'Ha! There'll be no home for me,' Long-Whiskers answered him with bitterness. 'And neither for my cubs.'

'You have cubs?' Stout Fox exclaimed. 'Then you're not the last.'

'My cubs die with me.'

The fox understood and, remembering all that had passed, a great sadness overcame him. He knew the foxes bore the blame for the present situation. 'Forgive us for bringing you to this plight,' he muttered brokenly.

Long-Whiskers didn't reply.

'I would like to help you if I can,' the fox resumed.

'I'm beyond help.'

'Perhaps not. Farthing Wood is close. We need you.'

'Oh yes,' the otter gasped with the irony. 'For giving you my knowledge. Ha! When we lived together, foxes and otters, you didn't want our knowledge. Only our extinction.'

This was horribly true and Stout Fox had no reply to give.

'Why should I, then, help *you*?' Long-Whiskers demanded.

'I have no right to ask.'

'Your mate is sick? What kind of sickness?'

Stout Fox explained.

Long-Whiskers was silent for a long while. Then she murmured, 'There is no help I can give you, even if I would. I was not one of the otters who fell sick from disease. It's true some of us who were sick were able to heal themselves. I don't know how.'

'You – you have no idea?' Stout Fox asked hopelessly.

'Perhaps a plant . . . I can't say . . .' The otter's head drooped. She seemed about to expire.

'Please, what can I do for you?' the fox beseeched her earnestly.

Several moments passed. The otter rallied. 'As we're . . . no longer enemies,' she said weakly, 'maybe you could stay with me until . . .' She left the rest unsaid; it wasn't necessary to finish.

Stout Fox was in a dilemma. He greatly wished to make recompense for the tragedy he had brought about. On the other hand time was running out for his vixen and he was desperate to get back to her. The otter bitch looked as if she couldn't last much longer. He tried to be patient. 'I'll wait with you,' he said softly.

★

Some of the other animals who were searching – the swiftest runners – had covered a lot of ground in very little time. Lightning Weasel was the fastest of these. He detected the musky odour of fox. He looked around. He saw Stout Fox lying, nose to tail, a little way ahead. Was he asleep? The weasel crept forward. He saw that there was another animal by the fox's side.

Stout Fox opened one eye. 'You have nothing to fear from me,' he said. 'I'm not hunting, although *you* clearly are. Why have you come so far?'

'To look for the otters,' Lightning Weasel squeaked.

Stout Fox's ears pricked. 'Then your search is at an end,' he said.

The weasel began to understand. 'You – you have found one?'

'Come nearer.'

Lightning Weasel trotted up. 'Is the otter dead?'

'Not quite. And why are you searching now? You didn't want to come with me when I asked you.'

The weasel explained about the hole in Farthing Wood, the dead foxes and the rabbits.

Stout Fox sat bolt upright. 'Which foxes were killed?' he demanded.

The weasel told him. Stout Fox sank back. 'Well, you and the other beasts and myself, too – we're all too late. The otters have been wiped out. I tried to save this one here, but failed. She told me she's the last. When she dies perhaps Farthing Wood will begin to die too.'

Lightning Weasel sniffed at Long-Whiskers. She was quite still and, seeing this, the weasel for once became still too. He and Stout Fox waited together quietly and, later, other animals found their way to the spot. Sly Stoat and Kindly Badger were among them. Together they waited in silence as though doing penance for the demise of the Farthing Wood otters.

18

THE OTTERS' SECRET

Before dawn all the animals were on their way home. Subdued and down-hearted, they drifted back in ones and twos to their dens and burrows. The significance of Long-Whiskers' death weighed heavily on all of them.

As light began to fill the sky, Stout Fox headed for the stream in a last effort to unlock the secret of the otters' knowledge. He felt that somewhere along the water's edge where they had chosen their holts, there might be a clue waiting to be discovered. He cast his eyes along the bank and around the territory. Then he swam the stream and did the same on the side bordering the Wood. He stared at each plant, trying to assess its value and hoping for enlightenment. Nothing struck him as being unusual.

'Oh, those otters,' he moaned to himself. 'Even now they're dead and gone they still haunt me. How was it they were able to do things we other animals can't? What made them so different?' He ran along the bank, shaking his head. All at once an idea came into his mind. 'There was one thing that made them different from us,' he murmured. 'Their love of water, their wonderful skill in diving and swimming. Perhaps there's something in the water that's beneficial . . .' He bent and lapped experimentally, but there was nothing to taste then, any more than the hundreds of other times he had drunk from it.

'I hate to return to the vixen with no hope,' he muttered. 'But I mustn't leave her any longer. I've tried to find the cure. I've done all I can.'

He ran on into the Wood, eager to see Stout Vixen again, yet dreading to find her worse than before. He came upon her asleep in their earth. He was loth to wake her, but she sensed his company.

'You're back then,' she whispered. 'I – I managed to hold on.'

'You look so weak . . .'

'Did you learn anything?' she asked with a glimmer of hope.

Stout Fox looked down. 'The otters are all dead. Their secret died with them.'

The vixen heaved a long sigh as if finally she was letting go. But Stout Fox said quickly, 'Listen. Can you walk? I want you to come to the stream. Try to drink some water. It may do some good.'

'What's the point?' she asked him hoarsely. 'I might as well die here as there.'

'There's just a chance. Please – for me and our cubs.'

'Our cubs will never be born.'

'You mustn't say that! You *must* try.'

Wearily, painfully, the vixen got to her feet. Stout Fox nuzzled her and nudged her to the entrance hole. She swayed, unused to any kind of exertion. Patiently and with sympathy he encouraged her to walk. For the vixen, it seemed each step was more difficult than the last.

The edge of the Wood was a long way off. They paused often to allow her to rest. The noise of machinery echoed through the woodland, emphasizing the peril that each creature now recognized was its inheritance. Even Jay's screeches of alarm were drowned by the brutality of the bulldozers. Stout Fox had no need to explain the state of affairs to his mate. She knew enough to realize that, if ever their cubs were born, they would be born into a hostile world.

Somehow Stout Vixen got herself to the fringes of Farthing Wood. By then it was growing dark again. She gasped, 'Where is the nearest water? My legs won't take me any farther.'

'Here. Just over here,' the fox called. The rain at last had ceased and the pale moon was reflected in the dark swollen stream.

The vixen crawled on her belly to the bank and let her muzzle drop into the water.

'There's a lot of growth there.' Stout Fox pointed out a mass of cressy plants tangled underwater. 'Come to where I'm standing. The stream runs clearer here.'

Stout Vixen raised her head. Strands of the plants

were draped over her muzzle. 'Growth or no growth,' she panted, 'this is where I stop.' She bent and drank greedily. The water was cold and, while drinking it, she swallowed some cress. She sucked in a good mouthful of the plant and chewed it, relishing its clean peppery taste. Then she lay her head on her paws and fell asleep where she was.

Later the vixen awoke and noticed at once that the dull ache in the pit of her stomach which had troubled her for so long had disappeared. She felt less listless than she had done for many days. She looked up. Stout Fox was absent. She scrambled to her feet, still weak but tremendously hungry. As she savoured her new feeling of well-being her mate came trotting from the Wood. A dead rabbit dangled from his jaws. He had scarcely dropped it before Stout Vixen seized it ravenously and began to tear off mouthfuls.

'Well, this is a transformation,' the fox commented delightedly. 'The water, then, has been of some help.'

'I think it was the plant,' Stout Vixen mumbled, her mouth full. 'It's purged me.'

'The plant?' Stout Fox whispered, recalling Long-Whiskers' words. 'So that's it! Yes,' he cried, 'of course. That's how the otters were healed. Water-plants!' He peered into the stream. 'Will you take some more?' he asked eagerly.

'Certainly,' the vixen replied. 'I intend to make a full recovery. I shall need to build up my strength again quickly.'

'The cubs!'

'Yes. You have been a good mate. You made me struggle here almost against my will. The stream did hold the clue and you were right to insist.'

Stout Fox was jubilant. He had saved his vixen and, in that joyful knowledge, the fate of Farthing Wood was for a while forgotten.

Two days later Stout Vixen gave birth to four cubs. The poison that had infected her caused three of them to be still-born. The fourth, a male cub, by way of compensation looked to be robust. Stout Vixen removed the rest of her litter from the earth with resignation.

'One little cub to face an uncertain future,' Stout Fox murmured sadly.

'But a future with some hope if he has your wits,' Stout Vixen remarked.

EPILOGUE

As the little animal grew, the building works took shape. Most of the grassland was swallowed up. Life in Farthing Wood continued as always. There were births and deaths, fights and quarrels. Prey was hunted, homes were excavated. There was nowhere else for the inhabitants of the Wood to go.

One day a large tree was felled. It toppled with a terrifying crash that seemed to shake the Wood to its foundations. In the eerie stillness that followed one creature, the old hedgehog, thought he heard again the mocking taunts of the otters.

'Well, Farthing Wood, we hope you like your neighbours! You didn't want us here, but look who came instead. We were your surety. Without us you are lost. Who will save you now?'

Sage Hedgehog stared into the distance as though looking beyond his surroundings and the present time to something that was yet to happen. 'A leader will come along,' he said, answering those ghostly voices with a sudden conviction. 'Everyone will unite to follow him. And *that's* how we shall be saved.'

ABOUT THE AUTHORS IN THIS BOOK

COLIN DANN

Colin Dann always had an ambition to be a writer and he developed his passion for wildlife at an early age. His first Farthing Wood story was published in 1979 and there are now many wonderful books in the series: IN THE GRIP OF WINTER, FOX'S FEUD, THE FOX CUB BOLD, THE SEIGE OF WHITE DEER PARK, IN THE PATH OF THE STORM, BATTLE FOR THE PARK.

Also by Colin Dann the City Cats Trilogy: KING OF THE VAGABONDS, CITY CATS, and COPYCAT.

BETSY BYARS

Betsy Byars is an American author who lives in South Carolina. She has written many novels for children including MCMUMMY, THE CARTOONIST, COMPUTER NUT, CRACKER JACKSON, THE SEVEN TREASURE HUNTS, THE TV KID.

BENEDICT BLATHWAYT

Benedict Blathwayt is known mainly as an outstanding picture book author and illustrator and this is his only writing for older children so far. His other books, include TANGLE AND THE FIRESTICKS, and THE RUNAWAY TRAIN.

IF YOU HAVE ENJOYED READING THE STORIES IN THIS COLLECTION WHY NOT TRY SOME OF THESE OTHER TITLES BY THE SAME AUTHORS?